SECRETS
OF WINDWOOD

JACK REESE

CELEST
A CAYELLE IMPRINT

SECRETS OF WINDWOOD

For permission requests, contact the publisher below:

Cayélle Publishing/Celest Imprint
Lancaster, California USA
www.CayellePublishing.com

Orders by U.S. trade bookstores and wholesalers, please contact Freadom Distribution at:
Freadom@Cayelle.com

Categories: 1. Fantasy   2. Paranormal   3. Vampires/Witches/Werewolves
Printed in the United States of America

Cover Art by Robin Ludwig Design, Inc.
Interior Design & Typesetting by Ampersand Book Interiors
Edited by Cayélle Publishing LLC

ISBN: 978-1-952404-63-4 [paperback]
ISBN: 978-1-952404-50-4 [ebook]
Library of Congress Control Number: 2021936995

CELEST

A CAYÉLLE IMPRINT

For Lynne Foosaner, friend, mentor
and fellow writer, this is for you.

**Brittney Dennis, for the photo of me
at my niece's wedding and for all the
people who've helped me along the way.**

BURIED SECRETS

Windwood Plantation
Solomon's Wake, South Carolina
1985

ANDREA LORD AWOKE EARLY THAT morning. The wedding was just hours away, and she was excited. This was the first wedding to be held at Windwood in almost thirty years. As she got out of bed, she tried to be quiet so she wouldn't wake her husband, Calvin, who was across from her, slumped in his favorite leather recliner. He had fallen asleep with his glasses on again.

She tiptoed over to her closet to look at the pale green sequined gown she had decided to wear, and then at Calvin's black tux. Simon was finally getting married. Until a month ago, no one thought it would ever happen, but a certain Georgia Blake had changed all of that.

Andrea wanted this day to be a happy one for the family, especially because joy had eluded them of late. She pulled out a large photo album from the bottom nightstand drawer, and then sat on her upholstered bed bench as she stared at one of the many baby photos of Simon.

"Would you stop doing that to yourself? You're gonna get all worked up again," Calvin closed the recliner and slid into his slippers.

"Do you want me to go downstairs and see if Sutton's got your breakfast ready?" she said, still looking at the pictures.

"No. I have to go downstairs anyway." He kissed her on the forehead.

"I'll be down in a few minutes," she said to her husband, whose hand was on the doorknob.

Unlike all the previous mornings, and the ones that would follow, Simon would remember this one for the rest of his life. The sky was bluer, the air sweeter, and his life would be perfect the moment he heard *I do.*

His alarm went off at 8:15, and "Walking on Sunshine" by Katrina and the Waves played. He smacked the clock's Off button, flung the blankets aside, and lay there for a few more moments, staring at the ceiling.

"Are you going to lie there all day, or are you going to get up?" Andrea entered the room with a cup of coffee in her jeweled hand.

"Good morning, Ma!" Simon kissed her smooth cheek, took the coffee and sipped, then sat at the edge of the bed to put on his red-striped tube socks.

Andrea began to pick up his dirty clothes, which were strewn everywhere, and put them in the hamper. She straightened up his dresser, went into his closet to retrieve his tuxedo, and then laid it out beside him.

"You don't have to do that." He finished the coffee and left the mug on the floor in front of him.

"I know." Her lips quivered, and the waterworks started again.

"No more tears. It's a happy day." He got up and took the small woman in his arms. "I will always need you, just like I did in first grade when I fell off the monkey bars and chipped my tooth. Just like I did when I was eleven and got the chicken pox, and you stayed with me for days, playing Sorry, Life, and Mouse Trap with me to keep me busy. Who was it that was so sick with the flu, but still managed to make batch upon batch of chocolate chip cookies for my birthday party at school? I don't care how old I get, I will always need you."

"I am so proud of you. You've grown into such a fine man." She squeezed his shoulders.

"That's because I had you and Pop to guide me."

"You have room for one more?" said an older woman with graying black hair and a stern face, from the open bedroom door.

"Good morning, Nana." Simon pulled an old red Van Halen T-shirt over his head.

"That Georgia's a lucky gal." Rosa Lord beamed as she kissed her grandson's cheek.

"I'm the lucky one." He walked between the two women and stepped out the door.

The moment he left, Rosa's face turned dark, and she fixed an icy glare on her daughter-in-law.

"Now remember our deal. The minute Simon and Georgia say *I do*, you must leave this house at once, or I'll tell Calvin about the abortion."

"How could I forget? You've reminded me every day for the past fifteen years!" Andrea continued to tidy the room. "I can't just pack up and leave in one night." She began to make her son's bed.

"A deal is a deal. Our arrangement was that I'd keep my mouth shut so the boys could grow up in a nurturing, loving home. Which they have. As of today, Joshua's enrolled in his second semester at Clemson, and Simon is getting married in a few hours. The hourglass is empty, and you're out of excuses. I want you out by the time I wake up tomorrow! Are we clear?"

"Why do you hate me so much?" Andrea said, when Rosa was halfway into the hall.

"Because you're trash," Rosa spat, through clenched teeth, as she whirled back around. "You aren't worth the shit on the bottom of my shoe. You're not good enough for my son, you're not fit to carry the Lord name, and after tonight, the thorn in my side will finally be removed."

Rosa stormed away, leaving her daughter-in-law in tears.

Toni Corsini awoke early to take her little Maltese, Trixie, for a walk along the Aurora River like she had done every day for the past three years. Last night's brutal summer storm had left a mess of debris up and down the river line. As Trixie sniffed everything from the sand to the cattails that sprang up along the Aurora, Toni looked out at the river, took a deep breath, and tilted her head back so she could feel the sun on her face while the cool water cascaded over her bare feet.

Trixie began to bark at the river. Then the canine's bark turned into a ferocious growl as she began pawing at something in the water. When Toni tried to get a closer look at the object, Trixie took it between her jaws and ran. Toni chased after her for what seemed like an eternity.

Finally, out of breath, Toni stopped as she remembered the dog biscuits in her pocket. She retrieved the little sandwich bag full of colorful bones and shook it. Trixie released the object, dashed over to her master, sat and begged for a treat.

"That's Mommy's girl." She placed one in Trixie's mouth, and patted the dog on her furry little black head.

Toni dropped a couple more on the ground to keep Trixie busy while she went to inspect the piece of timber.

Upon further scrutiny, she saw the word *MARY* carved into it and realized that the long-sought-after *Mary Agnes*, which had sunk over a hundred fifty years ago, had been unearthed. Soon, every treasure hunter, diver, and hotshot would be down at the site to desecrate the graves of hundreds of souls, remove the Lord family's mythical missing jewels from within the ship's hull, and, upon doing so, discover the family's darkest secret.

However, Toni knew that what lay beneath the waters of the Aurora was meant to remain there. It should never be let out for any reason whatsoever. Toni possessed special powers—powers that she sometimes wished she never had—and she would use them to stop evil in its tracks.

The Corsini family began residing in Solomon's Wake soon after it had been founded, back in the 1700s. They were the descendants of an evil, shapeshifting witch named Luna, who had been put on trial for witchcraft and later hanged on the grounds of Windwood. It had taken decades to undo the damage she had inflicted on the family name, but she had eventually been forgotten. The Corsinis had since become the pinnacle of society—the saviors of a town that had been beset by witches, supernatural beings, and other forces of the unknown. The protectors of the town's secrets, sinister desires. And the indentured servants of the House of Lord.

Joshua and the other groomsmen had made lunch reservations at the pricy Corsini House. The two-story brick inn, which had been built in 1783, was the best place in town to get a home-cooked Italian meal. The guys would relax on the river deck with some adult beverages, and then retire to one of the many fine rooms that the inn offered.

During the Revolution, George Washington had spent the night there. And sometime later, President Reagan had lunched in the very room the groomsmen had reserved for the afternoon.

"To my brother, Simon, and the beautiful Georgia, who I shall treat as a sister ... I wish nothing but happiness and longevity for you both," Joshua raised his glass and spilled a little champagne on his hand.

Simon stood by his side and patted him on the back.

The room filled with cheers as the men burst out singing "Glory Days," while stuffing pizza, fries, and onion rings into their mouths. The dark room was filled with cigar and cigarette smoke, and smelled of beer and rum.

Simon leaned down. "Thanks for standing up for me," he whispered to Joshua, who was sitting at the end of the table, looking relaxed.

"No problem," Joshua said "But next time, could you go easy on the mousse? Your hair has so many spikes you look like a porcupine."

"Well, with that mullet of yours, you look like a wedding singer."

The two men laughed and hugged each other. "Love you, bro."

"If y'all don't stop carrying on like a bunch of frat boys," Toni said, "you're going to miss the wedding!"

"Don't be jealous 'cause I'm not marrying you." Simon grabbed her and waltzed between the tables and across the open floor.

"Simon Lord! You stop that now, before I tell your mama." Toni hit him with a green dish towel. "I'm going to close down early and be there as soon as I can." She chuckled and then fixed his collar. "I wouldn't miss it for the world. Tell Rosa I'll see her there." She swatted both men on their rear ends before heading back into the kitchen.

"Let's go get married," Simon said, as the crowd dispersed.

2

THE CALM BEFORE THE STORM

GIDEON BLAKE AND HIS FRIEND NOLA
O'Grady were taking their morning jog around Sumter
Square, in the heart of downtown Solomon's Wake. It had
been only a half-hour, but sweat was already pouring off
them, and they had to stop to drink some water. It was
about ten o'clock, and the thermometer registered nine-
ty-five degrees. Nola sat on a wrought iron bench in front
of the Fountain of Solomon Lord, namesake of the town's
founder, while Gideon did lunges next to her.

"Is there anything in this town not named after that
family?" He looked up at the bronze statue of Solomon.

"No. But you already knew that." Nola rubbed the cold
bottle of spring water across her forehead.

"Well, I would've thought that after a hundred years,
their influence would've waned." Gideon stuck his hands
into the fountain and splashed the water on his face.

"That was very unsanitary," Nola said.

"Oh, please! I've lived this long. It's gonna take more than a little dirty water to kill me."

"Do you regret coming back?" She sipped some of her water.

"Yes. If I hadn't come back, my daughter wouldn't be marrying into that family." Gideon began to stretch.

"But once upon a time, they were good enough for you, weren't they?" Nola stared at him with steel-gray eyes.

Standing six-feet tall, she had a tight, slim body, and her bobbed platinum hair, which did not move, was kept neat.

"Are we gonna start this again?" He continued stretching.

"Yes. Have you forgotten how you fell in love with that Lord woman? How when she found out that her husband was a werewolf, she got the whole town to come after us? We barely escaped with our lives, and then you brought us back to the very place where we let our brothers and sisters die."

"How could I forget? We fled the great famine that swept through our beloved Ireland, killing thousands. We had no choice but to seek a new life in America. We took jobs at the quarry and lived in shacks as small as those we were accustomed to in Millarney. The pack thrived and grew, and I met and fell in love with Iris. She brought out the best in me and helped me forget that a beast lived within me. Everything was perfect until the town turned against us. I can still see the townsfolk trudging down the path, with their torches raised and their pitchforks aimed at us. They trapped the pack in the quarry, collapsed it, and then flooded it. It wasn't Iris's fault—she accepted me for me. It was Marshall who found out what we were. He followed us back to the quarry and witnessed us changing firsthand." Gideon was still looking at Nola. "Iris came back to warn us about her father's plan, and she begged me to leave. I protested, but she and the other members of the clan made me go. I ran off and found you snared in a bear trap. After I freed you, I went back to see our brothers and sisters being driven farther and farther into the mine as the mighty Aurora rushed at them. Iris was furious at her father for what they had done, so she ran into the mine."

"How did Marshall know about us unless someone put it in his ear?" Nola said. "It was Iris! I know it was."

"You're wrong. I don't want to talk about Iris anymore. Let's just agree to disagree!" Gideon growled.

"Touchy, aren't we? Perhaps we should discuss the wedding." Nola jogged down the street, and Gideon caught up to her in no time.

"There will be no wedding," he said, as they continued down Windwood Way.

"What are you up to?"

"I heard from a reliable source that there's a book inside Windwood that can help me contact the spirit of Luna."

"Why would you want to do that? Don't we have bigger things to worry about, like making sure none of our brothers or sisters get out of that cave? After all, isn't that what we came back for?"

"Trust me. They're not getting out anytime soon."

"Besides, do you think they're gonna just let you walk into the mansion and take the book?"

"No. That's why I have to cause a distraction." He gave her a wry smile.

The quiet afternoon erupted with the sounds of exploding dynamite, and the two changed into two wolves—one charcoal black, the other silver. They darted off toward the echoes, and within minutes saw that the water that had once disguised the prison housing most of the pack had been drained, exposing the door to the cavern.

"Oh, my God, Gideon! What're we going to do?"

They stopped by the fence that surrounded the former quarry, and Nola was the first to change back to human form. The two stared down at the giant hole that had been created, and at the enormous crack in the cement, right over the prison. Then they hid behind a red, rusty Chevy truck so no one would see them naked.

"I'm gonna see if I can listen in," Gideon said.

At first, he heard nothing. But eventually he picked up the conversation the foreman was having with one of the workers.

"I don't care if it takes all night, two weeks, or two months!" the big-bellied, gray-haired man yelled over the sound of the equipment in the background. "Now that the water's gone, we need to fill the hole in. Mister Lord wants it done ASAP so we can begin laying the groundwork for the mall. If we finish on time, there'll be a bonus."

The worker, who had blond hair and blue eyes, and was no more than twenty-five, saluted the foreman and went back to work.

"Well, they're not going to open the cavern." Gideon heaved out a long sigh and leaned back against the truck.

"There's still a crack in the ground, Gideon, and they can still get out."

"For years they said the polar ice caps were melting, and eventually the earth would flood and we would die. But we haven't. Hell, we even survived Jimmy Carter. So I think it's safe to say none of them got out."

"Gideon, this is not a joke. I'm scared."

When he saw the tears in her eyes, he knew she was serious.

"There has to be something we can do," Nola said.

"I'm not gonna let anything happen to you." He wrapped his strong arms around her and kissed the top of her head.

"All right, already. You're making a scene." She pushed him off.

"If it'll make you sleep better, I can go see Toni Corsini and have her place a seal on the door to lock them in."

"You surprise me sometimes, you big lug." Nola pecked him on the lips, which turned into a passionate kiss, until she smacked him. "Never take advantage of a woman when she's vulnerable."

She turned back into the silver wolf and dashed into the woods.

"That's not fair." He changed and gave chase. Neither was aware of the bigger wolf that had escaped from the hole blown open by the blast.

All along the Aurora, young couples, children, elderly, and everyone in between, crammed the shores of the river to escape the heat that gripped the entire country. Up and down the river, folks were enjoying swimming, tubing, and sunbathing.

A young girl, asleep on the beach, with Walkman headphones on her ears, awoke to her hippy boyfriend shaking his long brown hair out all over her back.

"What the hell's wrong with you, Andre? I was in the middle of Aha's new song." She pushed him away.

"There's plenty of time to hear your song later. You'll never believe what I found under the water," he whispered, then reached into the girl's purse to pull out a Marlboro, and lit it.

"I don't know—a snork?" She threw her arms up, then took a drag for herself.

"No, Kara. You're a smart-ass. I don't know why I even bother. You've got a cocky response for everything I say."

She looked at all the tattoos Andre had up and down his arms, and at the big, ugly skull on his back.

"Relax. It was a joke," she said, when he started off toward the car.

He smiled and ran back. "If you weren't so damn hot and great in the sack, I would've gotten rid of you like yesterday."

Kara glared at him.

"Relax. It was just a joke."

She flipped him the bird.

"Will you tell me what you found down there?" She handed Andre a bottle of baby oil to rub on her back.

"Do you remember back in Missus Blackmore's history class, when she told us about a clipper that sank in 1853, during a freak hurricane?"

"Oh, God, that feels so good. Don't stop," she said as Andre rubbed her shoulders.

"C'mon, Kar, I'm serious."

"Yes, I remember. Why?"

"I found it about halfway downstream, in the deepest part of the Aurora, embedded in the riverbed. All sorts of fishing lines and nets were wrapped around it. And if I'm not mistaken, there were skeletons trapped in the hull."

Kara turned around and kissed him. "People have been looking for that wreck for years, and never found it!" she said so loud people turned to look. "You swim out there and find it on the first try. I don't buy it." She grabbed a can of Tab from the cooler.

"It is the *Mary Agnes*. I saw it with my own eyes. That massive storm we had the other night must've stirred the riverbed enough to dislodge the vessel. And that, my beautiful doubter, is why I was able to find it." He pecked her cheek.

"This is the break we've been looking for to blow this town. When I was dating Joshua Lord, he told me that one of his ancestor's wives was on board when the ship went down. She perished with the crew, and all her rubies, emeralds, and diamonds were lost." Kara's violet eyes lit up like polished marble at the thought of getting her hands on the loot.

"My buddy Sammy takes his boat to Jamaica for the summer and carts people out to the reefs to snorkel. I'll ask if we can borrow the oxygen tanks and all the other crap we need. We'll come back tonight, dive down to the wreck and take anything we can get our hands on."

"I love it when you go all James Bond on me." She kissed him again, knocked him over and straddled him, with her big bosom in his face.

"Get a room!" a father of three yelled from across the way.

"Why don't we?" Kara said.

They grabbed their towels and cooler, and took off toward Andre's beat-up green Gremlin.

"Andrea, the band and caterers are here." Calvin entered the room, looking suave in his black tuxedo.

His silver hair and blue eyes complemented the ensemble.

"Talk to Sutton," Andrea replied. "He knows exactly what I want done."

Calvin had to pick his tongue up off the floor as his wife came back into the bedroom.

"You look absolutely ravishing."

Andrea wore a pale green gown, with a simple diamond necklace and matching earrings. Her ash blonde hair was held together in a figure-eight bun, instead of wild and free like she preferred.

"I've got something for you." Calvin reached into his tuxedo pocket to pull out a little box, and gave it to her.

"What's this?"

Andrea gasped after she opened it and found her wedding ring, inset with the birthstones of Simon, Joshua, and even her little girl, Melanie, who had died at the tender age of five.

"Where did you find it?" she said.

"I had Sutton steal it when you were in the shower."

"All this time, I thought I had lost it. Thank you, Cal!" She gave him a peck on the lips.

He then pulled her into a passionate kiss.

"I love you, Missus L."

Andrea buried her face in his chest to keep him from seeing her tears.

How could she leave now?

Georgia Blake stared around the large four-bedroom colonial house she shared with her father, Gideon, and her sister Virginia, lovingly referred to as *Ginny*. It was the house they grew up in. The house where their mother, Tara, had lived and died. And the house where Georgia first changed. In just a few short hours, she would leave this house for the last time as Georgia Blake.

"Is there anything I can do to change your mind? Georgia, he's not right for you." Gideon entered the long, narrow kitchen with the rust-colored rug with lime-green squares.

"Daddy, how many times do we have to go over this? I love him, and that's it." She stood at the sink, looking out the window, at the Koi pond in the backyard.

"What's this, Daddy, the Spanish Inquisition?" Ginny said. "Leave her alone. The wedding's today. If you wanted to change her mind, you should've done it weeks ago." She kissed him on the forehead.

"Are you just getting in?" Gideon said, after he saw the Cindy Lauper getup Ginny had on.

"I had to work a double. Lanny didn't show up again. I'm not complaining, though. I made a killing at the bar." She opened the refrigerator to grab the Five Alive from the door, then reached for a glass out of the cabinet near the sink.

"I still don't like you working downtown, all hours." He kept his gaze on the paper.

"Daddy, I'm fine." She put the glass in the sink. "Enough about me. It's Georgia's day. What time are the girls getting here?"

"About a half-hour," Georgia said.

"We better start getting you dressed." Ginny took her by the hand and led her upstairs.

Gideon sat at the table, reading the paper, bouncing his left knee, when he heard the doorbell, followed by feet scampering down the stairs, along with giggles, as the bridesmaids showed up.

"You okay?" Ginny poked her head into the kitchen when she noticed his frown.

"Yeah. I was just thinking about your mother and wishing she was here."

"She is, Daddy. She is." Ginny blew him a kiss, then ran upstairs to attend her sister.

He went up the stairs and watched the girls from the open bedroom door, laughing and singing "Girls Just Want to Have Fun," into their brushes while they did Georgia's hair and nails. She looked happy for the first time in years.

Then he looked at Ginny, who jumped up onto the bed, taking the lead. Her auburn hair was wild, and her blue eyes sparkled as she really got into the song.

"Daddy, hurry up and get ready. We only have an hour," Georgia said, through the open door, with half her copper locks in curlers, and the other half ready for the hot-pink curling iron.

"All right, all right, I'm going." Gideon shook his head and snickered as he went into his bedroom.

Once Georgia's bedroom door closed, he raced down the stairs and out the front door.

3

THE EYES OF THE BEAST

TONI HAD SO MUCH TO DO BEFORE THE
wedding. She did not have the time to meet with him, but
because Gideon was a council member, she had no choice.

As Toni approached Aurora Point Cemetery, she could
see the massive Lord mausoleum towering above everything else. She parked her Dodge Caravan outside, by
the gate next to the silver Audi she assumed belonged to
Gideon.

A woodpecker was doing some damage to a magnolia tree, and toward the back of the cemetery, someone
was busy mowing the lawn while another did the weed
whacking. Toni walked through the gate, down a long
path, past all the older graves, to a lone grave underneath
a flowering dogwood.

"Hello, darling." She crouched down to stare at the
tombstone of her husband, Gianni. "I know it's been a

while since I've come to see you. Things have been so busy at the inn, I'm lucky if I'm able to sit down." She removed the dead the flowers she had brought the last time.

"I don't mean to intrude, but can we move this along?" Gideon walked up behind her.

"I'll be back as soon as Mister Grouchy Pants and I are done."

"We have a problem." Gideon strode through the cemetery.

"Nice to see you, too, Gideon." She followed him through row upon row of headstones. "If your problem is at the quarry, why are we in the cemetery?"

"The quarry and the cemetery border each other. It was a lot easier this way, so we're not seen." He contin-ued to move without looking at her.

"Well, now that you have me here, you gonna tell me what this is about?"

They came up to a cut-open fence.
"The lake has been emptied, and the quarry uncov-ered," Gideon said.

He could feel the glare of Toni's dark brown eyes cutting into his back, and the anger radiating from her like a funeral pyre, as they approached the empty lake.

"That was the one job you had, and you can't even do that," she said. "I stuck my neck out to get you allowed back into Solomon's Wake, and you blow it. All you had to do was guard that hole in the ground."

She was getting so angry the birds began to stir and the wind kicked up.

"Toni, calm yourself before you bust a gut. It's only cracked. Not open. If you put one of your spells on it, everything will stay as it is and no one needs to know."

"Why should I go out of my way for you again?"

"Because we're all in danger if one of those rabid creatures gets out. The werewolves were almost wiped out by this virus when it first appeared. Only a vampire bite could cure it, and now they've all gone extinct. And if any of you witches are bitten, you lose all your powers. We both know what will happen if the Monarchs find out we failed to keep them in."

"I will do it," Toni said, "because as a member of The Order, I took an oath to protect this town. However, it will cost you. And one day, I expect to be paid back. When I put the seal on, only a Corsini witch can open it."

She spouted off some Latin words, and the crack began to seal. In a matter of seconds, it disappeared.

Gideon was so excited he kissed her on the cheek and smacked her on the rear.

"I owe you big time."

"Yes, you do. Now let's get to the wedding before your daughter gets married without you."

"I'll see you there in a few minutes." Gideon waved to Toni as she pulled out of the cemetery.

He was so busy paying attention to everything around him that he dropped his keys when trying to unlock the car. When he bent down to pick them up, he saw the green eyes of a wolf staring through the trees. It pounced on him, knocking Gideon to the ground, and climbed on top of him. The wolf glared at him with tortured pale green eyes, and sniffed him like he was a clean towel from the dryer. Then it licked him across the face. Gideon froze underneath the beast, unable to find his voice. He looked into those sad eyes and knew his son Channing was free.

"Hello, Pop. Did you miss me?" he said, in a gruff voice.

Gideon reached for a rock to the side, and the wolf jumped off and sprinted into the woods.

Gideon stared after it for a few moments.

"God help us all." He got in the car and sped off.

A tiny but beautiful chapel on the outskirts of town had been chosen for the nuptials. The same chapel Gideon and his wife, Tara, had been married in years before. To make the event complete, Georgia had chosen to wear the same dress her mother had.

By seven o'clock, everyone was getting ready at the chapel. And at seven-thirty, the place was packed. Georgia was so jittery she had trouble getting into her dress and putting on her veil. Ginny had to do it for her.

The candles by the pews were all lit. The floral arrangements at the altar were made of orchids, hyacinths, and lilies. The chandelier was draped in pearls that stretched across every corner of the ceiling to give it a romantic ambiance. A red carpet was laid as a runway. The organ music began, and the bridesmaids came out from the back, followed by Ginny, then Georgia, escorted by Gideon.

The marriage vows were spoken with such love there wasn't a dry eye in the house. At long last, they were pronounced man and wife.

Back at Windwood, the ballroom was prepared for the reception, including the band, waiters, and cooks. It was to be the perfect evening.

As the festivities began, Andrea was mortified when her sister in-law, Helena who had recently come home after being banished by her father Theodore, thanks to a scandal involving a prominent South Carolina senator, entered the room wearing the same sequined gown. Helena took a bottle of champagne from the bar and sauntered across the room as Georgia and Gideon took to the dance floor.

"How dare you wear my dress?" Andrea caught Helena by the arm. "For Christ's sake, you even copied my hairdo."

"What's the matter? You jealous it looks better on me?" Andrea attacked Helena and wrestled her to the ground. Round and round they went, kicking and biting, pulling hair. And then Helena got the upper hand and put a death grip on Andrea's throat.

Finally, Calvin thrust through the mob that had gathered around the women, to pull them apart. The two ladies continued to shout at each other.

"What's everyone gawking at?" Calvin gripped them by the arms and dragged them across the room, into his office. "What the hell is wrong with you two?" He slammed his office doors shut. "Have you gone mad? It's Simon's wedding day. Why would you carry on like animals in front of the most prominent people in the country? I'd expect this from you, Helena. But not my wife. Things were fine until you came back, Sister. After the reception, I want you gone from here for good." He turned his back to her.

Helena picked up a paperweight from his desk and threw it at her brother. He moved just before it hit him in the back of the head, and it smashed into the portrait of Rosa that hung above his desk.

She ran out of the room in tears, right past her mother, who had been talking with Helena's great-great-aunt Eugenie, who seemed to be fading in and out of consciousness.

"Don't Calvin and Andrea make a nice couple?" Aunt Eugenie said, before falling back asleep.

One of the white flowers she wore in her long hair had fallen off, and she had begun to snore. Rosa wrapped a shawl around her and got up from the table to follow Helena.

"In my younger years, they used to tell me I looked like Mae West." Aunt Eugenie grabbed Rosa's hand. "Nowadays, I'd say it's more like Grandma Clammpet." She chuckled, then dozed again.

Rosa caught up with her daughter by the old birch tree Helena loved to climb as a girl.

"Honey, what happened?" Rosa said, from behind her, as she brushed Helena's chestnut hair out of her face.

"It wasn't me! It was Andrea. Calvin's making me leave. What kind of man puts his own sister out? I don't care. I'm leaving and not coming back." Helena wailed as she ran back toward the house.

"Damn you, Andrea." Rosa walked through the miles and miles of cars, back to the party, and noticed the full moon.

For years, Rosa had protected Simon from the curse he had no way of controlling. When he was thirteen, Rosa knew he was a werewolf when she found him naked in the stable. The horses were mutilated, and Simon was bloody. When he was eighteen, she was called up to the summer camp, where he had been a counselor, after he was found naked once again, in the chicken coop. The chickens were all dead.

Rosa and Calvin had a secret room in the basement, which consisted of a silver cage strong enough to hold him when he changed. No one else knew it was there.

A yellow Porsche backfired right next to her and scared the bejesus out of her. As she entered the house, she could still hear ringing in her ears.

Simon and Georgia finished their dance when Simon gripped her hand like a vise, then collapsed, writhing in pain.

"It's starting! You must get me to the secret room and into the cage I told you about, before it's too late."

People began to stop and stare. Simon kept on smiling as Georgia scooped him up.

"No need to be alarmed!" Georgia shouted. "It seems my husband has had a little too much to drink. So please continue to enjoy the party."

She looked out the window. A full moon glimmered in the dark sky.

It took all her strength to drag Simon downstairs. A second more, and the beast would have been unstoppable.

She couldn't get him in the cage, but was at least able to lock him in the room. The beast pounded and snarled as he tried to batter down the door. Georgia hurried back upstairs, dropping the key in her haste.

Helena had followed her, and hid under the stairs until Georgia was upstairs. She took the key and banged on the door.

"Simon, you all right in there?" She continued to pound on the door.

Once Rosa saw Georgia come out from the basement, she crept down the stairs and watched in horror as the woman she perceived to be Andrea was about to learn her darkest secret. Just as Helena unlocked the door, Rosa shoved her in and slammed the door.

A few moments later, the most horrifying scream came from within the room. Calvin and Gideon raced downstairs and kicked open the door. The beast pushed past them, and Calvin managed to fire two shots at it, but missed. He then rushed in for Helena.

When she came out, her hair had turned stark white. She was delirious and trembling, and would remain so for the rest of her life.

"What happened, Mama?" Calvin said to Rosa. "What happened!"

When she didn't respond, Calvin shook her.

Rosa took one look at Helena and screamed, "No!!!!!"

4

FULL MOON MADNESS

ANDREA WEPT QUIETLY AS SHE SAT IN THE library, which was silent and far from prying eyes—the one place the mother of the groom could collect herself. As she stared out the window, looking over the grounds, the door opened and Gideon came in and sat at the long cherry desk.

He picked up the receiver. "Nola, I'm in the library. I wasn't able to locate the book, nor was I able to stop the wedding." He slammed the receiver down.

"Why would you want to stop the wedding?" Andrea came out from behind a large bookcase and ran for the door.

"I wouldn't do that if I were you." Gideon gripped her arm.

"Let go before I scream." Andrea winced as she tried to wriggle out of his grip.

"Scream all you want! There are hundreds of people down there, and loud music. No one will hear you."

They heard what sounded like an animal howling nearby. The sound of splintering wood and shattered glass filled the library. Both stood still.

They heard it again, from the back of the room.

Gideon pulled out his revolver with silver bullets, and crept toward the commotion. On the floor was glass and bits of wood.

Andrea moved closer to get a better look, when she felt the warmth of its breath on her neck. She turned and shrieked. Before her stood a giant silver and white wolf snarling as it eyed its prey. The beast growled and swatted her. Its fangs were bared, and drool dripped down the sides of the monster's mouth.

Again, she screamed as she backed away, but the animal continued to pursue her. Gideon fired again but missed, and put a hole in the wall. Before he could manage another shot, the wolf pounced, and the gun dropped to the floor.

The creature stopped as if it recognized its victim, and Andrea picked up the gun and fired into its back. The wolf arched and yelped before collapsing on top of Gideon. Andrea watched in disgust as the beast transformed into a woman.

"What the hell's going on?" Andrea said.

"Take a good look at dear, sweet Aunt Eugenie." Gideon shoved the old woman off him.

Andrea stared down at the wrinkled, naked woman lying on the hardwood floor.

"You just shot an old lady."

Andrea looked at Gideon as if she had taken the bullet.

"This can't be." With her hand to her mouth, Andrea stumbled back into the desk.

"Oh, but it is. All the answers to your questions are right here in black and white." He held up a large daybook. "For centuries, this family has lived under a curse. A curse that transforms every first-born child, whether man or woman, into bloodthirsty wolves. Just look at poor Aunt Eugenie."

"That's my husband's dossier."

Andrea tried to catch her breath. She felt like she had been slapped in the face.

"Read the file and then talk to your husband. Let's just say, there's more than one wolf on the loose tonight. By morning, we'll see if you still look at your son with the same love and affection." Gideon left her alone with the file.

A few seconds later, he turned into a beautiful, leggy blonde.

"That was almost too easy." She waltzed down the hall.

A small fishing boat cut through the murky river at about twelve knots, with only a few dim deck lights ablaze. At exactly ten o'clock in the evening, they had returned with Sammy, who offered his services for a cut of their profit. The whole way to the wreck site, Sammy went over all the safety precautions, how to use the gear, and how much air they had left in the tanks.

"You've got about a half-hour of air," he said. "Use it wisely."

Kara and Andre suited up, and were in the water in seconds. Beneath the surface, they saw only darkness, even with the flashlight on.

Out of the shadows, the ship's silhouette emerged, broken and busted, skeletal, except for the hull. For some reason it remained intact.

Kara squeezed Andre's hand in excitement as they swam toward the wreck. They had to be careful as they headed inside the hull. One wrong move could snag them on one of the fishing lines, and it would be curtains.

Andre went first, shining the light through the hole to find skeletons with their hands still locked on doors, beds, and tables. Kara got scared and tried to swim away, but Andre grabbed her arm and calmed her enough to continue.

The deeper into the ship they went, the more amazed the duo became. All sorts of silver and gold goblets, plates, and candelabras littered the boat floor. Andre dove down and gathered as many gold pieces as he could, and stuffed them into a bag. Kara continued to monitor the oxygen tank while Andre stuffed her bag, too, when she saw an object sparkle from under a broken ladder. She swam down into the hold, her mind racing with hopes of it being the lost jewels they came for. Instead, she came upon the horrific remains of a body. A stake had been driven through its heart, and shoved through its mouth was a silver dagger with all sorts of gems embedded in the handle.

Kara pulled the dagger out and noticed an inscription on the handle. Before she could figure out what it said, Andre startled her and she dropped it through a hole in the floor. She tried to reach for it, but Andre pointed up toward the surface to signal time was up.

"How'd we do?" Sammy reached for Kara's hand and pulled her back on deck.

"That's okay, Sammy. I don't need any help," Andre quipped, as he climbed up the ladder.

"We would've had a lot more if Andre hadn't made me drop that dagger. You should've seen this thing, Sammy. It had to be pure silver, with an ivory handle embedded with emeralds and sapphires." She sat on a hatch to take off her flippers.

"Bite me, Kara! Next time, I'll let you suffocate." Andre dove back into the water.

Without Kara, the dive would take less time, so he calculated that he had enough oxygen to get down and back. With any luck, he'd get his hands on the dagger and a few other goodies.

As Andre neared the cargo hold, he noticed that the body had disappeared. Panicked, he began to swim around in circles. Once he reached the outside wall of the ship, he got snared in the fishing lines. As he feverishly worked to free himself, he looked up and screamed. The skeleton locked eyes on him, and Andre was compelled to stand still. By the time he saw the fangs, it was too late.

"Where the hell is he? It's been over twenty minutes." Kara peered over the railing, into the water.

Sammy came up behind her to shine the flashlight into the bleak river just as Andre's cracked scuba mask floated to the surface.

"We're getting the hell out of here," he said to Kara, who fell into his arms. "Stay put. I'm going to raise the anchor and get us out of here after I radio River Patrol."

"Don't leave me!" Kara shrieked.

"I'll be back in a flash. I promise it'll only take a minute."

Inside the bridge, Sammy tried to radio for help, but there was no signal. When he tried the engine, it was dead.

"I swear to Christ, if that generator's broken again, someone's ass is mine." Sammy hurried down into the engine room, only to find the engines in perfect working order. "What the fuck!"

He turned to face what looked like a deformed woman with scraggly hair, rotted flesh and small brown eyes. As with Andre, Sammy never saw it coming.

"Sam, answer me. I'm scared. Please, say something. Anything, Sammy."

Kara grabbed a harpoon that hung on the wall by the bridge, and inched around the boat, the harpoon pointed forward. When she made it back to starboard, she shrieked at the sight of a beautiful woman with long raven hair, mysterious eyes, and almost translucent skin, standing naked by the bow.

"Please don't be frightened. I won't harm you. I'm so very cold. Could I trouble you for a blanket? Sammy fished me from the water. A group of friends and I were tubing. Somehow we were separated, and the next thing I knew, I woke up on this boat. Sammy's supposed to get me some clothes."

Kara continued to scrutinize the buxom beauty. Fixated by her eyes, Kara handed the woman a wool blanket from under one of the benches, and she pulled Kara closer.

"This won't hurt a bit."

Joshua wanted to get away from the chaos, but he was still in the partying mood. So he invited some of his closest friends back to the Corsini House to continue the reception. Toni was more than willing to open up the place for one of her favorite clients.

"Don't think I'm gonna do this for y'all every day," she said. "It just so happens I have a fondness for you and your brother." She opened the door and turned on the lights.

"We appreciate it," Joshua said. "Don't we, guys?"

The room filled with slurs and drunken jabber.

Soon the jukebox was playing, the darts were flying, and the girls were dancing. And Toni was making a fortune. Not bad for less than a half-night's work. She normally made less than this on Mondays. A couple hundred more dollars, and she could finally get that industrial dishwasher she wanted for the restaurant.

"Hey, Toni, can we get some more champagne?" said some twenty-something-year-old man with red hair, freckles, and a cigarette hanging out his mouth.

"Gotta check the basement. If I have it, it's going to cost you seven-fifty a bottle."

"Bring me four." Joshua watched the Carolina Panthers on the 20-inch screen above the bar.

Toni left the bar through a small side door that led to the Corsini House's large kitchen, and from there opened another door at the back of the room, down a narrow flight of stairs to a damp and dimly lit basement that ran the entire length of the inn.

She needed to do some spring cleaning. There were boxes of old menus, crates of broken and mismatched plates, along with some glasses that she hadn't used since 1969. Near the back of the cellar were some tables and chairs that her grandfather had made with his bare hands. After the remodel, there was no room for them.

Somewhere amid all the clutter, she found the crate of champagne, and there were exactly four bottles left. Toni lifted it up and started upstairs, when she realized she wasn't alone.

"Who's there?" She put the crate down on top of a large plastic column they used during Halloween.

No one answered, but she could see the shadowy figure under the window.

"Don't be frightened, child. Show yourself."

Out of the darkness came the naked body of the woman from the boat. She had her fangs bared and was about to attack Toni, but she lifted her hand and froze the vampire in its tracks.

"What are you?" the vampire said, still unable to move.

"Someone who can help you. Meet me upstairs in the kitchen. I have a small party upstairs that I must tend to."

"What did you do, Toni? Go to Rome to find it?" Joshua moved down the stairs.

She motioned the young girl to hide behind an old refrigerator.

"Ha-ha. Just make yourself useful and carry this upstairs." She shoved the crate at him.

"I love it when you get assertive." He took the crate and charged upstairs.

"That's why you're still single, 'cause you're so fresh." Toni chased after him. "No Southern belle wants to be talked to like that."

A few hours later, the party finally wound down, leaving a mess behind. Bottles and glasses scattered all over. Cigarette butts littered the floor, and plates with half-eaten food lay on the tables. It was already after two. At this rate, she'd be lucky if she got to bed by five.

"I didn't mean to scare you earlier." The vampire came out from the cellar.

"I'm sorry. I forgot you were down there. Honey, I don't scare easy," Toni loaded some of the glasses in the dishwasher. "Why'd you come here?"

"I don't know. I just felt like I should."

Toni stared at her. "You're not gonna get anywhere in your birthday suit. Go up the stairs off the pantry. The first door at the top of the stairs is my granddaughter Carla's room. Something of hers is bound to fit you." She tied her jet-black hair back before grabbing the trash to take it out back to the dumpsters.

"Why are you helping me?" the vampire said.

"Just get dressed. I'll fill you in on everything."

When she stepped outside, the air was cool on her face, and the scent of sweet flowering tobacco filled her senses. Along the paved walkway around back, she admired her beautiful flower garden. Her hydrangea bushes did exceptionally well this season.

"Damn it! Who left the gate open? Every stinking stray animal in the neighborhood's gonna be nosing in the trash." Toni yanked back the other gate and screamed so loud the light next door came on. "For the love of Pete, Josh, you scared the hell out of me." She held her chest. "What are you still doing here?"

"I was looking for my car. Thought I left it in the garage."

"All right, big fella. Let's go get some coffee." She wrapped her thin arms around his broad shoulders, and led him back to the inn. "How much did you drink tonight?"

A few cups of coffee and a Western omelet later, Joshua finally began to sober up. As Toni cleaned up the grill and put the glasses from the dishwasher away, Joshua yammered on about the wedding and school.

"I don't know. I was thinking about trying to get into Brown or Yale, or maybe study abroad. I just want to get out of this dead-end town." He got up and took the rest of the coffee.

"You don't have to make that kind of decision tonight," Toni wiped down the counter.

"I found this in the closet. It fits perfectly." The vampire entered the room. "Julian?" Her eyes lit up like the sky on the Fourth of July.

"No, my name is Joshua. Joshua Lord. However, I can be Julian—or anyone else, for that matter—if you like." He stumbled into the chair, and then the table, sending the silverware and an unlucky mug to the floor. "Sorry. I'll get that."

He couldn't take his eyes off the woman standing in the doorway, dressed in tight stonewashed jeans and a pastel-blue sleeveless shirt, with feathered hair.

He was in danger. Toni had to get him out of there.

5

THE PATH OF FATE

A VISION OF A DIFFERENT TIME BEGAN TO replay in the recesses of his mind. Joshua tried to wipe it out of his psyche, but the harder he tried, the more the memory took hold. He saw himself in button boots and a formal black frock coat with silk-faced lapels, on a sinking clipper in the midst of a violent storm.

"Josh, could you do me a favor?" Toni said. "Can you go into the restaurant and check the salt-and-pepper shakers for me? I asked Jesse to do it, but everything goes in one ear and out the other with him."

"Sure. But I expect to see you when I get back." He flashed a smile, then cocked his finger at the woman before vanishing through the swinging doors.

"Okay, Martha." Toni motioned her to sit.

"How do you know my name? Why are you helping me?" The vampire sat in the seat vacated by Joshua.

"I know everything about you and your family. As for helping you, I really didn't have a choice." Toni looked at Martha, who sat expressionless, with her hands in her lap.

"Do you want me to fill the sugar, too?" Joshua called from the other room.

"That would be a great help," Toni hollered back.

"What do you mean, you don't have a choice?" Martha rested her elbows on the table, her pale skin lustrous under the overhead kitchen lights.

"My ancestor Luna was the cause of your curse. When she spoke those words she nearly damned my family to death, as the town hunted us all down. In a last ditch effort, the patriarch of our family at the time, Umberto, used his magic to save Solomon Lord's nephew, Richard, who was dying from tuberculosis. Had Richard died, the Lord line would have died with him. Even though Solomon saw this miracle with his own eyes, it was not enough for him. The only way he would let my family live was if he signed a letter stating that the Corsinis would help the Lord family in perpetuity."

Toni got up from the chair and peeked out at Joshua through the swinging door to find him passed out at the table, his head resting on the back of the chair.

"Then you know all about my family's cursed blood-line, and the secrets that have troubled us for years?" Martha relaxed a little.

"Yes. And a great deal more. You were one of the biggest secrets I and the other members of The Order were sworn to protect." Toni sat back down and poured herself a cup of coffee from the pot that sat on a warmer in front of her.

"The Order? What's that?" Martha leaned back against the table.

"We are an ancient organization of supernatural beings that has existed since the days of Atlantis. Each panel of three is ruled by the monarch, who is always a vampire—or was, until they were almost obliterated by a virus that also claimed hundreds of werewolves, to the point of extinction."

"So that means I am one of the last?" Martha said, wide-eyed as she stared at Toni, who got up to heat her mug in the microwave. "How can a virus kill what is already dead?"

"Vampire blood could cure the virus, but it also made the vampires sterile. Once the werewolves learned this, they waged war on the vampires until those who survived what became known as the Crimson Rising went underground, and the monarchs that survived have been in hibernation state ever since. The werewolves have pretty much been decimated, but you're still not safe. There are Weres out there who will want your blood to save their kind. I am putting myself in danger by helping you, but I believe I can stop your vampirism by making you human." Toni got up to fetch her coffee.

"I suppose you'll tell me next that women can vote and blacks are free?" Martha chuckled.

"Actually, we can, and they are." Toni sat back down and sipped from a mug that had *World's Greatest Grand Mom* on it.

Martha seemed happy to hear of such progress in a country that had barely been born when she was a girl.

"If I am human, they won't need my blood." A smile washed across her creamy complexion at the thought of living again, being able to love, and most of all, reuniting with her beloved Julian.

"I'm more than willing to help you, but you must be completely honest with me. What is your connection with Joshua? It's obvious you've met before. It was written all over your face."

Martha got up from the table to look through the swinging door, at Joshua, who was still passed out at one of the tables in the dining room. This man had the same impish smile, the same soft blue eyes, and the same birthmark on his cheek, only noticeable to those who knew it was there. Could it be that after a hundred thirty years, they had finally found each other again?

"My father could not destroy me, nor could my cousin Richard. While I slept in my coffin, they decided to bury me in hopes that it would be forever. A severe storm in 1853 flooded the town, forcing coffins out of the ground. It destroyed crops, houses, and anything in its path. I was freed from my prison, and set eyes for the first time on my Julian. I knew that someday fate would bring us back to each other."

"I am going to stop you there. That man is not Julian, and never can be. If Joshua were to remember anything, it would expose both of us to danger, and it could very well tip the Weres off as well."

"What am I supposed to do? I can't just forget him." Martha began to cry, and droplets of blood trickled down her cheek.

"Then he must forget you. I will hypnotize him and make him forget, ensuring both our safety. Take this pill and get into your coffin. By the next moon, your new life will begin." Toni reached into her pocket and gave her a green pill. "We need a new name to go with your fresh look. No one can know you were once Martha Lord." She looked around the room, and her gaze fell on the Donatella almond cookies on the table. "We'll call you, Donna."

Toni reached for a cookie and took a bite out of it.

Andrea sat in the library and began to skim through the pages of the family annals. A lifetime of pain and suffering sprang to life. It all began in the late 18th century, when Prince William died after falling from his horse and hitting his head. He was the only child of the exiled Grand Duke and Duchess of Marin, Solomon and Flora Lord. The Grand Duchess was so devastated she turned to the one woman who could help her—the witch Luna, who, lived in the woods by the swamp.

The pale light from desk lamp was too weak for Andrea's eyes so she grabbed the journal to take it back to Calvin's office to get a better look at it, when out fell a hand-painted parchment of a repulsive woman with long jet-black hair, a white stripe down the left side of her head, dark eyes, olive skin, a lazy eye, and snaggletooth which protruded from her bottom lip. The stereotypical witch.

"Andrea," a faraway voice called.

"Who's there?"

"Come to the attic. Follow my voice, Andrea. Follow my voice."

Andrea left the book on the desk and stuck the gun under her dress. She rushed out to the foyer, straight past Sutton, who was busy directing the servants with the cleanup. Charlene, the youngest of the staff, and her sister Darcy, were in charge of the kitchen. Tucker and Rafe, lovers from Atlanta, had the grounds, and Miss Mabel Carter and her granddaughter Bonnie Sue had the upstairs, leaving the ground floor to Sutton.

"Missus Lord, can I get you anything?" Sutton called.

She ignored him and continued to climb the stairs.

"Everyone has their orders," Sutton said. "Let's try to have this place in order by the time Mister Lord returns."

The crowd dispersed.

"Charlene, fix your skirt. And Tucker, no champagne until the work's done."

Tucker sighed and put the glass down. Sutton shook his head.

Andrea found her way up to the attic. She could smell the musty odor of years gone by as she reached blindly for the light switch, whose location was committed to memory. The light shone brightly, reflecting off a million floating dust particles. Andrea waved her hands frantically in front of her face. She tried to take in the various boxes and unused furniture. She moved from the stairwell, and an unusual cold surrounded her as she proceeded to the center of the room.

The woman's voice called out again. *"Lift the sheet from the mirror."*

Andrea raced through the mazes of forgotten treasures and didn't find a mirror until she reached the end of the room. Nestled against the wall was an oblong mirror, covered by a white sheet.

"I've never seen this before." She yanked the sheet off.

The mirror began to swirl, and an image emerged.

"Take a good look at the image, Missus Lord. Gaze at the figure before you and see what happens to those doomed to carry the Lord name."

Andrea fixed her eyes on Simon writhing on the ground. His back was arched, and he was screaming in agony.

"What's wrong with my son?" she shrieked at the mirror.

"Just watch, Missus Lord."

As Andrea turned her attention back to the mirror, a large werewolf howled and beat at its chest. He was so close and lifelike she could feel his breath on her face, and she put her hands up to shield her face.

"Behold your loving Simon."

The voice screeched with laughter as Andrea crumpled to the floor.

6

BROKEN

WHEN CALVIN RETURNED FROM THE HOS-
pital, the house was silent except for a servant mulling
about every now and then. He sat in one of the folding
chairs, looking around at all the damage that had been
done. Then he bent down to pick up a baby-blue carna-
tion from the floor. He sniffed the flower and leaned back
into the chair when he felt a hand on his shoulders.

"Can I get you anything, sir?" Sutton said, his hand
still on Calvin's shoulder.

"How about a magic wand to make this day disappear? This was supposed to be a happy occasion, yet
all we managed to do was raise suspicion on our family
again. Sutton, I gotta wonder sometimes if it's all worth it.
I think I would give up the cars, the money, the house—
all of it—if we could live like everyone else."

Sutton put the clipboard down and began to massage Calvin's shoulders.

"That feels wonderful." Calvin closed his eyes as Sutton worked his magic. "Where did you learn to do that?"

"When I worked in the infirmary during Nam, a lot of fellas needed their muscles worked out. How are Miss Rosa and Miss Helena?"

"Mama's locked herself in her room. My sister's gone certifiably mad. And my boys are who knows where. What do you say we hop on the Lord jet and fly to Maui and get away from this lunacy?" Calvin said, his eyes still closed.

"I'd follow you anywhere, sir." Sutton held on to his boss a little longer than intended.

He released his grip and picked the clipboard back up.

"I can't go anywhere right now, though. This mess isn't going to clean itself up." He began to head back towards the central hall. "You might want to check on Missus Lord. She's gone up to the attic."

"Geez ... Andrea. I've been so busy taking care of everyone else, I forgot about her."

Calvin bolted from the chair and charged out into the central hall and up the stairs. He threw open the attic door, his heart racing as he searched the room for his wife.

After what seemed an eternity, his mind was put at ease when he found the cupola door open. He climbed the stairs to see his wife seated in a rocker, staring out the window, sobbing and speaking gibberish.

"Andrea, thank God. Are you hurt?" He came up behind her.

The moon's glow shed light on all of Andrea's wrinkles, imperfections, and grays. She stood to face him, with the gun in her hand. She pointed it at Calvin. His beautiful, loving wife now seemed to be in the grips of madness as an unfathomable rage festered behind her eyes.

"Darling, please put the gun down. You don't want to hurt anyone."

"Come any closer, and I'll shoot."

"Okay, just calm down. Let's not be hasty." He backed into the wall, with his hands out in front of him.

"When were you going to tell me about the curse placed on this family? Or that our son's a bloodthirsty were-wolf?" she screeched.

"You were never supposed to know." Calvin looked down.

"So that makes it right? All the years we've been married, and you couldn't tell me the truth? You let me have children, knowing damn well one of them would turn into a monster."

"I did it to protect you and Josh from the truth. No one has to know. We can go back to the way things were before you found out. We can lock Simon in the basement on nights there's a full moon, like Mama and I have done since he was fourteen."

Calvin brushed her hand with his, and Andrea slapped him across the face with her free hand.

"Your cow of a mother knew before me? Since every-one has a secret, here's mine. Fifteen years ago, I had an abortion because I didn't want any more children, but you kept insisting we try for a girl, despite my protests. That mother of yours knew and kept silent. How does it feel to know that Mama isn't so innocent?"

Calvin looked like he had been stabbed through the heart.

"We can never go back. Our marriage is over," she spat, staring blankly at him.

Calvin lunged for the gun.

A naked Simon came out of the woods and lumbered toward the house. Georgia had been sitting on the gallery, in one of the wicker chairs, for the past two hours, waiting for him to return. Her eyes were becoming heavy as she gazed across the lawn in hopes of catching a glimpse of her new husband. She even had his jeans and favorite T-shirt ready for him to throw on the moment he stepped on the porch.

"Hurry up, Simon." Her head began to droop.

"You're gonna go to sleep now." He stood before her in all his glory.

"Not when I have a sight like that to keep me up." She licked her lips. "Here!" She threw the clothes at him.

As Simon slipped the blue Clemson T-shirt over his head, a bullet shot out from the cupola window. He pulled Georgia down behind a large stone planter.

"What was that?" She gripped his arm.

"I don't know."

Simon crept out from behind the urn and slid down the steps to crawl along the grass until he was a good distance away from the house. He looked up to the third floor, from behind a marble fountain, and saw his parents wrestling over a gun.

"What's happening?" Georgia whispered, still behind the ancient pot.

"It's Mom and Dad." He sprinted back toward the house.

"Where are you going?" Georgia grabbed him by the sleeve when he got to the front door.

"I have to see what's going on." He saw the concern on her face. "I'll be fine. Be back before you can say *honeymoon*. Wait out here. I don't want you getting hurt." He pecked her cheek and hurried inside.

Georgia sat back down in the same wicker chair and put her feet up on the table.

"Please hurry, Simon." She gazed at the front door.

Any remnants of the much-anticipated wedding had been wiped clean as Windwood returned to normal, and the day's celebrations faded into history. Simon stood at the bottom of the stairs, looking toward the third floor, when the gun went off again. With his acute hearing, he heard his father moan and collapse. Simon vaulted the stairs, hurdled over the Victorian furniture in the upstairs hallway, and dashed up to the attic.

Andrea sobbed as she hunched over the body of her husband. She felt like she would vomit at any moment.

"What did you do to Pa?" Simon spun her around to face him.

Andrea tried to turn away, and Simon could see the terror in her eyes. His mother's body trembled.

"Why are you afraid of me? Look at what you did!" he yelled, in her face.

"Get off me. Stop touching me," she cried, as he continued to try to force her to look at Calvin.

Andrea shoved him, and he fell into a group of boxes and trunks. As Simon got to his feet, she trained the gun on him.

"I'm so sorry," she said.

"I want you to get a good look at my face so that when you go to sleep, I'll be there. And then while you daydream about your perfect life, I'll creep in and smash that wonderful world."

"Andrea, he's your son," Calvin moaned, as he came to.

She fired into Simon's chest. He stumbled back and stared at his mother in disbelief. He reached for her, but she yanked back, causing him to lose his balance and fall through the cupola window.

After about twenty minutes, Georgia popped up from the chair and strode toward the front door, when she saw a brown Dodge Caravan pull up to the gate, with the window rolled down.

Toni Corsini poked her head out.

"He's pretty bad off," she shouted, as the sun began to appear over the skyline. "You might want to come help me get him up to the house,"

Georgia looked at the cupola, then to Joshua, who had a hard time getting the back door open.

"I thought he'd sober up by now. Rosa would be furious with me for letting him leave my bar in this state." Toni got out and opened his back door.

"Georgia, you're still here?" he slurred, and reached out to touch her face.

"I'm glad to see you, too." She put an arm around his waist, and his arm around her neck.

"Thanks, Toni," Georgia said. "I got it from here."

"You sure? He's awful heavy." Toni hesitated before getting back into the car.

"I'm fine. Go home, get some sleep."

Toni waved and then shot off toward the street.

"Donna," Joshua murmured, as Georgia dragged him across the lawn.

"Donna? Is she another one of the girls you met at the bar?"

"She's the woman I'm gonna marry." He laughed, then turned his head to throw up all over Andrea's prized Carolina lilies.

"Let it out," Georgia whispered, as she patted her brother in-law's back.

Crash! They looked up to see Simon plummeting from the cupola window. He landed in a lavender butterfly bush.

Georgia screamed.

Joshua looked up to see his mother in the window frame.

Nola wanted to kill Gideon for making her come back to this place. She found the old root cellar exactly where he said it would be. Nola placed the lantern she carried on the ground so she could see while she removed all the vines and dead leaves from the door. The flimsy timber door gave her no problem. She raised the lantern and saw nothing but darkness before her.

"I swear to God, if he jumps out at me, he's dead." Nola descended the stairs.

The small room was empty and stifling, its contents removed long ago. Nola felt along the hard dirt walls and found nothing out of the ordinary. Even the lantern seemed ineffective in penetrating the darkness.

"This is ridiculous. I'm gonna be here all night," she moaned, as she moved across the floor.

She tripped over a rock or a root and put her hands out to shield herself, and crashed right through the wall. The lantern broke and the wick extinguished, leaving her dazed and bruised. And right beneath Windwood.

"It's about time." Gideon extended his hand to help her up.

"Well, maybe if you had told me exactly where the passage was, instead of having me find it with my head, I could've been here sooner." She held onto Gideon's arm to kick some debris off her shoe. "Where are we, anyway?" She looked around at the endless maze of corridors.

"We are right underneath Windwood's parlor. From here, you could take any of these passages to the lake, to the old slave quarters, or to the cemetery. One pathway is said to lead straight to the center of town," He aimed the flashlight ahead of them.

"What was the point of all these passageways?" Nola looked at one tunnel after the other.

"Solomon Lord had them built as escape routes. After the Grand Duchy was annexed in 1792, by Austria, the former Grand Duke, the grand ducal family, and some of the staff, settled here in Solomon's Wake. With them, they took the royal jewels, some gold, silver, precious stones, and anything else of value, and stored it down here. During the Revolution and the Civil War, they used these tunnels to escape with their treasures."

"When did you become such an expert on Lord family history?" Nola followed close.

"I was a Lord through marriage, remember?"

"I don't know why they'd keep anything down here. It smells like wet dog and vomit." She shook her head in disgust and stuck out her tongue.

Nola put her hand on the limestone wall and felt the moisture on her fingers.

"Between the lake and the river, they get a lot of water down here." Gideon continued along the left side of the cellar, then turned right, down another tunnel.

"Did you bring me down here to play explorer, or are you just wasting my time?" Nola scoffed as she held onto one of his belt loops.

"There!" He pointed to what looked like a make-shift jail cell with Italian words all over the wall—words written in blood. "This was the prison of the witch Luna."

"And how do you know that? Were you here then, too?" Nola slapped him on the back.

"It says so on the wall."

"You're just full of surprises tonight. Italian?"

"I settled in Tuscany for a few years after I lost Iris. After a while, the language just came naturally. The Italian language is so beautiful. Everything sounds better. Even werewolf has a romantic undertone to it."

"Okay, big talker. Put your money where your mouth is and tell me what it says. A hundred bucks says you can't." She reached into the pocket of her black Jordache jeans and pulled out a Ben to wave in his face.

"The next thing you know, you'll have me stick my tongue to a freezing pole." He snatched the hundred-dollar bill from her. "It says, *I have spilt my own blood to curse you, Solomon, and your house. My blood is now part of the very soil on which this house rests. As long as Windwood stands, so shall I. From this day forward, every last Lord, from now through eternity, will be struck down. Horrible torments and terrible tribulations await all of you."*

"Okay, so you know what it says."

Gideon gave her an I-told-you-so smile.

"I know you didn't bring me here for a history lesson, or to teach me Italian, so tell me the real reason I'm here."

"We are going to contact Luna ourselves. She was kept in this room, which should make contact with her all the easier. I snuck into Calvin's office during the reception and found this." He showed her a tattered leather book with a large gold pentacle engraved on its cover.

"And she'd help you, why?"

"I'll promise to restore her body. In exchange, she gets rid of Simon for me." Gideon smiled.

"You know what? I think you're insane. I want no part of this. You're so obsessed with Simon, I'm beginning to think you're in love with him." She began to walk away.

"Nola, please. I need your help. I can't do this alone. I have to stop Simon and Georgia from having children, or the curse Luna placed on Solomon will pass to my grandchildren." He caught her by the arm and pulled her into a kiss.

"All right, I'll help you. Just stop begging. It's very unflattering. God, I need my head examined."

7

PAYBACK TIME

GIDEON SMILED AND DROPPED TO THE floor. Sitting Indian style, he pulled Nola down by the wrists. He opened the book, which was also written in Italian, and began to search for the right spell.

Halfway through the book, he said, "Here we go!"

In a thunderous voice, Gideon began the incantation, which seemed to be a mix of different dialects. Nola began to get chills and felt uneasy as a mass of cold air enveloped them.

"Stop it, Gideon! I can't breathe. Feels like something's clawing at my chest, trying to get inside me." She shrieked, and her eyes became black as coal.

"Nola, Nola." He stared at her in awe.

"Hello, Gideon. It's been a long time," a distorted voice said.

"Who are you?" he said, his eyes wide.

"You don't remember me? I was only your father-in-law," the spirit said, staring blankly.

"Marshall?"

"I've waited almost a hundred years to face you again."

"I didn't summon you," Gideon scratched his head.

"You might want to brush up on your spirit summoning, for you're going to need more than a book to reach her."

"I don't understand."

"You cast an amateur spell that called on every spirit that could hear it, and I was the strongest and able to break through." He cackled. "A hundred years ago, you took something that meant more to me than anything in the world. I find it only fair that I return the favor."

"What are you going to do?"

"You'll see."

The room became warmer.

Blinking, and shaking her head, Nola said, "Gideon, what happened?"

"I'm not sure."

Ginny heard the gunshots. She heard Georgia scream, and saw the police take Andrea into custody. Yet through it all, her father was nowhere to be found. Once again, the house fell eerily silent.

Ginny stood before the dresser, staring at the mirror, and began to take out the baby's breath to let her hair down. Now all she wanted to do was get into a nice hot bath, relax, and forget about everything that happened tonight.

"I've drawn you a bath and left some fresh towels for you on the hamper," Charlene said. "If you need anything else, I'll be out in the hall." She smiled from the doorway. "For the record, it was a beautiful wedding."

Her young face was vibrant. Her golden hair shone, and her smile was worth a million bucks.

"Thank you, Charlene."

The young girl nodded and closed the door.

Ginny unzipped her teal gown and let it slide to the floor. After stepping out of it, she drifted to the bathroom, where she dropped her black panties and left the matching bra on the doorknob.

"That's more like it." She eased into the warm water in the clawfoot bathtub. "Ahhh. I could get used to this." Eyes closed, she laid her head against the back of the tub.

Her mind was working overtime as the events of the evening replayed over and over again. Where was her father? Where was her sister? And most important, who got shot?

Exhausted, she began to fall asleep, when something tried to pull her underwater.

"Someone help me!" she screamed, holding onto the sides of the tub.

The force continued to tug at her feet, harder and harder, until her hands finally slipped, sending her beneath the water.

Water splashed over the sides of the tub, soaking the linoleum floor and trickling out into the bedroom as she thrashed toward the top. Ginny could no longer hold her breath or fight this being off. She had accepted her fate, when a hand reached down and pulled her out by the hair.

"Miss Blake, are you all right?" Charlene reached for a towel.

"Something's trying to kill me." She gasped while gripping Charlene's arm.

"Hurry up. Let's get you out of here." Charlene held open a large mint-green towel.

"Thank you!"

As Ginny went to step out of the tub, the force pulled her all the way under until she disappeared.

"Miss Blake! Miss Blake!" Charlene reached into the tub.

Still unable to grasp what she just saw, she ran out of the room, screaming.

Gideon rushed down the hall. "Charlene, what's the matter?"

"She's gone! Mister Blake, your daughter's gone." The girl was trembling.

"What do you mean, *gone?*" He looked into the bedroom.

"The bathtub swallowed her," she whispered. "I heard her screaming, and I rushed in to find her underwater. I thought she'd fallen asleep and slipped. I helped her up and then watched her vanish before my eyes. I'm sorry, Mister Blake. I've had enough of this loony bin. I'm going back to Mobile." She turned and ran down the hall.

"Ginny!" Gideon called out into the bedroom.

"She's gone someplace you'll never find her," Marshall said.

With his hands in his face, Gideon sank to his knees and bawled. If only his hatred for the Lord family hadn't got the best of him, his daughter would still be here. What if Marshall wanted to go after Georgia, too? He had to cut Georgia out of his life completely to save her from a similar fate.

"Nola!" he screamed out into the hallway. "Nola, please hurry." He stepped back into the bedroom.

"What is it? You look like you've ate some bad sushi."

"Marshall's done something to Ginny," he whispered, as he strode over to the nightstand.

He pulled out a stationery and a pen, and shoved it at her.

"Here. I need you to write a letter to Georgia. Convince her that she and Simon are in danger. But most importantly, make her leave Solomon's Wake."

"Isn't this a bit drastic?" Nola pushed a strand of blonde hair out of her face.

Gideon glared at her with his cold, dark eyes, and left the room without saying a word.

The blonde woman drove her gold Tempo down I-73, toward Channing's compound in West Virginia. Most of the cars flew by her with ease, a good number of the drivers honking or flipping her the bird. It wasn't her fault the transmission went out and the car wouldn't go past forty.

She reached for her car phone and dialed the number. A man answered on the second ring.

"It's done," she said. "Gideon released the spirit of Marshall. Andrea Lord has discovered her son Simon's secret, and I have Nola in the trunk."

"Very good, my dear. You shall be handsomely rewarded." He hung up.

"You're welcome."

As she continued to drive, she couldn't help but feel like she had seen that house before, even the people in it. Only, she couldn't remember anything about her past. And every time she tried, she became more frustrated. For all she knew, her name wasn't even Lila.

Rather than get upset, she turned the radio on to hear her favorite song, Madonna's "Crazy for You," and began to sing at the top of her lungs as the other cars whizzed by.

8

SINS OF THE FATHER

IT WAS ALMOST SIX, AND TONI WAS STILL wide awake. That her granddaughter, Carla, still wasn't home didn't help her insomnia. Instead of lying there, she got up, strode over to a large closet with sliding mirror doors, and yanked back a bunch of dresses, coats, and stoles to reveal a door made of Scottish silver, the strongest metal known to man—nothing supernatural could penetrate it.

Toni began to look at some of the things she had in the vault. Clothes hung on a long metal rack by the door. They included a flapper gown, a wedding dress from 1735, and a pair of gloves worn by Grigori Rasputin. She even kept the mallet that Dr. Van Helsing had used to finally destroy Count Dracula, locked in a glass case. This stuff was all trivial compared to the other objects in the room.

One of her more spine-chilling oddities was kept under a velvet shroud in a huge, enchanted glass box. She had not laid eyes on it in years because it frightened her and raised too many questions about her own lineage.

Toni moved around the large case and stepped on her shoelace. To keep her balance, she grabbed the shroud, pulling it off, and revealed the severed head of a beautiful woman.

"Now you've done it. You won't sleep for days."

Toni put the cover back over the case, and couldn't help but stare at the name engraved on a silver plate at the bottom of the glass—*Ivana, Baroness of Zorn.*

Ivana Zorn and her entire family were the scourge of the earth. They reveled in the ways of black magic, devilry, and vampirism, and they terrorized Bavaria for years. Yes, the Zorn's were a bad brood whose ferocious bloodlust led to their undoing. They were so wicked while alive that they continued to haunt the living after death.

One night, in the late 17th century, a brave man set out to rid Bavaria of these demons once and for all. He trapped and decapitated every last Zorn in the cemetery except two, Ivana and her brother, Xander, who could not be found. The surviving vampires sought refuge in the castle, but the man burned it down with them in it. One by one, they came out and he finished them off. Eventually, Ivana met her demise, but Xander had never surfaced.

Toni hurried up with the cover and crossed the room.

She reached for a switch that turned on a bunch of monitors she had built into the wall. One showed her the driveway out in front of the house. Another showed the hallway, kitchen, and living room. And the other three showed the underwater prison of her fallen comrades.

One room in particular was of great interest—the one that contained the golden sarcophagus and the only thing capable of destroying the vampires, witches, and were-wolves. As long as that coffin remained sealed, the threat was minimized. Thankfully, as she scrutinized the surroundings on the screen, there were no signs of it opening anytime soon.

Toni let out a sigh of relief and was glad Carla had talked her into getting the cameras, or she'd have to travel out to the lake every night and open the door to make sure the coffin was secure and that there were no intruders inside the chamber. The accursed object had been in the possession of the Monarchs since it ended up in the ocean after the Titanic sank.

Toni continued to stare at the screens as she thought of the other evil trinket stored in the vault. Also buried in it was another small box made of the same silver of the door, and lined with black satin. She plucked the box from the shelf, opened it and reached inside to pull out a beautiful blue diamond pendant. She held it up to the light and watched as it glistened and danced under the fluorescents. She gasped as the ugly face of Luna appeared inside the gem.

"You will not win this time. Your spirit will never rise again to hurt anyone." Toni dropped the necklace in her pocket and took off toward the river.

This pendant was also known as the Zorn necklace. It had belonged to Ivana, her mother, and Luna, who was a Zorn by birth. The necklace was the cause of great turmoil through the centuries, as it brought misery and destruction to anyone who wore it.

On the edge of the embankment, Toni reached into her pocket, pulled out the long chain, and with all her might, hurled the pendant into the Aurora.

"Game over, Luna." Toni smiled as she watched the diamond sink until she could no longer see it in the murky water.

"Dare I ask what that was?" Gideon came up behind her, wearing gray sweatpants and a white undershirt.

"Nothing you need to be concerned with." She turned around and saw the condition he was in. "What happened to you? Have you been crying?"

As Toni looked at his puffy eyes and disheveled hair, as well as the condition of his clothes, the Gideon she knew was nowhere to be found.

"I'm leaving, and I suggest you do, too." He reached behind his ear to pull out a Marlboro, lit it, and took such a long drag it made her chest hurt.

"We can't leave, and you know this. As the only two members of The Order remaining, we're bound by duty to stay. The Monarchs will behead us for high treason, burn us at the stake, or throw us down the mine with the others. Have you forgotten what we were all sent here to do?"

"No, I haven't!" He put his cigarette out. "Look around you, Toni!" He spun around. "The Monarchs are in slumber, Lord knows where. And who knows if they'll ever wake up. The last vampire member of The Order is long gone. The werewolves are scattered, and their numbers dwindled. And you witches are down to a few. Why on earth would you want to stay?"

"The golden sarcophagus with the face of a young pharaoh on it, that's why. Your pack master and his followers tried to open it, and that's why you got the job of watching over it."

"It was also the day the virus first manifested and infected my whole pack, and started a war that almost killed all of us."

"Then you know we cannot leave." Toni sat on the grass and motioned him to follow. "Our whole purpose for being here is to protect that tomb and keep it out of the hands of those who want to do us harm. The Monarchs instructed us to—

"Our beloved Monarchs are the reason for all this!" He jumped up. "They brought that coffin here, believing that inside was a talisman that would enable someone to bring the dead back to life. Instead, we found Pandora's Box. Like the legend says, it unleashed evil on the world the first time. However, if it's opened again, it'll put evil back. And in doing so, take every magical, mythical, and supernatural being with it."

"We still don't know if that's true. Regardless of how it came about, we are responsible for it until we are informed otherwise."

"I'm done with all of this. I don't care if that tomb opens, or if the Commies find it. Channing is back, and he's coming for us. I must protect my family. So as far as Georgia believes, I'm dead." He looked at Toni with tears streaming down his face.

"I knew it! He escaped from the tomb earlier, didn't he?" She stood and moved closer to him.

"Yes, but I didn't know until much later." He wouldn't look at her.

"You're still a lying son of a bitch, and as selfish as ever." She grabbed him and spun him around to face her. "He's your son, and the reason for half this mess. I helped you trap him down there, and you were going to leave without telling me he was out and about, leaving me to fend for myself? This is how you repay me for saving your ass with the Monarchs, and for telling you about that book?"

"Toni, we've done all we can. Everything has been secured. There's nothing left for us to do, and no one to guide us. Channing is not going to be happy with us. You know as well as I do what he's capable of. Don't make the mistake I did and wait around for him to make a move." He took Toni's hands and looked her in the eyes. "I'm gonna sorta miss this place, and your nagging." He tipped her chin and strode off down the beach.

Slowly, she made her way back to the inn, taking to heart everything Gideon had told her. What if Channing did come for Carla, or he managed to get into the tomb? There was no way she could defend herself alone, or protect the town.

A group of schoolchildren whizzed by on their bikes and waved to Toni. As she continued on, she got a cold chill down her back, which caused her to stop and turn around. She looked up to see Windwood, the imposing monument of timber and stone looming over Solomon's Wake. Right then, she realized that everything going on in town was caused by that house and the people that had inhabited it for over two hundred years.

"You are right, Gideon. It's time for me to go. The sins of our fathers will not fall on our children."

Toni kept on moving and didn't look back.

9

A HOMECOMING

Present Day

OLD WINDWOOD WAS QUIET AS AARON Sutton cleared the dinner dishes from the dining room table like he had done for the past thirty-something years. He was the only servant to remain at the manor. The others had left long ago, along with most of the family.

The elderly servant shuffled to the back of the house, toward the kitchen, passing all the empty walls where Picassos and Monets once hung, with only the white silhouettes of distant memories left behind. Aaron placed the dishes in the sink and began to clear away the night's dinner. He wrapped up what was left of the catfish and put the slaw in a round container next to the cornbread in the refrigerator. He helped himself to some sweet tea, sat at the small table and was ready to have a biscuit with honey, when a crash down the hall scared him half to death.

By the time he reached the first-floor office, he found the master of the house, Calvin Lord, in a rage, overturning furniture, breaking heirlooms, and throwing anything not nailed down.

"Excuse me, sir. Is everything all right?"

Calvin's face was flushed. "No, it's not. I've just been informed by the board that I've been removed as CEO of Lord Shipbuilding, effective immediately." He ran his hands through his thick silver hair, then sat in a ripped-up Victorian chair with rose-patterned upholstery.

"Oh, sir, I'm so sorry. Can I get you anything?"

"My family built that company from the ground up. We poured our blood, sweat, and tears into it. And how do I get repaid? By being fired by the very people I appointed." Calvin tossed an empty glass at the fireplace, and it shattered into a million pieces. "I would like to be alone for a while."

"If you need anything at all, you know where to find me." Sutton left, closing the door behind him.

Calvin reached into the bottom left desk drawer to pull out a half-finished bottle of whiskey, and drank it right from the head. He looked around the small, cluttered office.

His desk sat directly in front of a large window overlooking the grounds. On the other side of the room was a fireplace flanked with books on almost every topic. Pictures and certificates lined the walls.

Calvin looked up at the portrait of his father, Theodore Lord, and sighed.

"It's all gone, Pa." He grunted as he poured another drink. "I'm sure wherever you are, you're relishing my failure. After all, you predicted it would happen by my hand. We both know I really had no control over my path of fate. Your ancestors saw to that some two hundred years ago, didn't they?" He raised his glass to the oil painting of a man with silver hair, large gray eyes, and a gaunt face. "Congratulations, dear old Dad, for you got to preside over the fall of the House of Lord."

He threw the tumbler at the painting, placing a huge gash on Theodore's face.

Calvin wept some more after seeing the array of photos on the mantle—his eldest son, Simon, and his wife, Georgia, posing for the camera on their wedding day. Another photo of his daughter Peyton, when she won the Academy Award for Best Actress, followed by Joshua, the middle child, who favored Calvin in every way, posing for the lens after winning the Pulitzer Prize for the biography he wrote about their ancestor Caleb Lord. Behind Joshua was a small, framed photo of his first little girl, Melanie, who lost her life at the age of five, from leukemia. It almost destroyed Andrea, and Calvin often wondered if that was the beginning of the end for her.

He looked around the room and continued to sob as he saw more photos of his grandchildren, parents, and siblings everywhere. He reached into his pocket and pulled out a small photo he kept of his second wife, Vivian, taken outside the stable.

"Even though I was found not guilty, everyone around here still thinks I did it. They don't have to tell me. I can see it in their eyes." He brushed his finger across the photo. "I could never hurt you."

A few hours later, a shot rang out, and Calvin Lord was dead, clutching a photo of his first wife, Andrea.

For the life of him, he could not remember the way to the house. When he had been a boy, he knew every shortcut, hidden path, and gravel road that surrounded the estate. In the dark, everything looked the same as the hybrid Lexus SUV cut through the obscurity, its lights focused on the path before him. The past few hours were driven in silence as his wife, Donna, slept in the passenger seat. Their eleven-year-old daughter, Jenna, dozed in the back, and their teenage son, Brandon, played his Nintendo DS while listening to his MP3 player cranked all the way up.

"Face it, Josh, we're lost." Donna sat up, stretched, and reached for her half-empty bottle of spring water from the console.

"No, we're not. The turn has to be around here." Joshua leaned forward to peer through the windshield.

"Could you please turn around and go back to that gas station on the highway, and ask for directions? It's getting late. Jenna's tired. I'm bushed, and Brandon's gonna go blind if he doesn't give that game of his a break. C'mon. We've been at this for hours. If you won't ask for directions, then let me. At this rate, we'll never make it in time for the reading of your father's will." Donna turned and looked back to check on the kids, her chestnut hair wild and free.

"I don't need to stop for directions."

"Really, Dad? It's way past midnight, and I need to use the john. If we don't make it soon, I'm gonna go all over the backseat," Brandon said loudly, as he bobbed his head to the music.

"Didn't I tell you to go in Mont Clare?" Joshua said.

His son continued to move his head up and down.

"Brandon!" Joshua yelled.

"What?"

"Didn't you go at the last rest stop?"

"Yeah, but I had all that Mountain Dew." Brandon began using the back of his dad's seat as a drum set.

"Hon, just stop. I need to stretch my legs, anyway." Donna rubbed lotion on her hands, looking out the window.

"Oh, for God's sake. I'm too tired to fight both of you."

The SUV squealed and jerked as Joshua accelerated to turn around.

When the car pulled into the Quick Stop, only a small white Volkswagen Bug was parked by the entrance. A heavyset middle-aged man with thinning hair looked up from his newspaper long enough to stare at them through the large window.

"Could you get me a cup of coffee?" Donna opened the door to get out and stretch.

Joshua came around and gave her a kiss, when Brandon poked his head out.

"Dad, can you get me some beef jerky, another Mountain Dew, and more chips?" He pushed his head back in.

"Where were we?" Joshua gave his wife a big kiss.

"That's messed up, Dad," Brandon yelled, as Joshua entered the store.

The Quick Stop was tiny, outdated, and in need of repair. The smell of cigarettes filled the air even though the sign on the door clearly said no smoking. An old Conway Twitty song emanated from the small boombox on the counter. Joshua went to pour Donna a cup of coffee, when he noticed it was so thick he could use it to tar the driveway. Onto the snack aisle, everything he picked up had been expired two years.

Fed up, he went to the counter to get the directions.

"Excuse me. Could you tell me how to get to the Windwood Plantation?"

"You want directions, you have to buy something," the man said, in a strong Southern drawl.

"I'm sorry, Earl. That is your name, isn't it?" Joshua pointed to the name sewn on his blue shirt. "But the food you have here isn't fit for my dog."

"Listen Yank, don't come down here shooting off your mouth, acting like you're better than everybody else. Or we're gonna have a problem." Earl stood, and slammed a fist into his hand. "You want the directions or not?"

"For the record, I am no Yankee. I was born and raised here in South Carolina, and graduated from Clemson." Joshua grabbed a pack of gum from the rack in front of him and threw it down on the counter. "The directions, please."

"Where did you want to go again?" Earl rang the gum up.

"Windwood Plantation."

"Never heard of it." The cashier looked away.

Joshua could tell he was lying.

"Why won't you tell me where it is?"

"Do you know what that place does to people? From the moment it was built in the 1700s, that house has brought nothing but misery to everyone who enters it. Ghosts, murders, and suicides have plagued that poor family, and this town suffered for it. Just last week, the old patriarch of the family, Calvin Lord, was found dead in his office. Before that, his second wife, Vivian, turned up with her throat ripped out by the pool. And his first wife, Andrea, is a certified loon who's spent most of her life in the nut house. Trust me, run as far away from that house as you can get."

Earl got up and went to the back room. As he walked away, all Joshua could do was focus on the bald spot on the back of his head.

10

THE HEIR APPARENT

EARL HAD JOSHUA SO HEATED THAT WHEN he went back outside in the humid Southern air, it cooled him off.

"What took you so long? And where's my coffee?" Donna said through the opened window, when he came out empty-handed.

"Dad, how 'bout those chips?" Brandon leaned forward from the backseat.

"He was absolutely no help," Joshua said. "Says he's never heard of Windwood. As for the coffee, it would've put hair on your chest, or made it fall out. Not sure which. Brandon, you've had plenty to eat, and enough soda to keep you up a week." He buckled his seatbelt and pulled out onto the main road.

"What are we going to do? Drive around for hours again?" Donna moaned as she put her seat back and covered her eyes with a black silk mask she pulled out of her pocket.

"I'm sure I was on the right track."

"Can't we just go to a motel until tomorrow morning?" Brandon said.

"Can you stop complaining for more than five minutes?" Joshua replied. "Sit back. You're making me nervous."

"Why did I have to come to Solomon's Wake? I didn't even know Grandfather. South Carolina blows." Brandon huffed, settling back into the tan leather seat.

"Can the two of you stop bickering?" Donna bolted up and caught a glimpse of herself in the mirror.

Her vision blurred, and pupils dilated.

"We need to find a motel," she said.

"Don't you start, too," Joshua said, keeping his gaze on the road.

"I'm getting a migraine, and my medicine's in the trunk." She lay back on the headrest and closed her eyes.

Sighing, Joshua turned the car around once more and sped off toward the motel.

Earl came around the counter once he knew they were gone, pulled the shade down, and locked the door. He scurried back around the counter and dialed the number the stranger gave him the other day. It rang and rang. As Earl was about to hang up, a raspy voice answered.

"Hi, this is Earl at the Quick Stop in Solomon's Wake. You asked that I give you a call if anyone came around asking about Windwood. I had a gentleman in here about ten minutes ago, asking how to get there." Earl waited for a response, but only got heavy breathing. "Look, things have been quiet around here. We don't need any trouble."

The line went dead.

"You're welcome." Earl hung up and went back to his paper.

Once they checked in, Donna pushed past Joshua and hurried into the bathroom. She flicked the light on, which cast a faint glow across the mint-green tiled walls of the small bathroom consisting of one toilet, a shower, and a rusted sink. She turned on the hot water full blast, and the steam from the shower began to fog the mirror immediately. As she wiped away the condensation, her hands began to tremble, her mouth began to hurt, and that ferocious thirst for blood rose within her. She gripped the counter so hard she left an indention in the Formica.

Donna began to sweat, and she looked up into the mirror to see her eyes take on a feline appearance. Then her reflection began to disappear.

"Hold on, Donna. Hold on," she said, as her fangs began to show.

"Babe, you okay?" Joshua tapped the door.

"I'll be fine. Just need a few minutes for my medicine to kick in."

Her fangs were now fully exposed, and her hunger raged like a volcano. If she didn't get it under control, she could slaughter her whole family in a matter of seconds.

Donna took her purse and spilled its contents on the floor.

"Where the hell are they?" She searched for the little green pill that had to be taken every day to keep her vampirism at bay. "There you are, my little beauty." She popped it into her mouth. "That was close."

She could taste the concoction of garlic, blackthorn, mountain ash, and bloodroot as it pulsed through her.

"Do I have to break the door down?" Joshua grumbled.

"I told you I just needed a minute." Donna smiled as she opened the door, wearing nothing but a towel.

She dried her hair with a towel, then sat on the bed and motioned for Joshua to sit beside her.

"Thanks for stopping." She leaned in to kiss him.

"I kind of didn't have a choice," he said, their foreheads pressed together.

They stared into each other's eyes, and Donna ran her hands through his lush, dark hair as he pulled her closer to him.

"I love you," he whispered.

He began to remove the towel from her body, when Donna caught sight of Jenna standing in the doorway.

"I'm scared," the girl said. "Can I sleep with you tonight?"

"Of course you can, sweetheart." Donna adjusted her towel and pulled down the bedspread.

Jenna wasted no time and leapt headfirst onto the mattress.

"If you're sleeping in here, no funny business. Right to sleep, okay?"

"All right, Mommy."

"Daddy and I have to talk. We'll be in the next room if you need us."

Donna went out through a separator door that led to the next room, where Brandon was already passed out on one of the twin beds.

"Is she still having those nightmares?" Joshua sat in one of the cushioned wheeled chairs by the door.

"I don't know. It's not like we let her watch movies about vampires or werewolves, so I don't know where she gets it from. Most little girls dream of dolls, toys, or the boy they may someday marry, not about a witch being hung." Donna sat beside him in the other chair.

"Jenna just has a vivid imagination. At least she's not dreaming of murder and suicide, or sex. Maybe she'll put it to good use and become a writer like her old man, or an actress, when she's older." Joshua shrugged.

"I guess. Are you going to tell me what's been bothering you the past couple days? Ever since you got the call from your father's lawyer, you've been so far away. I'm not trying to be callous, but you haven't seen your dad in twenty years, so there has to be something else you're not telling me."

"You know me too well." Joshua sighed. "I got a call from a Loretta Thornton at the clinic in Rock Hill, where Mama's been for the past twenty-something years. She's going to be released to my care, and is coming home to Windwood." He slouched into the chair, resting his temple against the side of his hand.

"Why didn't you tell me this? You shouldn't have had to deal with that by yourself." Donna slid off the chair and climbed into his lap. "I'm your wife, and I'll do anything for you. And I mean *anything*. All you have to do ask."

"I don't know what I'm supposed to feel. The woman shot and killed my brother." Joshua wept as his wife opened her arms to him.

"Let it all out." She stroked his head.

After he composed himself, they sat silence. Rain began to sprinkle outside, and the glow from the exterior light crept under the dark red curtains.

"Mama's nurse, Loretta, told me she's been completely rehabilitated. No more fits of rage, homicidal tendencies, or paranoia. I just don't know about having her back in the house, or my life."

"It's late. Let's go to bed. And in the morning, we'll look at the situation with a clearer mind." Donna stood and offered her hand to him.

"What would I do without you?" He took her hand and let her lead him to the bedroom.

For over twenty years, a woman who kept her face hidden by a veil showed up at the hospital day in and day out to sit by the comatose body of Simon Lord. The woman never spoke or revealed her identity, which gave birth to all kinds of wild rumors—like, she was the woman who shot him. Or she was the wife of the mobster who gunned him down out of jealousy. But most people believed her to be the grief-stricken mother who prayed for her son to wake up.

All those rumors would be put to rest today.

"I've got to give her credit. I don't know if I could keep coming year after year, talking to someone who's never gonna wake up," the older black charge nurse said to the LPN beside her, when the mystery woman walked past them.

"She's right on schedule," the young brunette said. "Rain or shine, she's here at ten o'clock, and sits with him until visiting hours are over." She handed the charge nurse a clipboard.

"I only wish I had someone to love me like that." The charge nurse sighed as she signed the papers.

Simon's small room was bright as the sun bore down on the city of Denver. The mysterious woman laid her purse on a tray by the bed, and knelt down to kiss his cool lips. The IV endlessly pumped medications through his veins while the ventilator continued to propel air into his lungs as the blood pressure monitor beeped nonstop.

"This is the last time you'll see me, Simon. I thought maybe my being here would be enough to bring you back to me. Twenty years of my life are gone, and I have nothing to show for it. Even when the doctors told me to give up, I had enough faith to carry us both. But regretfully, I've come to the conclusion that they were right." Tears streamed down her face. "I'm going home to Solomon's Wake. Goodbye, my love."

The machines went haywire. Simon's blood pressure spiked, and his toes began to move. Soon, the nurses and doctors flooded the room and asked her to step outside.

"What's the matter? What're you doing to him?"

They all looked at her in disbelief. The mystery woman had found her voice.

"Just give us a few minutes." One of the nurses closed the door.

"Please, God, let him be all right."

She found a seat in the waiting room, by the TV. Some talk show discussing politics entertained the few people gathered around it. The minutes seemed like hours, and when she could no longer sit, she paced, then sat, and then paced some more. She was about to barge into the room, when Dr. Clewell came out with a puzzled expression.

"I can't explain how this happened, or how it's even possible. Mister Bishop's awake and alert. A little groggy, but awake, nonetheless. You may see him." He scratched his head and walked down the hall.

Georgia froze in the doorway while a young nurse took Simon's vitals as he sipped water from a Styrofoam cup. All she could think about was how she had dreamed of this moment. Now, though, her feet felt like lead as she tried to move toward his bed.

The nurse smiled at her when she passed by.

"You always knew he'd wake up." The nurse winked and patted her arm, then shut the door.

"The doctors told me you've been at my bedside for two decades, and now you have nothing to say," he croaked. "Come here. Let me see you. What's with the veil? Take it off so I can get a good look at you."

Hesitantly, she lifted the veil.

Simon remained silent, his gaze locked on an older Georgia. She had a few more wrinkles on her face and creases in her forehead, plus a couple gray hairs near her temples. Other than that, she was still the most beautiful woman he had ever seen.

"Like the song says, you will always be beautiful in my eyes." He smiled, and she just melted and couldn't fight back the tears.

"Am I dreaming?" Georgia said, her voice cracking, afraid to approach the bed.

"Come. Don't be scared." He motioned for her to come closer, all the while staring at her face. "You still look the same as the day I married you."

He pulled the sheet back and motioned her to lie beside him.

"What if I hurt you or pull one of those tubes out?"

"I'm a werewolf. I can't get hurt or die unless by silver. While I slept, my body regenerated. Besides, I don't care. I want to hold you again, feel you next to me. I've only waited a decade or two. C'mon!" He patted the spot alongside him.

Georgia melted as he wrapped his arms around her and pulled her close. His kiss sent a chill down her spine. Both cried tears of joy as their emotions took hold.

"I never gave up hope, Simon. Never." She sat up and wiped the tears from her face. "I was so lost without you. I brought you here to Colorado to keep you safe. I couldn't risk your mother finding you."

"Well, you don't have to worry about that, because I don't plan on leaving your side ever again."

WINDWOOD

IN THE MORNING, THE FAMILY DEPARTED the motel. Jenna prattled on and on about wanting to go swimming, going to a new school in the fall, and all the new friends she was going to make. Brandon continued battling through some mythical land being overrun by an unseen force, unable to focus on anything else.

Joshua concentrated on the road. As he'd predicted last night, he found the turn right away. Some overgrown shrubs blocked the path, and there was no way he would have seen it them in the dark.

"I told you it was here." Joshua sounded like a child who just got a trivia question right.

"It only took you all night to find it." Donna adjusted the flow of the air conditioner.

"How much farther?" Jenna grabbed her mother's headrest.

"We're almost there," Donna said. "Sit back and put your seatbelt on."

Jenna huffed and buckled in.

The car traveled under a black wrought iron gate with *WINDWOOD* scrolled in gold letters across the top. Along the drive, live oaks lined the entire route to the house, blanketing the area with an awning of emerald green foliage. Jasmine, magnolia, oleander, and honeysuckle greeted the travelers with their heavy scents. The rain washed the earth clean, making everything fresh. Even the humidity fell, allowing a cool breeze in from the Aurora River.

After driving down the dirt road for about two miles, they came out from the shaded path provided by the live oaks, into a formal garden with gold and marble fountains scattered throughout. Southern magnolias, weeping willows, blue asters, pink and white azaleas, and five-foot pale-green royal ferns were strategically placed all over the property, adding to the estate's beauty.

Joshua drove up to the front gallery through a circular drive. After getting out of the car, the quartet stared in awe at the opulent antebellum mansion. The property, including the palatial white stucco house, took up a whole city block. Four giant Corinthian fluted columns supported a two-story portico that occupied the front entrance. Iron lace railings adorned both levels of the gallery, including the two-story gallery on the east side of the house. The enormous windows were imported from Italy and capped by dark-green shutters. Atop the roof rested a cupola with two rounded openings on each side.

"I feel like I'm in *Gone with the Wind*," Donna closed the Lexus door.

"This is our new house!?" Brandon said.

"Yup. She's not much of a looker now," Joshua said, "but you should've seen her back in her heyday. Windwood's one of the only plantations left in the South that has her original owners."

From years of neglect, the great house had fallen into ruin, a shadow of its former glory. Shingles were falling from all sides of the vast roof. Windowpanes were shattered on the third floor. Water damage could be seen on all sides of the mansion, and some of the balustrades needed repair.

When they walked up the cement steps to the front gallery, they saw the Lord family crest carved into a green front door. They stepped inside the central hall, which was fifteen-feet wide and seventy-feet long. Every door on the first floor had heavy Greek frames. The five downstairs mantels were made from white marble carved with the Lord family crest, and gold chandeliers hung from plastered rosettes in each room. Also on display was a faded mural of the gods of Olympus. Hand-painted doorknobs, etched glass, and immense gold-framed mirrors greeted them, making the room look never-ending.

The first floor afforded a ballroom, music room, double parlor, dining room, and library. A service wing at the back of the house contained an apartment, bathroom, kitchen, and office. Upstairs encompassed eight bedrooms, a sitting room with a view of the Aurora, more bathrooms, black marble mantles, and hand-painted wallpaper.

One of the side doors opened, and an elderly man shuffled forward, wearing a black suit. His white hair and soft blue eyes complemented the ensemble. His jawline was pronounced, and his face was smooth for his age. Sutton was about sixty-five, but looked eighty, thanks to emphysema caused from years of heavy smoking.

"Welcome home, Master Joshua." His Southern accent was heavy. "I am at your service." He bowed slightly, and almost fell over.

"Thank you, Aaron. This is my wife, Donna; our daughter, Jenna; and son, Brandon."

"I am very pleased to meet y'all. Please call me Sutton. Come into the parlor and relax." He opened the sliding doors.

Maroon satin wallpaper enhanced the walls, and a portrait of a beautiful blonde woman hung over the marble fireplace. A worn Chinese throw rug with threads showing covered the pine floor. A small loveseat, two mismatched chairs, and a bigger sofa were not enough to fill the impressive room.

"I'm sorry I don't have much to offer you. As you can see, there's not much left. Your father, though, till the day he died, kept this house going. I don't know how many times someone's come around offering to buy the place. Your father would have none of it. He'd chase them off with his rifle. Lord Shipbuilding's fallen on hard times, too. It got so bad they removed him as CEO. That hurt him almost as bad as losing your mother."

"Sounds like Dad—always too proud to ask for help." Joshua stared at the portrait.

"Who's she? Some ancestor?" Donna said to him.

"That's my mama, Andrea Sullivan Lord."

"She's beautiful," Donna said.

"Sutton, could you have someone bring the bags in?" Joshua said.

"I'm the only one left at Windwood. Your father let the others go years ago."

"All right. Brandon, help me get the bags." Joshua wiped a bead of sweat from his brow.

He started for the door before realizing Brandon was still sitting on the couch, playing his game.

"Hello? Brandon? Bags. Move it!"

"Why do I always have to be the one to help you?"

"'Cause you're so good at it." His father smiled.

Brandon rolled his eyes, threw up his arms and followed.

"Do you hear that, Mommy?" Jenna said, from the window.

"Hear what, honey?" Donna came up behind her and caught a view of a beautiful pond. A gazebo sat a few feet away.

"The woman!" Jenna screamed. "She's in pain. She needs my help. Don't you hear her?"

"If you don't stop with this, Daddy will make you go to that doctor again. Do you want that?"

"Mommy, but I heard them!"

"Enough already, Jenna, or no riding lessons."

"What's wrong with your eyes?" The girl cocked her head.

"What do you mean?" Donna hurried over to a mirror and saw her eyes begin to change. "Jenna, tell Daddy I had to go upstairs."

She ran out into the hall and up the wooden staircase.

While Joshua and Brandon gathered the luggage, another car came up the drive and parked right next to them. The car door opened, and a middle-aged woman with auburn hair and a tiny frame got out to open the back door and help a gray-haired lady out.

"Missus Lord, we're here." Loretta went around to the trunk to get the woman's walker.

Andrea Lord hobbled forward. Her long steel-gray hair clung to her face. As she looked over Windwood, tears formed as she saw the dilapidated state the house had fallen into.

She stopped as soon as she saw her son. They locked eyes until Joshua turned away.

"Hello, Joshy." She inched closer to him.

"Mama, you look well," he said, without looking at her.

"So do you." Andrea moved to embrace him, but Joshua turned away. "You must be my grandson. You're handsome. And like your grandfather, you've got the same large amber eyes and bronze skin." She pulled a string off his green polo shirt.

"I do? I've never seen a picture of him."

"Brandon, the bags?" Joshua said.

"We'll talk later." Andrea waved after them.

"Would you like to go inside?" Loretta said.

"Not yet. I think I'd like to walk around a bit." Her gaze darted all over the property. "See that magnolia tree? I planted it myself when it was a sapling. Now look how big it's gotten. Most of the flowers I planted, too. I'm glad to see Calvin took good care of them."

A gun fired in the distance, and they both jumped.

"Up there in the cupola room is where I shot my son." She pointed toward the attic.

"We don't have to do this now." Loretta walked beside her.

"We should go inside."

SHADOWS OF YESTERDAY

AFTER DONNA TOOK ONE OF THE LAST OF her pills, she decided to check out her former home to see how it had changed. The sun shone into the hall so bright she could tell the outline where certain pictures had been taken down.

Windwood smelled like centuries-old must and dust. Cream wallpaper peeled from corners up and down the hallway. Every piece of furniture had been taken away, and the pine floor was in desperate need of waxing.

She found that most of the doors had been locked. A room at the end of the hall was opened slightly. Donna entered the sizable space to find it had been perfectly preserved. The nineteenth-century rosewood roll-top desk where her mother, Flora, wrote letters to her father during the War of 1812, sat in front of one of the large windows that overlooked the grounds. A queen-sized bed with a blue bedspread lay against the wall, and a white marble fireplace with an array of framed photographs occupied the wall across from the bed.

On the nightstand lay a photo album titled *Our Family.* Donna sat on the bed and began to sift through the pages. There were so many pictures of Andrea and Calvin smiling, laughing, and very much in love. She chuckled when she saw a photo of Joshua when he was about a year old, standing naked in a silver tub. Another picture showed him at about ten, wearing a plastic Dracula mask for Halloween, next to an older boy dressed as the Wolf Man.

"That must be Simon," she said.

"It is, dear."

Donna looked up to see Andrea in the doorway.

"I'm sorry. I didn't mean to intrude, Missus Lord."

"Nonsense. You are the mistress of Windwood. I'm the intruder," Andrea scooted over to the desk and opened the righthand drawer. "I have a lot more pictures here, if you'd like to see them. And please, call me Mama. After all, you are married to my son." She sat beside Donna. "That was taken Christmas of '79, right before we headed out on the annual Lord Christmas cruise. Ah, that was Calvin at the Admiral's Ball, when Lord Shipbuilding won the coveted Tuggy Award for the best cruise line. We were really happy then."

"Is this Windwood?" Donna said.

"Oh, yes. Looked like a different place, didn't it? We had such grand parties. People from all over the world came to get a taste of Windwood's famous Southern hos-pitality. My garden was one of the finest in the South, winning award after award for its beauty and landscape." Andrea smiled as an abyss of memories swallowed her.

"How old is the house?" Donna said, after finding a black and white photo of the house when it looked new.

"The original house was started by Solomon Lord in 1790. He floated every piece of brick, iron, and marble down the Aurora. The house has been rebuilt 3 times, and upgraded and enlarged over the years. It sustained minor damage during the Civil war. A wing was added to the south part of the house in the 1800's, but in 1912 after years of flooding due to a primitive drainage system, that section of the house sank into the ground."

"The basement and the stairs leading to it are part of the original house?" Donna said.

"Why, yes, they are. How did you know that?" "Time for your rest, Miss Lord." Loretta entered the room.

"Thanks for talking with me. Joshua's past has always been vague to me." Donna got to her feet to extend her hand.

"I hope we'll get to be good friends." Andrea stood up to embrace her. "You make my son happy, and I'll forever be grateful."

"You've had an eventful day." Loretta pulled back the blankets and helped Andrea get into bed.

Then she handed Andrea a small Dixie cup full of water, and a yellow tablet of Risperdal.

"Go on. Swallow it." She watched with raised eyebrows as Andrea popped the pill and downed the water.

"See!" Andrea opened her mouth to show that she took it.

"Good girl. Now lie down and get some rest. I'll be back to check on you later." Loretta threw the blankets over her.

When the door closed, Andrea ripped the blankets off and got out of bed. She spit the pill out in her hand and tiptoed over to the door to crack it slightly. She watched until Loretta rounded a corner at the end of the hall, then hurried back over to the bed, put her blue flats back on, and rushed down the servant's staircase.

Loretta returned to the parlor, where Donna, Brandon, and Jenna sat playing Monopoly. From the looks of it, Jenna was buying up the board. Joshua stood by the window, lost in his thoughts, oblivious to the goings-on around him.

"Excuse me, Mister Lord," Loretta said. "I just thought you'd like to know that your mother has settled into her room."

"Miss Thornton, may I speak with you outside?"

"Sure." She smiled as she followed him through the large front door, out onto the gallery. "I know you have your reservations about your mother, but I can assure you she poses no danger to anyone." She leaned against one of the railings.

"Reservations? Do you know what that woman did?" Blood rushed to his face.

"I am aware of what she has done." Loretta folded her arms and sat on a white rocking chair. "That was a lifetime ago. I'm not telling you to forgive or forget, but your mother's had to live with what she's done. She's undergone shock treatment and a barrage of medicine, and has finally admitted there are no such things as werewolves."

"She did? Wow. The one thing she always insisted on was that she shot Simon because he was a bloodthirsty werewolf." Joshua sat in the matching rocker beside her.

"Your mother no longer exhibits any signs of paranoia, delusions, or fits of violence. Once she let go of the fantasy she'd created to justify shooting her son, she became a completely different person."

"You do realize she tried this before about ten years ago, when she pretended to suffer from multiple personality disorder."

"Her doctor figured her scam out and put a stop to it. This time it's different. She passed all the tests with flying colors."

"I hope you're right." Joshua got up from the rocker and went back inside.

Andrea was elated to be back at Windwood. The more she wandered around, the more exhilarated she became.

The peach trees she had planted had grown and yielded such a harvest that they could not only feed Solomon's Wake, but also the next two counties over. This made her heart proud. Even all the fish she'd stocked in the pond had thrived.

Before she knew it, Andrea was at Raven's Peak Cemetery, standing in front of the Lord mausoleum. The mammoth tomb of marble and granite housed every member of the Lord family. From the late 1700s, members of the family were buried in the lower level. And from 1851 on, they were placed on the second floor. Green marble statues adorned the inside. A skylight stretched across the roof, while a stained-glass window depicting a blond angel surrounded by other cherubs, guarded the entranceway. Near that window lay the larger than life pink tomb of her daughter Melanie. Andrea smiled as she placed a yellow rose she had picked earlier on top of the coffin. She patted the marble lid, then turned to her husband's tomb, directly across from Melanie's.

"Hello, Cal." She ran her hand across his plaque. "I've come home, and this time you cannot stop me. All of this is on your hands, Husband. You allowed me to have children, knowing all along that one day one of them would become a beast. You kept me locked up to keep me silent. Well, no more. I must kill Brandon and stop this poison from spreading anymore. I finally got to see him today. He looks just like you. And as he is the firstborn, we both know what will happen, because he carries the gene just like Simon, and we can't have that. No, the curse of the werewolf must end with Brandon, for all our sakes."

Tears welled in her eyes as she hurried out of the gate.

Once he had a moment to himself, Joshua looked around the mansion. He found himself upstairs and outside the room that was his brother Simon's. He sighed and stared at the door for a while before opening it, afraid that Simon would jump out from behind it, like he did when they were kids playing Hide and Seek.

Joshua felt his heart race as he turned the doorknob and pushed. Simon's room looked as it did the day their mother shot him—a museum to everything 1980s.

The curtains were drawn. The bed was made with the same blue and black bedspread, with the Panthers throw pillow. Above the bed hung a poster of supermodel Carol Alt. Across from his bed, on top of his chest of drawers, were all his trophies from soccer, football, hockey, and even one for chess champion of 1982. Yes, Simon Lord was a Jack of all trades, and Joshua's idol.

When he was little, he followed Simon everywhere and wanted to be just like him when he grew up. Most older brothers would've minded, but not Simon. He doted over Josh, even took him along on a few dates.

Joshua continued to look around the room until his gaze fell on the framed engagement photo of Simon and

Georgia. He sat on the bed and stared at the picture as he wiped the dust off with his shirt. Tears formed as he remembered happier times.

Andrea passed by the room and saw the door open, but couldn't bring herself to go in. She watched for a few moments, before shuffling down the hall.

The ex-Mrs. Lord was about to return to her room, when she heard Jenna playing Barbie in Melanie's old room. She stopped and caught a glimpse of the past. It was as if Melanie was alive again through Jenna. She could see her clearly, as if it was yesterday. If Jenna hadn't called for her, she probably would've stood there all day.

"Are you okay, lady?" The girl glanced up, then returned to brushing her doll's golden hair.

"I'll be fine." Andrea entered to gaze about the room she hadn't seen since the night she left.

"You're the woman hanging in the painting above the fireplace?"

"I am," Andrea said, with her back toward the child.

She reached for a tissue in her pocket and dabbed at her eyes.

"No, you're not. You're too old and wrinkly."

Andrea broke out in a fit of laughter. "I find it hard to believe myself sometimes. I can assure you that's me. You can ask your father if you don't believe me. I was in my twenties then, and had just moved into this house."

"Then you're my grandmother?" Jenna looked at her.

"That's right. And this was the room of my little girl, and your dad's sister Melanie." Andrea could feel the tears forming again.

"What happened to her?" Jenna looked up at her grandmother with these big blue puppy dog eyes and Kewpie doll cheeks.

"She died a long time ago." Andrea sighed as her gaze settled on a picture Melanie had drawn at school on Parent's Day. On red paper, she had drawn rainbows, kittens, and two stick figures with jumbo letters underneath—ME AND MOMMY.

"What happened to her?" Jenna reached for a polka dot stuffed elephant from a shelf on the wall.

"Jenna, I thought I told you to take a nap," Joshua entered the room, not realizing his mother was there.

"She's a beautiful girl, Son."

Before Joshua could respond, Loretta came by.

"Okay, lady, off to bed. You still have an hour before you're supposed to be up. Let's go!"

Andrea felt like a prisoner as she marched her out of the room.

"Wait!" Jenna cried, when they were halfway down the hall.

"What is it, sweetheart?" Andrea said.

Again, she was brought to tears as the little girl ran up to her and gave her a big hug.

13

THE RUNAWAYS

AROUND NINE IN THE MORNING, SIMON
was released from the hospital. As the nurse wheeled him
down the long corridor he clung to Georgia's hand until
they reached the front entrance. Outside, the hustle and
bustle of the city reminded him of Charleston when his
father took him and Joshua there when they were boys.

Georgia led him across the street, to the hospital
parking garage and over to a black sedan parked toward
the middle of the lot. For a brief moment, Simon thought
he sensed some other being near.

"What's wrong?" Georgia opened the trunk to toss in
the few bags Simon had.

"Did you feel that?" He scanned the garage.

"Feel what?" She opened the passenger door and threw
her purse in the backseat.

"I don't know. It felt like a power surge pulsated through my body. The only other creatures that can do that are other vampires, witches, and other Weres. I haven't seen a vampire in years. My bet is it's another Were." He stiffened his spine and growled as he prepared for battle.

"Calm down, killer. It was probably a shadow. It's dark in here. Simon, I think you need to relax and give yourself time to adjust. You just woke from a twenty-five-year coma. Look at it like a light suddenly coming on inside after being in the dark for so long. Your eyes have to acclimate to that light, so now your brain has to adjust to being used again."

Simon took her words to heart, but still felt like they were being watched as the car pulled out of the garage. After the sedan cleared the gate, a man in a black leather trench and sunglasses came out into the light to watch them.

"Where are we going?" Simon said, as trees and light posts whizzed by.

"To my father's lodge in the Rockies. It's the perfect place for you to recuperate, and far enough away from Solomon's Wake and your family."

"How is Gideon these days?"

Georgia looked like she had been punched in the gut, and she burst into tears.

"Sweetheart, what's the matter?"

"He's dead." She sobbed.

"I am so sorry." Simon rubbed her back. "How?"

"I don't know. I got a telegram. All it said was, *I regret to inform you of the passing of your father,* and that we were in danger. When I saw you weren't getting any better and needed serious care, with Sutton's help I moved you to Denver, hoping no one would find us. I even changed your name. Your family believes you're dead."

"That's is a lot to take in. Other than my mother, who'd want to hurt us?"

Georgia turned off onto I-70.

Jenna crept into the large master bedroom where Joshua and Donna slept. The morning light penetrated the lace curtains while a pair of hummingbirds sang out loud to welcome the dawn. The little girl tiptoed across the floor, toward the king bed, which seemed to devour her parents in its overstuffed mattress. Jenna poked her mom until she finally stirred.

"What's the matter? Did you have another bad dream?" Donna rolled over and noticed the clock on the night-stand read 6:20.

"I need to show you something." Jenna whispered, to not wake her dad.

"Right now?" Donna glared with tired eyes.

"Uh-huh!" The little girl nodded so hard it looked like her head would break off.

"All right." Donna put on her slippers and white satin robe, and followed Jenna out into the stuffy hallway, down the back staircase, and into the library. "You better have a good reason for waking me up this early and bringing me here."

"I found this in the back of the room, with a whole bunch of other pictures." Jenna lifted what looked like a painting, nestled against one of the long tables.

She held up the canvas to reveal the portrait of Edwina Lord, who had lived at Windwood in 1853.

Donna blanched and turned away.

"It's me, Mommy."

"That can't be you, sweetie. That woman died over a century ago, and she's a lot older than you."

Jenna was oblivious to the quivering in her mother's voice.

"That's not all. I found this book in this desk drawer, and it has another picture of me." Jenna hurried over to the drawer, opened the book and found the page she was looking for. "See!" She shoved the book at her mom.

Donna felt sick as she stared at the photo of a portrait of a woman who sat with a smile, in a navy-blue velvet dress. A tiara sat atop mounds of black hair. Her hazel eyes glistened, and a teardrop diamond necklace rested between her breasts.

"Her name was Eleanor Lord," Jenna said. "She lived back in the 1800s, and she was a princess. Mommy, could I be related to both these women? That woman I see in my dreams looks exactly like these ladies."

Donna kept her back turned to her daughter.

"There is also another woman named Iris, who looks like these other women. She lived here in 1912, and is hanging in the upstairs hallway."

"It's very possible. I don't know much about Daddy's ancestry." Donna sat in one of the desk chairs. "Jenna, come here." She opened her arms, and her daughter went right into them. "Turn around and look at me."

She had not attempted hypnotism in a long time, but felt it necessary to keep her family safe. Jenna looked up at her with wide eyes full of love.

"You will forget all about these pictures. You came down to show me the library."

"Isn't this place huge?" Jenna said.

"It sure is. Why don't you go get ready for breakfast? Then later, I'll take you for some ice cream."

Donna was glad to see she was still able to use her mind control. Most of her other powers ceased when she started the pills.

She ripped the picture out of the book and stared at it. The girl in the picture smiled back at her. Only, Donna knew the grin was a farce. Behind those bright hazel eyes was pure evil. After all these years, Donna found that she was still afraid of her sister.

"Your ugly jealousy always got the best of you, Eleanor. After Mamma died, and Aunt Regina took the reins, you poisoned her gloves. Then you went as far as accusing me of sleeping with your husband. You cursed him and his descendants by turning them into bloodthirsty were-wolves. But instead of it being my offspring you cursed, it was your bloodline that you damned. You couldn't live with what you'd done, so you took your own life. Then your real mother, Luna, took her revenge on me and our entire family. Sister, you belong to the past, and have no business being in the future."

Donna felt her rage boil over as she tore the picture into little pieces. She grabbed the book, and went to the kitchen to stuff the remaining bits of the picture into the garbage disposal. She turned on the disposal with a grin, and then headed upstairs to the bedroom.

When she saw Joshua had gone, she hurried into the bedroom, opened the nightstand drawer to throw the book in it, and reached for her cell phone before slamming the drawer shut.

"It's me. I need to see you."

14

SIMON'S TORMENT

THE MILES PASSED BY WITHOUT THEM seeing so much as a store, a gas station, or another car. Then out of the blue, the little town that held Gideon's lodge came into view. In the town square, a carnival was underway. Seemed busy for a Wednesday night. The fair offered such things as the crocodile boy, the bearded lady, and the littlest woman in the world. But the thing that got their attention was Octavia's Tent of Wonder, where they saw an old woman reading fortunes, the tarot, and a crystal ball.

"Simon, can we stop?" Georgia said.

He was reluctant at first. But his curiosity got the best of him, and he agreed to see what Octavia could tell them. Maybe this time the old woman could tell them something about his family's accursed existence.

Butterflies fluttered in their stomachs as they drew closer to the tent, which was smack in between the Tunnel of Love and the Fun House.

"I don't know about this. Something about her scares the hell out of me." Georgia stopped in the middle of the road to admire the Ferris wheel, with its yellow and white lights that seemed to shimmer off the polished red seats to light up the night sky.

"Georgia, never mind about that wheel." Simon grabbed Georgia by the arm and dragged her toward Octavia's tent.

"I'm scared. Maybe we should just go to the lodge. I almost lost you, Simon. I'm not ready to lose you again."

"My mother shot me, and I lost twenty-five years of my life because of that bullet. I owe it to myself to find out how this all started, and why, for centuries this curse has destroyed my family. I told you at the hospital, you're stuck with me now." He pulled her into a passionate kiss, then charged toward the tent.

Georgia was at his heels, but paused when she saw the man in the black trench coat and sunglasses standing by the ticket booth.

"Simon, see that guy over there?" She pointed at the ticket counter.

"Now you're seeing things. There's no one there."

"He was just there!" She scanned the fairgrounds with her scotopic vision, but found no threat. "A man was standing over there, watching us." She strode toward the Tilt-a-Whirl.

People all around them were smiling and laughing, without a care in the world.

"What's the story, bright eyes?" Octavia said, in a domineering tone, as they approached her makeshift table, complete with a crystal ball. "Never mind. I'll tell you." She motioned them to sit in front of her on two wooden crates, and then asked to see Georgia's hand. "Hmm ... someone is looking for you." She leaned in closer to get a better look at Georgia's hand.

All Georgia could think about was the awful smell of patchouli oil and ribs cooking.

The gaudy silver earrings Octavia wore had a hypnotic effect on Georgia, who felt dizzy.

"That star behind your ear ... when did you get it?"

Georgia was about to answer, when Simon pushed Georgia's hand away and replaced it with his.

"My turn."

Octavia placed her hand on his, and felt a pulse unlike any other.

"You come from an old family. A bloodline that goes back centuries. This clan has seen plenty of heartache, and has a bounty of dark secrets. Secrets that threaten all who share your blood. I see her surrounded by death, her eyes full of darkness. Beware of this woman, for she cast the spell that troubles you all." Octavia remained fixated by the ball before her.

"What woman?" Simon stared at the fortune teller.

"She's a witch whose origins trace back to your roots. I see a large house haunted by its past. Be cautious of this place, for its walls hold many skeletons. A scar on your family name could pave the way to your ruin." Octavia raised her hand to her mouth and turned from them.

"What's the matter?" Georgia said.

"You're werewolves. I knew it when I saw that star behind your ear." Octavia went over to a trunk behind her.

"Werewolves?" Simon fidgeted. "Us? You must be mistaken."

Octavia stood and pointed the barrel of a rifle in their faces.

"I don't want any trouble. The last time a werewolf attacked was in 1912. I put silver bullets in here, so I'm going to give you until the count of three to make tracks. One..."

Simon scooped Georgia into his arms and bolted.

"Two..."

He turned to see Octavia waving the rifle in the air. Her yellow headdress fell off, and her snow-white hair was wild. The unbalanced woman fired at them as they raced toward the sedan. She chased them out onto the fairgrounds as people screamed and ducked for cover.

A bullet grazed Georgia's neck. Simon threw her into the backseat and zoomed away from the fairgrounds as Octavia continued to shoot and yell obscenities.

"I don't know where to go." He sped down the street.

"After you pass the corner, follow the road until you can't. Make a right, and it's the lonely house by the creek.

Hurry—it burns," Georgia cried, as smoke rose off the nick in her neck.

"We're almost there."

At last, Simon passed through a clearing in the woods, and came to the little lodge. He bounded up the front stairs, kicked open the door, threw Georgia on the couch and began to lick her wound.

"You could at least wait until the bleeding stops before you try to have your way with me."

"Hush up. My saliva will heal your neck."

"It feels better already." She lifted her long copper locks so Simon could fully see her wound. "I hope it doesn't leave a scar." She got off the couch and went into the bathroom to fetch a bottle of Iodine.

"It's only a little nick. Your hair will cover it." He looked at her through the doorway as he took his shirt off and draped it across the back of the couch.

Georgia stood in front of the medicine cabinet mirror as she slid the thin nightgown over her head, onto her ruddy skin. She possessed a natural beauty and confidence that intoxicated anyone who met her. Many men found themselves eating out of her hand, something which always got Simon's dander up.

Georgia began to sob, and Simon was beside her in a second.

"What's the matter? Are you hurt somewhere else?" He inspected the wound on her neck again.

"I thought you were gone forever. When you left us, I wanted to die. But I never believed you weren't coming back, and now you're here." She choked up as a flood of tears burst forth, and she buried her face in his chest.

"I promise I'll never leave you again."

Georgia shifted her green-eyed gaze to Simon's shirt-less body, and to the trail of hair that went from his navel to his waist.

"Welcome home!" She slipped her hands into his trousers and undid the button of his pants, which slid to the floor.

Without taking her gaze off Simon, Georgia slipped her gown off. Her perky breasts stared him right in the face as she pushed him down onto the floor and climbed onto his lap. Simon encircled her back with his strong hands as he thrust his hips up and down. Georgia moaned each time he pushed harder. Soon, they climaxed at the same time, and released their canine side with a fierce howl.

They remained silent for a while in the dim light of the living room, all sweaty and tired from their lovemaking. Georgia still sat on his lap.

"I love you." Simon kissed the top of her head. She looked up into those big blue eyes of his and pulled him into another kiss.

"And I, you." She hopped off his lap and headed for the kitchen.

Simon watched her sashay across the room, and whistled. Georgia turned around to blow him a kiss. He smiled a smile so bright they could see it in China.

The alarm clock on the end table went off, and Sheriff's "When I'm With You" drifted out of the speakers. A day planner next to the radio was opened to July 10, 2012.

"It's our anniversary. Georgia, come in here, please." He grabbed a silk purple rose from a vase on the desk by the bed.

"What's the matter?"

"May I have this dance?" He bowed, with the rose in his mouth.

"It's our song." She grinned as he spun her around the room, singing the song word for word.

"Twenty-five years ago today, I married you," Simon whispered, nuzzling her ear with his nose as they swayed to the music.

"Ah. Even back then, you were my knight in shining armor. You found me shot on the side of the road, in werewolf form. You thought I was a wounded dog, so you brought me back to the house, where I almost died. When you woke up the next day, you found a naked woman in your bed."

"Thankfully, I did find you. I never knew there were others like me out there. I don't know where I'd be if you hadn't saved me. Just hours before our paths crossed, I was ready to end it all. Then you appeared and instantly made me a better person."

Georgia smiled, fighting back more tears.

"Windwood was so crazy that morning," she said. "I remember your grandfather's Aunt Eugenie—who had to be like a hundred and twelve—came to my room to tell me about the birds and the bees. I didn't have the heart to tell her I already knew." She chuckled.

Classical music followed. They continued to dance and reminisce about their big day.

"You had those teal bridesmaid dresses with the Dynasty shoulder pads, and then the Olivia-Newton-John-like headband veil."

"Me? Really? If I hadn't put my foot down, you would've come to the ceremony looking like Don Johnson or George Michael."

The two laughed, followed by an uneasy silence.

"Then that bitch shot me." Simon drifted out onto the porch, still naked.

After years of waking up on some lawn or street, it was an afterthought to him. Half the people in South Carolina had seen him in the buff.

Simon looked up and saw a shooting star streak across the night sky.

"Make a wish." Georgia came up behind him to cover his eyes.

Her naked skin felt cool on his exposed back as they stood in front of the wooden rail.

"I have everything I want right here." He pulled her into another kiss.

"Happy anniversary, my love," Georgia said, as they stared at the night sky.

"I think I want to go home."

"Are you sure you want to go back to Windwood? Your mother could be there."

"I'm counting on it."

He had that intent look in his eyes, which he always got when he was determined to do something his wife would not approve of.

"Simon, please don't do anything rash."

15

FAMILY TIES

AFTER HE MADE SURE NO ONE HAD FOL-
lowed him, the man with the sunglasses and trench coat
returned to his motel room. He was still in shock. After
years of searching every hospital, morgue, and police
station, as well as several continents, he'd found his daughter, thanks to Earl, who had called to tell him Joshua Lord
was back in town.

Sure enough once Joshua settled into his role as master
of the house, Sutton called Georgia to let her know they
had come home. Gideon camped out day and night outside
the house until his heightened hearing picked up the call
that finally revealed Georgia's whereabouts.

He took his coat off, hung it on a hanger, then put his
glasses on the nightstand before he reached into the mini-
fridge for a beer. He lay against the headboard, staring

at the ceiling as he savored his brew. Gideon reached for his wallet and pulled out a tiny photo of two little girls. One had copper hair and green eyes, and wore a pale yellow dress while sitting on a swing, with a tiny smile on her face. The other girl was smaller, with brown hair and green eyes, wearing a matching short set with Minnie Mouse on it. She was crying because she wanted to use the swing.

"I am so sorry for what I've done and the pain I've caused you, Georgia. I promise I will make it up to you, if it takes till the day I die." Gideon brushed his finger across her face. "Now, if I could only find Ginny."

Twenty–something years had passed since he'd lost both his girls. Georgia, he knew was safe. But Ginny seemed to have vanished without a trace.

He put the picture back in his wallet and turned on the TV to find *Curse of The Werewolf* playing on AMC. A quarter of the way into it, Gideon fell fast asleep.

Joshua watched his mother in the greenhouse, amongst all her plants. For a moment, he caught a glimpse of the woman he once loved while she hummed and pruned her begonias. Andrea had been home a few weeks, and already she had the conservatory back in tip-top shape.

All the different-sized pots were stacked on a shelf behind her. The garden tools hung from largest to smallest, underneath the pots. Even the seed packets were arranged alphabetically in cardboard trays on the table in front of her.

"She's very happy today." Loretta paused outside the conservatory door.

Joshua continued to stare at his mother through the glass.

"Excuse me, sir." Sutton entered the hall from the butler's pantry. "You wanted me to inform you when Missus Lord returned."

"Yes. Thanks, Sutton." Joshua nodded at them both before cutting across the hall and through the pantry.

"Before I forget, Miss Thornton, one of the trunks you sent for has arrived. I've taken the liberty of having it delivered to your room."

"Thank you, Sutton. You're a lifesaver. I don't know what I'd do if I had to keep wearing the same three things over and over." She thanked him and scurried off.

Sutton approached the greenhouse. He stood in the doorway for a moment, glaring at the former mistress of the house, who appeared ignorant of his presence.

"I know what you're up to." He inched in.

"Do you?"

"You may have everyone else in this house fooled into believing you've been rehabilitated. But I know better." He stood with his arms folded, watching her.

Andrea jumped up from the stool, slammed the shears down, and caught Sutton by the throat.

"Listen up, you washed-up faggot. I know you were in love with my husband. I overlooked it because I knew it was one-sided. But if you stand in my way, I will kill you." She reached behind her for the shears. "Are we clear?" She relaxed her grip a little and aimed the shears at his gut.

"If you hurt them in any way—"

"You'll what? You couldn't even save them last time." She finally let go of his throat. "Now run along," she hissed, and sat back down on the stool as if nothing had happened.

Sutton staggered off, dazed from the chokehold she'd had on him. Andrea appeared to be old and frail, but she was as strong as an ox.

She just had to throw in his face how he had done nothing to stop her the night of the wedding. Sutton had followed the master of the house up to the attic and watched as Andrea fired at Calvin and pushed Simon out the window. Memories of Nam and all the death and carnage he'd witnessed came back to him in a split second, paralyzing him and preventing him from doing anything.

Sutton stopped to catch his breath near the end of the hallway, holding onto the ivory rail. His heart continued to race as he gasped for air, each breath getting deeper and deeper. Having asthma didn't help.

"Ah, but I did save him from you, psycho," he spat, as he regained his composure enough to walk down the stairs. "Simon's alive, and you don't even know it."

Toni looked toward the great house and couldn't shake the feeling of evil. Staring at the cupola, she saw the specter of a young woman. At first she didn't know what to make of it, until she realized something even stronger than that poor, helpless girl waited in their midst.

The sun was shining down on Toni, giving her dark black hair the luster of jet. Her bronze skin glistened, and her clothes were brightly colored.

"It's so sad." She walked with Donna, from the car. "Rosa would turn in her grave if she saw this."

Toni's gazed wandered here and there, and settled on the woods that surrounded the house and dominated the land. Arm in arm, they entered the foyer, where Toni saw the old, yellow-fringed red rug said to have come from the Sea Court Palace in Marin, brought here by Solomon himself. The rug was now faded, with holes in it. Like everything else around her, that too, had been robbed of its beauty.

Hanging high above her on the walls, the many portraits of all the Lords glared down from their perches, where they had rested for years. A stairway, its balustrade made of pure ivory, was in the center of the grand foyer, with a doorway built into it that led to the basement. Overhead, a chandelier hung from the high ceiling by a thread, ready for the perfect moment to come crashing down.

"Is that who I think it is?" Joshua called from the dining room.

"Joshy!" Toni hurried over to embrace him. "You're still as handsome as ever."

"Things haven't been the same since you left. Would you like a drink?" He went into the parlor and over to the liquor cabinet to pour a whiskey tonic.

"Vodka on the rocks, please. Easy on the ice." She sat on one of the chairs and took off her red silk headscarf, allowing her jet-black hair to flow. At almost eighty, she had not one gray hair, her sun-kissed skin was still flawless, and she looked about fifty.

"I see the Venetian air seems to agree with you." He handed her the drink.

"Venice is beautiful—not nearly as busy as Rome, and more laid back—but I miss my inn and my family so much that I may move back."

"We'd love to have you back." Joshua smiled as he sat next to Donna on the sofa.

"Nonna!" Jenna cried from the doorway, and ran into Toni's arms.

"There's my little principessa." She kissed the little girl all over the head and squeezed her tight.

"I didn't know you were coming," Jenna said.

"Surprise! I even brought you a doll made to look just like you." Toni tapped her on the nose with her finger.

"Really? Can I have it?"

"It's in the car, if you want to go get it."

Jenna jumped for joy and dashed out of the room.

"I'll go help her. That way, I can bring your bags in." Joshua followed after his daughter.

"We have a problem." Toni said, when Joshua and Jenna left the room.

Donna stared at her blankly as Toni got up to shut the parlor doors.

"I'm out of bloodroot. Some other supernatural force sent a fungus, causing the roots to wither and die."

"Oh, my God. What am I going to do? If I don't have those pills, everyone I love will be in danger."

"I won't let it come to that." She sat next to Donna on the sofa, and put an arm about her waist.

"How?" Donna sobbed as Toni brushed some of the dark hair from her brow.

"We'll have to get into the tomb."

"No. We can't. That tomb was sealed for a reason. If we open it again and one of those rabid Weres escapes, or that box gets open, we're all as good as dead."

"Would you rather have everyone know that you're really Martha Lord? I don't like it either, but the blood-root only grows in darkness and only thrives by streams, where werewolves are known to drink. That underwater prison is the only place we can be certain the blood-root will be."

"If we do this, we risk fulfilling Luna's curse." Donna got up from the sofa to pour herself another drink.

"I know, but it's a price I'm willing to pay."

"Well, I'm not. Just the thought of my little girl becoming that witch, or my handsome boy becoming a werewolf, makes me wanna die all over again."

"The thought of me losing you has the same effect on me. Y'all are not my kin, but I have grown to love all of you as much as any mother would. If opening that tomb gives me the chance to be your mother a little longer, then I'm willing to do that. I'm sorry if that's selfish, but that's how I feel."

"She's already begun to remember," Donna said.

"Okay. That doesn't mean she's going to be possessed by Luna. And I told you when Brandon was born that I took care of it. He won't become a werewolf as long as he continues to drink the orange juice laced with silver." She patted Donna on the hand and returned to her chair to fetch a cigarette from her purse.

"Yes, it does. I was there when she spat those wretched words from atop that beautiful four-hundred-year-old Southern live oak. I watched her shift her head toward my father as if she could see through the blindfold before the noose encircled her neck. Luna warned all of us that from this day forward, every century, a girl would be born into this family who would resemble Luna in every way, and that child would carry her memories and one day rise up to bring this family to their knees."

"That's been anticipated for many years, and nothing's ever happened." Toni went out onto the gallery to light her cigarette.

"That's because none of the women ever lived long enough for the curse to work. In 1853, Edwina Lord died from typhoid. And like Jenna, she had visions of the future and was the mirror image of Luna. In 1912, Iris Lord, another dead ringer for Luna, was sealed in that cave with the werewolves before we could find out if she was becoming Luna." She followed Toni outside into the warm Carolina air.

Donna looked across the lawn at the summer sun, which shone directly on the Southern live oak, and thought she saw Luna's lifeless body hanging from the tree branches.

"Whatcha looking at?" Joshua brought Toni's black leather luggage up the front stairs.

"I thought I saw something." Donna looked back at the tree, but nothing was there.

"It's this house. It gets you every time." He smiled and went into the house.

16

SIBLING RIVALRY

SIMON AND GEORGIA AWOKE EARLY TO take a jog around the property, something they had enjoyed every morning at Windwood. With just a quick cup of coffee, the duo headed outside to find a beautiful blue sky, a breeze, and lots of sunshine. Simon stared at Georgia in her gray jogging suit with pink stripes. Her hair was tied back, her face full of happiness.

"What, is there a wasp on me?" She almost twisted her neck off to check.

"I'm just admiring the view." He kept staring at her.

Georgia threw up her arms, hugged him, and kissed his face.

"I still can't believe you've come back to me," she said, as they came down the front steps.

Octavia was hiding underneath the stairs.

"Evil can never outrun a gypsy." Octavia cackled as she pointed her revolver at Georgia, then spat, "Our world is safer with the likes of you out of it."

Simon leapt in front of Georgia to shield her, sending them to the ground as Octavia fired and hit the front door. She moved closer and fired again, hitting Simon in the leg. The silver bullet burned, and his insides felt like they were on fire.

"Lights out." Octavia pointed the revolver at his head.

Simon closed his eyes, said a prayer, and squeezed Georgia, who was still beneath him.

A charcoal black wolf the size of a pony jumped out of the woods and attacked Octavia, tearing off the arm she held the gun with. Then it decapitated her.

Simon got off Georgia and grabbed the gun from the severed arm to aim it at the beast.

"Daddy?" Georgia used her elbow to knock the gun out of Simon's hand.

"Hello, Georgey," the wolf half-barked.

Georgia reached out and touched his face. The wolf pushed his muzzle into her hand while he rubbed up against her waist.

Georgia wept with joy at being reunited with her father. Simon watched from a short distance.

Then Gideon pushed Georgia, sending her into a potted bush and scratching her right arm and cheek in the process. He jumped up and caught a quail in his jaws and tore it to shreds.

Simon helped Georgia up and out of the brush.

"If you were hungry," he said, "all you had to do was ask. I would've gotten you something to eat."

"That was no quail. That was your everyday Changer." Gideon moved out of the way to reveal a mangled young redheaded woman lying naked and dead a few feet away from him.

"Why'd you have to kill her?" Georgia ran into the house.

"Believe me, Simon. I have my reasons. Can you bring me some of your clothes so I can morph back to myself? I really don't think you or my daughter want to see me without clothes on. I promise I'll explain everything."

"Fair enough." The screen door banged shut as Simon entered the cabin.

Gideon climbed onto the front porch and lay down at the top of the stairs. There was another Changer, but it managed to get away. Others would soon show up, and he would be ready for them. He just got his family back, and no one, supernatural or otherwise, was going to take them apart again.

Channing paced on the front porch of his compound, known as Wolves Den, nestled in a forest somewhere in West Virginia, anxiously awaiting the return of his two scouts, who should have been back hours ago.

While he was imprisoned beneath Solomon's Wake, he had plenty of time to plot his revenge. Gideon would live to regret locking him down there, and Toni would pay the price for helping him.

He reached into his pocket to pull out his cell phone, and began dialing the number, when another call came through. It was Lila, his best scout.

"We lost Ingrid. Gideon spotted us, and before we could do anything, he caught Ingrid and just..." She choked up. "Anyway, I'm a bit banged up myself. I don't think I can make it back to Wolves Den."

"Did he find my sister?" Channing sat on the loveseat next to his Siamese cat, Ming, and pet her.

"Yes, he did."

Channing closed his phone, then chucked Ming across the lawn and howled. He slammed the sliding glass door so hard it shattered. His harem curtsied as he flew past them and down the stairs to the prison where he kept Nola.

"Daddy bested you again, didn't he?" She stepped up to the bars of the jail cell.

"I'm really getting sick and tired of your smugness."

Nola looked at the giant standing before her, with his broad shoulders, enormous arms, and thick neck. The pack leader was easy on the eyes and had his sweet moments. But for the most part, he was a cunning killing machine that would squash anything in his path to get what he wanted.

"What are you going to do? You've already imprisoned me. You gonna behead me or throw me down in the quarry with the others next?" She sat down on a cot that was positioned against the wall.

"That's exactly what I'm going to do." He stared at her through the bars like she was lunch.

"Your father will stop you before he'll let that happen."

"I'm gonna use you as bait. Gideon will have no choice but to rescue you. We are going into that pit and freeing my mother. We will be the happy family we were always meant to be."

"You're delusional!" Nola yelled. "If any one of those creatures get out, we could have another epidemic on our hands."

"Maybe. Lucky for you, I have a vaccine. Only, I haven't used it yet, so I'm not sure what its effects will be. You get to be my guinea pig. Inject her. "He left.

The guard looked at her, stone-faced. He moved toward her with the pace of a cheetah, the syringe in his hand. Nola froze as he unlocked the barred door. She knew the syringe was full of the virus.

"Stay away from me!" she wailed, as she backed into the corner of the cell.

"I'm sorry, Nola. I have my orders." The guard continued to advance. "Let's not make this any harder than it has to be, huh?"

She kicked him and punched at him until he grabbed her by the hair and dragged her out of the cell.

"Please, Colum. I used to babysit you. I took you on your first kill when you first morphed."

"If I go against Channing, he will be so angry there's no telling what he'll do to me or my family."

Before she knew it, he had the needle against her arm.

"I'm sorry, too." She kicked him right between the legs.

Colum doubled over in pain, and the syringe slid across the floor.

"You bitch!" he said, through clenched teeth.

Nola shoved him into the cell, and snatched the keys and locked the door.

"No, no! You can't do this to me. Nola, I'm sorry. Please. I have a wife and kids at home. Do you know what he does to those who fail him?" Colum's golden-brown eyes began to water.

Her emotions were always her downfall. Nola stared at the once-strong man who now cowered and begged to be released. Pitiful.

"Very well." She found the right key.

Colum seized the opportunity and caught her once again by the hair.

"You should've run when you had the chance." He gripped her platinum locks. "I can hold you here all night."

Her scalp hurt so bad it brought tears to her eyes. She was powerless as her face got closer and closer to the bars.

Nola stretched her foot out, and with the tip of her boot, was able to reach the syringe. Then she bit down on Colum's big hand.

"Ouch! That hurt. You're going to pay for that." He let go of her hair.

"Tell someone who cares." She injected him with the syringe, then ran out into the outer hall and shut the Scottish metal door behind her.

This silver door was so strong that without the key, no werewolf, witch, or vamp could open it.

Be strong, Nola. She slipped out of the compound via a trash chute used to shuttle the bones of the pack's numerous victims into Barkers Creek.

17

TAINTED LEGACY

FROM THE MOMENT DONNA SET FOOT BACK inside her ancestral home, Windwood's dilapidated state broke her heart. Everything her father had worked hard to build, and all he'd smuggled out of the Grand Duchy, was gone. That morning, at breakfast, before the reading of the will, she approached Joshua with the idea of restoring the house.

"If it means that much to you, then you have my blessing. But are you sure you want to restore the house, and not modernize it?" Joshua sipped from his coffee mug.

"No, this house is too full of history and antebellum charm. I could never do that. I like it the way it is." She stared over the large dining room, and out at the faded mural of Olympus. "I'll start with Olympus." She pointed toward the hall.

"I know of a great painter in town." Andrea reached for the butter. "I would love to help. It's a project I've always wanted to tackle. This house needs to shine like the showcase it was destined to be." She smiled.

"That would be great," Donna said. "I could use all the help I can get."

"Mom, I can go on eBay and see if Grandfather sold any heirlooms?" Brandon said. "If so, I could try and get them back." He then stuffed his mouth full of scrambled eggs.

Donna patted him on the head and pulled away, because God forbid if she messed up the hair.

"Can I watch?" Jenna said.

Being the fussy eater that Jenna was, Donna was not at all surprised by the full plate in front of her.

"Of course you can," Donna replied. "But only if you try to eat a little more."

Jenna scoffed and groaned.

"Excuse me, sir." Sutton entered the dining room. "Mister Westbrook is ready for you in the office."

"Thank you, Sutton. Tell him we'll be there in a few minutes." Joshua finished his orange juice.

"Oh, come on, Jenna. Eat something, already," Donna said, as the girl continued to turn her nose up at the plate before her.

"Can I get you anything else, Missus Lord, before I go?" Sutton shuffled over to the table, giving Andrea an icy stare.

"Yes. Could you just put a plate aside for Missus Corsini when she comes down?" Donna tried to put a forkful of scrambled eggs into Jenna's mouth. "Whaddya say we take a walk around the lake later, Brandon, and you can tell me all about school. Then later on, we can talk about your grandfather. I can even show you some pictures, if you'd like."

"That would be awesome." Brandon grinned.

"What about me?" Jenna said.

"You're not going anywhere until you finish that plate. I'm tired of telling you. You don't finish that food, then no cartoons, young lady."

"I promise, Jenna. You and I will do something later." Andrea winked at the little girl.

The office, although small, fit them all comfortably. Joshua and Donna sat in front of the desk, and Donna held her husband's hand. Andrea sat in the back, next to the door, with Jenna on her lap, and Brandon stood by the window. Sutton stood behind Joshua.

"Good afternoon, everyone," the family lawyer boomed.

Everyone sat quietly, waiting to hear what he had to say next.

"*I, Calvin Lord, hereby leave my estate to my son Joshua. I also leave to my son Joshua my business and all its holdings. To my daughter Peyton, fifteen shares. To my ex-wife, Andrea, I leave my Arabian horse and eighteen shares. Joshua, along with what you have already acquired, I leave fifty-one shares to hold until Brandon and Jenna turn twenty-one. I have also taken the liberty to appoint Daniel Westbrook as the new vice president of Lord Shipbuilding.* That's all. We're finished here now." Mr. Westbrook rose. "Here is a videotape Calvin left specifically for you, Joshua." He pulled it from his briefcase and handed it to the newly minted heir. "He left this for you as well, Miss Lord." He handed her a sealed envelope written in Calvin's hand. "I'll be on my way. Good day." He headed for the door.

"If you all would excuse me, I'd like to view the tape." Joshua opened the walnut armoire at the end of the room to put the tape in the VCR.

Everyone nodded and left him alone.

Calvin appeared on the screen. "Hi, Son. If you are viewing this, then I am no longer with you. Joshy, you and the others think I wanted to drive you out of Windwood, when that couldn't be further from the truth. I had no choice." Calvin's eyes began to water, and his lips quivered. "You kids meant the world to me. All I've done, including making you leave this house, was to protect you from the evil that lives within the confines of Windwood. From the moment your grandfather died and we moved here, our lives were changed forever. I regretted, for many years, my decision to uproot our family, because the price I had to pay was losing everything." He ran his hands through his thick mop of gray, as he often did when upset. "Whatever you think of me, know that everything I did, I did because I love all of you more that my own life. I had to protect you from the ghosts of our past. Don't make the mistake I did. Leave Windwood before—"

The VCR made a grinding noise, and the tape jammed before Joshua could hear the rest of Calvin's message. He began to cry, and hurled the tape at the wall.

"What are you trying to tell me, Dad?" He looked up at the portrait.

Joshua sat staring at the fuzzy screen. Before getting up to shut it off, he saw Sutton shuffle by the open door.

"Sutton, could you come in here, please?" he called out.

"Yes, sir?" Sutton closed the door.

"Have you heard anything from my sister Peyton?" Joshua sat behind the desk and tried to straighten it up.

"No one's heard from Miss Peyton since your stepmother died. Master Calvin hired all kinds of PIs to find her, and always came up short."

"I can't say I blame her. The trial took a toll on all of us. She was so young when Vivian was murdered. I can only imagine how it impacted her life."

"No matter what you've heard, or what people have said, your father was innocent. He was a kind, generous man who loved you. Never forget that."

Toni was glad to be with family again. She had forgotten what it was like to have people around her.

Most of her things had been unpacked and put away, except for her pictures, which she began to place about the room. She finally got to the last picture of a beautiful blonde-haired, dark-eyed young woman wearing a white cotton dress and standing on a porch.

"I miss you, Carla." She took the hem of her dress and wiped the glass before placing it on her nightstand.

"Nonna, why are you crying?"

"I was just thinking about your cousin Carla. Today's her birthday."

"If you miss her so much, why don't you call her?" The little girl came in and sat beside Toni on the bed.

"It's not that easy, little one." Toni wiped the tears from her eyes.

Later, Toni slipped out of the house to go to the one place she knew she could stop Luna—the inn. In the late 1800s, a passageway was built underneath Corsini House, which went directly to the secret room. If it was still there, she could get inside and find what she needed. To get to the passageway, she had to go across town, through the cemetery, and find the giant marble monument of a hooded woman kneeling as if she was in church. In her hand was a rose. Once removed, it would open the passage.

As Toni walked around, she couldn't get over how much had changed. The people in town now walked around half-naked. The family owned-and-operated bank had now become a chain. Same thing with the supermarket, laundromat, and movie theaters. Bars lined the street, and an adult store was in plain sight. Solomon's Wake sure wasn't the same town she remembered.

Toni passed the street that would take her to the inn, which had been her home for many years. She knew she wasn't ready to see it just yet, and walked straight past the turn-off. Before she knew it, she was in the cemetery. Thankfully, this was still kept clean and trimmed. Her husband's stone gleamed under the sun rays. The trees looked green as ever, and the birds were music to her ears. She sighed and took it all in.

"I'm sorry I don't have any flowers. I wasn't exactly planning to come here." She couldn't take her eyes off the stone. "Try not to be too mad at me for not coming sooner." She sat on a bench next to his grave. "I had to come back and make sure that whatever is coming after Donna and the others is stopped. I wasn't there for Carla. Lord knows I blame myself, so I cannot sit back and do nothing again."

As Toni sat in silence, she continued thinking about Carla, wondering where she was, and if she was even alive. Carla was all she had left now that her daughter, Marie, had died. The private detective she had hired to find her daughter informed her that she had died from an overdose in an alley in Chicago.

Finding her resolve, Toni got up and spotted the statue. She charged across the cemetery, through the rows of stones, until she was face to face with the giant relic.

"How am I supposed to move that?" She stared at every angle of the flower, unable to figure it out.

Frustrated, she reached underneath, and with all her might, pushed the flower up. She gasped as the mechanism moved and the statute slid open to reveal stairs in the base.

Toni inched down the stairs, into the unknown passageway.

After their walk around the lake, Andrea and Brandon returned to the house, where, as promised, the old woman retrieved her photo albums and gave Brandon his first look at the grandfather he never knew. Most of the pictures were black and white, with a few color ones placed sporadically through the book.

Calvin Lord stood about five-feet-eight-inches tall, with a soft face, amber eyes, dark hair and bronze skin. In the photo, he was flanked by two young boys, both with dark hair—one being Joshua, and the other Simon, who favored Andrea more.

"You weren't kidding," Brandon said. "It's like looking in the mirror." He continued to stare at the photo. "Who's the other boy?"

"That's your Uncle Simon." Andrea turned to hide her face, and caught a glimpse of Sutton in the hallway mirror, spying on them.

She pretended not to see him.

"What happened to him?" Brandon closed the book and laid it back on the desk.

"He died a long time ago. Why don't you show me how to play that Nintendo Box? I used to beat your dad at Pac-Man all the time. So much so, that he stopped playing with me." She chuckled.

"You're on." Her grandson flew out of the room so fast he was halfway down the hall before he realized she wasn't behind him. "Nana, you coming?" he said, through the doorway.

"Go get everything set up. I'll be there in a minute."

Once Brandon had gone into his room and shut the door, Andrea confronted Sutton, who was cowering behind a flower stand.

"Next time you wanna eavesdrop, you might want to make sure I don't see you."

She glowered at him, then continued to Brandon's room.

Jenna had fallen asleep shortly after the reading of the will. The moment she shut her eyes, the ugly witch came, as she always did. Only, this time, it was like looking through a cloudy window. She saw them bring the witch out from her cell in the basement. The heavens turned dark, and the sun vanished. A strong wind ensued, followed by a powerful storm.

Along the way, her feet scraped across many stones and branches, and a hornet flew up her burlap dress to sting her on the thigh. The witch fought her captors every step of the way. First, she tried to make her body limp to force them to carry her. She even tried to bite, but the blindfold around her head prevented her from doing so.

Once they came to the steps of the platform that led up to the large oak tree, the burly jailer yanked Luna up the stairs by her hair, causing her to scratch her legs even more.

"Luna of the House Corsini, do you have any last words?"

From his raspy tone, Luna envisioned the gray-haired priest to be old, in dark robes, glaring up at her with a smug face. She looked down toward the portico and knew they smiled at her.

"Do you have any last words?" he repeated.

Luna nodded and spoke so softly the priest could not hear her. The cleric moved his ear closer to the prisoner's mouth, and Luna tore his ear off with her teeth. The priest collapsed onto the wooden floor. Blood trickled down Luna's mouth as she held the old man's ear between her teeth. The sorceress bit her own lip before she spit the hunk of flesh out onto the lawn.

"From now until the end of time, a girl will be born in my image once a century, and that girl will sow the roots of your destruction. As for you, dear princess." She glared down at Solomon's daughter, Martha. "Your comeuppance will begin with the first full moon."

She cackled like a wild woman until the jailer pushed her from the scaffolding, snapping her neck.

The witch turned to look at Jenna. "You are my last hope, little one. Seek out my blue diamond pendant somewhere on this property. Find it, and I promise you all your dreams will come true."

The little girl jumped out of bed, ran over to the door, and peeked out into the hall. Seeing that it was empty, she hurried out and down the servant's stairwell, into the backyard, where she got a shovel and lantern from the garden shed.

Jenna Lord then set out to find the mysterious necklace.

When Toni came out of the passageway, she found everything still intact. It was dirty—cobwebs were everywhere, and inches of dust covered the furniture and some of the artifacts.

She went over to the wall with the monitors and turned them on, amazed at how crystal clear the pictures still were. As she scrutinized each monitor, she finally saw what she wanted on the last screen. The sarcophagus was still intact, and bloodroot was growing a few feet away from the door that held the coffin. It grew tall in the murky tomb, and in abundance—enough to last Donna a long while.

Smiling, Toni turned off the monitor and headed back outside.

18

FAMILY SECRETS

THE HOT SHOWER FELT GREAT. GIDEON hadn't had one in months—the one at the motel was always cold. As he stood there, letting the water cascade over his head, he tried to figure out how to tell Simon and Georgia what was going without giving away too much.

"Dad, you've been in there over forty-five minutes." Georgia tapped on the door. "Don't think that by procrastinating, I'm going to forget that you owe me an explanation." She turned around and went back out into the living room.

"If I knew he was going to avoid us, I never would've offered him the shower," Simon said from the sofa, flipping through the channels.

"Typical Dad." She filled a mug with water and placed it in the microwave. "Would you like a cup of tea?"

"No, but I'll take a beer if you have one."

"Me, too." Gideon stepped into the living room, wearing khaki shorts and a baby-blue T-shirt, both of which belonged to Simon and fit perfectly.

Georgia threw one to Simon, then shut the fridge door, leaving Gideon high and dry.

"Tomorrow, we're gonna have to go to the mall and get some more clothes," she said. "There isn't enough for the both of you to wear." She eyed her father before fetching her tea from the microwave.

"Thank you for lending them to me, Simon."

"Okay, enough with the pleasantries. Daddy, what's going on? Why were there Changers following you? And more importantly, why did you lead me to believe that you were dead?"

She grabbed the milk from the fridge and poured a little into her cup. Gideon sat at the little round table in the small dining room, still in eye-shot of Georgia.

"I did it to protect you," he said.

"Protect me from what?" She pulled out the chair next to him and sat.

"A spirit."

Georgia burst out laughing. "Really, Daddy? You couldn't come up with something better than that?"

"It's the truth." He reached for her hand, but Georgia snatched it away.

"You'll never change." She fled the room in tears, and slammed the bedroom door.

Simon finally took his gaze off the TV to look down the hallway, and then to his father in-law.

"I have to agree with her, Gideon. That sounded kind of lame." He turned back to the screen.

"I don't care how lame it sounds. That's exactly what happened." Gideon sat beside him on the lumpy sofa.

"Why would a spirit want to hurt you?" Simon pulled up the cable guide.

"Revenge."

"For?" Simon continued to scroll down the index page.

"He blames me for killing his daughter."

"Who does?" Simon put on some dance show.

"It's actually one of your ancestors—Marshall Lord." That got Simon's attention. "Marshall Lord died in 1922. There is no way you knew him." He returned his focus to the show.

"Simon, I am over three hundred years old, and I lived in Solomon's Wake in 1912."

"Now I get it! You hate me and my family because of a vendetta with a great-uncle of mine. All those times you've tried to talk Georgia out of marrying me were because of something Marshall did?"

"No. I don't like you because you're not a blue-blooded werewolf. You're a monstrosity born out of a curse that will poison the Blake bloodline when you two decide to have pups of your own."

Gideon seethed. Just the thought of grandchildren sent him into a rage.

"I know your family thinks so highly of themselves." He sneered. "They even named a town after themselves, as well as a highway and a library. But you will never be good enough for my little girl."

"Tell me how you really feel." Simon frowned. "You could never handle that your daughter was going to marry into the high and mighty Lord clan. For the record, we decided we weren't gonna have children."

"No, I couldn't, because I married into it myself. I saw firsthand what happens to those who do."

Simon looked at him like he had something stuck in his teeth, and broke into a fit of laughter.

"You almost had me fooled." He waved a finger in Gideon's face.

Then he saw the serious look on his father-in-law's face, and the sadness in his eyes.

"You're serious?"

"Her name was Iris Lord, the most delicate, beautiful, and intelligent woman I had ever met. I knew the moment I laid eyes on her that she was the one for me. However, her father, Marshall deemed me to be beneath the mighty Lord family, and did everything to separate us. His plan backfired, and Iris became a casualty in a war that needn't have been waged. Marshall was so angry that he waited over a century to pay me back."

"What did he do?" Simon said.

"He took my daughter Ginny. I haven't seen her since the night of your wedding. I never wanted to say goodbye to Georgey, but I had to, to save her, or else I risked losing her, too. I originally planned to meet up with her later, but I lost track of her." He looked at Simon, trying to fight back the tears.

"What do you mean he took Ginny?" Georgia said from the doorway, gaze fixed on her father.

"Exactly how it sounds. He took your sister. She just vanished into thin air."

Georgia felt nauseous. How could she not have known something was wrong with her sister?

She slid down to the floor and bawled. Gideon sat next to her and took her hand into his. The two stared straight ahead, not saying a word.

"So the Changer you took down this morning," Georgia used her sleeve to wipe her eyes, "was she responsible for Ginny's disappearance?"

"No, that was all my doing. Before your wedding, there was an explosion that opened the old quarry, allowing a man named Channing to escape. That man hates me so much he'd hurt you or your sister to get to me." He turned his head to look his daughter in the eyes.

"Why does he hate you?"

Gideon stood, took a deep breath, and realized he could no longer hide the truth from Georgia. He went back over to the table to pull the chair, and motioned his daughter to sit.

"Simon, you might as well hear this, too," he yelled into the living room. "Iris and I married in a secret ceremony. We had a son, who was a young boy when she died. I was young and not ready to raise a child on my own, so I left him with my father, who would groom him to be pack master in place of me. I should've known better, for my father was a vicious, self-loathing narcissist that didn't have a kind bone in his body. He exiled me after I stopped him from beating my mother within an inch of her life."

"You were going to be pack master?" she said.

"Yes, I was. But I never wanted to be. My father hated me for it, and did many things to try and toughen me up. One night, shortly before I left, I saw him breeding with a shapeshifter out by the barn—a big no-no in the wolf community. I used that to force him to take my son, because if the truth got out, the elders would've either banished him, or stripped him of everything." The pain Gideon had to endure was still as fresh as the morning dew in his mind.

"I have a brother?" Georgia didn't know if she should be happy or sad.

Simon stood behind her, not buying any of it.

"As the years went on, I saw him less and less, until I stopped seeing him altogether. I met your mother, fell madly in love with her, had you girls, and was happy for the first time in years. One day, I got a knock on the door. It was him. He had learned the truth from my father shortly before he died."

"Channing's my brother, isn't he?"

"Yes, he is." the admittance seemed to age Gideon a bit.

"I don't understand why you've kept this a secret for so many years." His daughter jumped up from the table.

"He's dangerous, Georgey. That's why Toni Corsini and I imprisoned him in the quarry with the others."

Gideon watched her face become cold, and her glare pierced his soul.

"That's horrible, Daddy! How could you do that to your own son? No wonder he hates you." She jumped up from the table and sent the chair flying into the wall.

Simon stood silent in the doorway, not sure what to think.

"Channing murdered your mother." Gideon felt relieved that his secret was out.

Georgia stopped halfway into the living room to turn around with a confused expression. Gideon almost wished he hadn't told her, for that look alone sent hundreds of silver bullets into his heart.

"I don't understand any of this. Why kill Mom? She couldn't hurt a fly. She cried when a goldfish died, or said fifty thousand Hail Mary's when you said the word *crap*. For God's sake, she covered Ginny's eyes when we passed the lingerie window at the mall." Georgia plopped down on the sofa.

"He came to visit me at the house. When he learned I'd remarried and had more children, he got jealous, resentful, and thought that because he was pack master, he was invincible. He blamed me for Iris's death, and begged me to set it right by opening the quarry so we could find his mom and become a family. I told him his mom could not be let out, but that he could become part of our family. Next thing I know, he hit me over the head. When I came to, your mom was an unrecognizable mangled mess on the floor. Ginny was sound asleep in her crib, but you were nowhere to be found." Gideon slid down on the sofa next to her.

Simon remained in the doorway, still dumbfounded over Gideon's tale.

"Where was I?" Georgia laid her head on her father's shoulder.

"He kidnapped you and took you out to the quarry. When I showed up, he held you under the water until I agreed to open the passage. After I opened it, he continued to carry you down into the mine, and threatened to feed you to the infected if I didn't stay by his side." A tear formed in the corner of his left eye.

"That had to be so awful for you. I can't imagine going through that all alone." She looked at Simon, who gave her a reassuring wink.

"If it weren't for Toni, you wouldn't be here now." Gideon kissed the top of his daughter's head.

"Sounds like Toni's always trying to help," Simon said, "and make someone's life a little easier."

"What did she do?" Georgia said.

"She used a cloaking spell, which allowed her to sneak up on Channing. She bashed him over the head with a stone, and I snatched you. We sprinted out of the quarry, and Toni put a seal on it that lasted until the explosion cracked it open."

"So Toni is a witch? I never would've believed it." Georgia chuckled.

"Now that he's out, he will exact revenge, and he will not stop until he kills you," Gideon whispered, afraid of what would happen if he said it too loud.

"He'll have to get through me first." Simon pumped out his chest like he was Tarzan.

"Why does he want to kill me?" She moved toward Simon.

"Because you look like your mother, and all he sees when he looks at you is a threat he has to eliminate so he can secure his happy family. He's taken Nola, too. And he won't rest until he completely breaks me."

"Well, then, we're just going to have to make sure that doesn't happen." Georgia got up and strode over to an armoire across the room.

She opened the heavy doors and pulled out a silver machete.

"We fight. I'm tired of losing people. I lost Simon. I lost you and Ginny—I'm done. This isn't Halloween, and I'm no Jamie Lee." She reached for the weapon.

"It's going to be dangerous, Georgey. Channing is going to hit us with everything the pack has." Gideon looked at the other goodies in the armoire.

"Then we hit them twice as hard." She smiled, put the machete down, and hugged her father.

"If only finding Ginny could be this easy," he sputtered.

"Can I say something here?" Simon raised his hand. "It seems to me that all this unpleasantness stems from Windwood. So I suggest we start there. If Ginny indeed vanished from the house, she may have left behind a clue. And if not her, then maybe Marshall."

"You would help me?" Gideon said.

"No. However, I love your daughter, and I will do it for her. I haven't forgotten that you tried to kill me."

"What?" Georgia said.

"I did nothing of the sort. I do hate you, Simon. That's no secret. But I would never try to kill you."

"Bullshit. I saw it with my own eyes. You were in the library with my mother. You had a gun pulled on her, and then you watched as she shot Aunt Eugenie. My mother hates me because you told her I was a werewolf!" Simon caught Gideon by the throat and choked him until he began to turn blue. "I lost everything because of you."

Gideon felt like he was going to lose consciousness at any moment.

"Let him go, Simon." Georgia tried to pull him off her father.

Gideon managed to kick Simon in the groin, causing him to let go.

"I didn't do it." He rubbed his neck. "Lord knows I hate you, Simon. Your family has done nothing but bring misery to everybody and everything you come in contact with. Yes, I tried to stop the wedding. And yes, I would've given everything I had to break you two up for good. I know about the curse and how it will affect your firstborn. I don't want any kin of mine carrying the Lord name, but I would never murder the one thing that has brought my daughter so much happiness."

"I saw you."

"I believe him, Simon." Georgia put a reassuring hand on her husband's shoulder.

"Well, I don't." He stormed out through the screen door, and into the night.

"I'm telling you, Georgey. It wasn't me."

Georgia knew her father told the truth. Whenever Gideon Blake was caught lying, he would bite his lower lip unconsciously.

"I know, Daddy. We'll talk about it in the morning. I think we all need some sleep."

She turned off the TV and went to the bedroom.

19

ECHOES FROM THE PAST

THE SUN WAS STARTING TO SLIP BENEATH the horizon, and little Jenna Lord still found no traces of the mythical pendent. She had looked all over the mausoleum, torn apart the stable, and dove into the pool, to no avail. Now, lost and in the dark, the little girl began to panic, for the one thing she feared most was the night.

"Why did I do this?" she wailed, turning round and round, trying to get her bearings straight.

All the trees on the estate looked the same now, and every path seemed identical. An owl perched high above in the trees hooted, sending the child into a tailspin, and she bolted, not knowing or caring where she was going. She just knew she had to get away.

A thorn bush caught the shoulder of her shirt. Screaming, Jenna pulled so hard she ripped her shirt and went flying. She fell down a hole and slid down a long shaft, hitting her head when she came out on a fireplace mantel. Unbeknownst to her, she had found the missing wing of the house, and landed smack dab in its drawing room.

As the little girl lay there unconscious, the apparitions of Lords past materialized and hovered above her.

It was getting late, and Jenna had not come out of her room since earlier this afternoon. Fearing that she was coming down with something, Donna went into the bathroom to get the Children's Tylenol, the VapoRub, and the thermometer from the medicine cabinet, and proceeded down the hall, when she saw the shadowy figure of a woman standing at the end of the corridor.

"You must save her," the spirit moaned.

"Who?" Donna looked right through the spirit, to the painting of some ancestor that hung on the wall.

"Save her." The specter vanished, leaving Donna to stare at the wall.

"Jenna!" She dropped the items and made a beeline for her daughter's room.

Her heart thumped and the tears streamed when she found her gone.

"Jenna!" Donna continued to call, as she went from room to room.

"What's the matter?" Back from the inn, Toni flew up the stairs.

"It's Jenna," Donna cried. "She's missing." She threw the door open and searched the upstairs parlor.

"I'm sure she's around here somewhere. It's a big house. She could be anywhere." Toni followed her into the parlor.

"No, it's Luna. I know it." Donna sobbed and plopped down in one of the chairs by the window.

"Just because she's missing doesn't automatically mean that Luna had something to do with it. If she did, I would feel it." Toni bent down to take Donna's hand. "I promise you, we will find her."

"I saw a ghost tonight, and she told me I had to save her," Donna said, choked up. "I knew we should never have come back."

"Running away isn't the answer, either. If that witch wanted to find you, she would, no matter where you went. Now let's stop feeling sorry for ourselves, and find your daughter," Toni yanked her out of the chair.

Soon, the whole house was searching for the child, and it was becoming clear that Donna and Joshua were living every parent's worst nightmare. The hours passed, and everything they did proved futile. They were almost out of options, and would have to involve the police.

Toni decided the best way to find the child was to contact the spirit Donna had seen earlier via a séance. It had been years since she'd performed one, but like a bike, once you know how to ride you never forget. Toni gathered the family in the upstairs parlor, the nicest room in the house, and only used for special occasions. Painted in pastel colors, and containing portraits of ancestors from the 1700s, this room didn't match the rest of the dingy house. A huge Ming vase nestled in a corner, and ferns and spider plants hung in pots from the ceiling. The carpet was pale peach, as was the upholstery. In the middle of the room was a long pine table that seated ten.

Andrea loved this room. It was the only thing she could call hers, as it contained items that had survived from her family. The room also had a balcony that overlooked the river.

"Please be seated so we may begin," Toni motioned for them all to sit. "Join hands, please, and then close your eyes. Now take three deep breaths. Everyone relax as I speak. Spirits of the dead, I summon you from your graves. All of the specters that haunt this land appear to me. We are in need of answers that are of great importance."

She stopped to catch her breath, when the candle flickered.

"Who's there?" Toni waited for a response. "Give me a signal."

The French doors to the balcony blew open, and a figure glided in.

"Who are you?" Toni said.

"I am Katherine Lord. Why have you disturbed my rest?" the apparition said, in a sorrowful tone.

"We need your help," Toni said.

"I know nothing. Let me go," Katherine whimpered.

"Tell me of the girl," Toni said.

"Let me go, now." The specter vanished as quickly as she'd come.

"I will tell you." They all turned to look at Andrea, who appeared to be possessed.

"Who are you?" Toni said.

"Annabelle Lord," Andrea said, in a voice not hers. "She's alive."

Andrea began to convulse as the table rocked, and the candle flame blew up toward the ceiling.

"Where is she?" Toni said.

"You must stop this séance before it is too late."

"Why?"

"The portal is open now because of you, allowing her to come forward. She can't be stopped once she's free."

"Who?" Toni said, in a calm tone.

"You don't realize the evil you're about to unleash," Annabelle whispered.

"I don't understand."

"I have to go now. I think she saw me."

Everything went dark. All the windows in the room shattered, sending glass into the air. Every portrait on the walls came to life. The horses dashed across the meadow. The oil painting of the Lords' first liner, *Odyssey,* which set sail in 1922, whistled three times as passengers waved and cheered goodbye to their loved ones on land, the smell of saltwater hanging in the air.

"What's happening?" Andrea said, apparently recovered from her possession.

"She's here." Donna stared at the fireplace, whose embers burned bright until a fireball shot out, revealing the twisted manifestation of the witch Luna, who cackled as loud as a siren. She hovered above the table, bringing with her an unfathomable cold.

"You, the descendants of Solomon, will endure my wrath. You may think I'm a nuisance now, but soon you shall feel my full fury as my prophecy reaches fruition." She shifted her beady-eyed gaze to Donna. "Remember what happens to those who dare to love in my house."

She pointed her crooked talon-like finger at Donna, who jumped up from the chair to stare at her nemesis.

The lights came on, and their ghostly visitor vanished.

"Jenna's gone, and she's never coming back," Donna wailed, as she fled the room.

Joshua hurried after her, but Andrea stopped him.

"I'll go. Stay here and continue to look for Jenna." She shuffled out of the room.

"Who is this Luna?" Sutton rose from the chair to start cleaning up the mess the specter had left.

"She was a powerful shapeshifting witch hung right out that window." Joshua pointed toward the broken window a few feet away from them. "Family lore has it that she cursed Solomon Lord. Throughout my family's history, stories of witches, supernatural beings, and other unknown forces have beset my ancestors. I always dismissed the stories as myths, but now I'm not sure." He went over to the sideboard to pour a drink.

"Tell me of the events that took place in this house back in 1912," Toni said. "I see blood everywhere, bodies hacked to pieces, and the dead returned from the grave."

"How'd you know about that?" Joshua's voice trembled. "Nobody but a Lord's supposed to know the true origins of this accursed house."

Toni motioned for him to sit across from her on a green loveseat.

"Marshall Lord went mad and butchered everyone in this house," he said. "India Lord, the sole survivor, blamed it on the witch and mistakenly killed a woman in her hysteria. She lived out the rest of her life in the asylum. Marshall never got over what he had done, even though he had no recollection of it. My father often said that when that wing of the house sank into the ground, it trapped the souls of the dead inside forever."

"If we could find the sealed-off rooms," Toni said, "we might be able to free the souls locked in."

At last, Jenna came to. It took her a few moments to adjust her eyes to the darkness, which seemed to swallow everything. The murky quarters were covered in cobwebs. Floorboards were rotted, as well as certain parts of the walls. Broken rafters fell from the ceiling, and the whole first floor smelled like mud.

"I need to get out of here," she whined, standing in the center of the drawing room.

"*Find the necklace, Jenna,*" that familiar voice called, from nowhere.

"Where? I don't know where to look." She spun around to look for the voice.

"*Follow your instincts, little one. Follow your instincts.*"

"Wow, that was a big help."

The girl found that she was not as scared as she thought she'd be, and began to move about the room as her eyes adjusted to her surroundings. After opening the double doors, she stepped out into the foyer, which was in worse shape than the drawing room. She had to get up the stairs to search the second floor, but the stairwell to the upstairs rooms had collapsed, and as far she could tell there was no other way up.

"How am I supposed to get up there?"

She sat in the middle of floor and tried to figure out her next move.

Sutton passed Brandon's bedroom and found Andrea sitting on the edge of his bed, playing some video game. From the looks of it, she had mastered the level. Sutton took this opportunity to search her room, in hopes of finding something that would tell him exactly what she was up to. The moment Andrea Sullivan came home to Windwood, he knew she would be nothing but trouble.

After switching on the lights, Sutton rummaged through all her drawers, and her desk. He moved on to the closet and looked through all the shoeboxes, garment bags, coats, and hats but found nothing. While searching, he made sure he left everything exactly as he'd found it.

After closing the closet door, out of the corner of his eye he spotted something yellow sticking out of the ficus tree by the window. Sutton hurried over to the tree and found her Risperdal tablets buried in the soil.

"I knew it!" He rushed over to the desk phone.

Thankfully he didn't move too fast, or he would have fallen flat on his face when he tripped over a barbell under the bed.

"What are you doing in here?" Loretta barked, from the door.

"Your job." Sutton showed her a yellow pill.

"Where did you get that?" Loretta entered the room.

"From the fica tree." He pointed at it. "She had them hidden in the soil."

Loretta's eyes widened, and then she scowled at having the wool pulled over her eyes.

"Son of a bitch." She sat on the bed.

"Time and time again, I've warned you people not to let her out. She's unstable and should not be allowed to roam free. Yet you didn't listen, and now she places everyone in this house in danger."

"I think you're overreacting. Just because she didn't take her medicine a few times doesn't make her a homicidal maniac."

"Then what do you call this?" He picked up the barbell to show her. "Seems to me like somebody's been working out. If she isn't up to something, then why does she have this?"

"I'm going to have to call this in. You might want to get out of here before she gets back." Loretta got up and strode over to the phone.

"Let me tell you something, Miss Thornton. If anything happens to this family because of your negligence, it'll be your head." He stormed out.

How could they have been so blind? Andrea had been put on a strict medication regimen, and given aftercare services. Hell, she'd even fooled the facility's top psychiatrists.

"Operator, can you connect me to Riverview Sanitarium in Rock Hill."

Loretta had her back to the door, unaware that Andrea was listening from the hallway.

20

THRILL OF THE HUNT

IT HAD BEEN DAYS SINCE NOLA HAD SEEN anyone, and from what she could tell, no one had followed her. Her feet ached, and her stomach growled as she pressed on through the woods, trying to get as far away from Wolves Den as possible. She figured she was somewhere in North Carolina, but she wasn't certain. Even though she wanted to stop, she knew better, because the moment she did, Channing's goons would be on her.

The whole time Nola had been running, she felt so bad for what she'd done to Colum that she almost turned back to check on him. If she wasn't in love with Gideon, she would have. Finding Gideon was all that mattered, and stopping Channing and the pack from hurting him was her number-one goal.

The sun was beating down on her. The humidity was unbearable and wreaked havoc on her pale skin, and did even worse damage to her hair. She leaned against a sourwood tree to find some relief from the sun, when she heard the sound of running water a few feet away. Nola sprinted until she came through a clearing and to a pond. She dove headfirst into the cool water and felt refreshed as she splashed, flipped, and floated on the water. The tranquility of it all relaxed her enough that she almost fell asleep while she lay with her head back, staring at the sky. But she noticed a hawk circling above.

"Great. They found me." She bolted out of the water and back into the woods.

The hawk gave chase. Knowing she could never outrun it, Nola shifted into a silver wolf and outran the hawk in minutes.

Bo and Reginald came to Franklin County once a month to hunt coyote and take a break from life. They were best friends who'd grown up together, and now worked together and lived on the same block. They hiked through the woods while keeping an eye on their surroundings. It had been years since they'd caught anything.

"I don't know why I let you talk me into coming," Reginald said.

"Wow. If I wanted to hear bitching, I would've stayed home with my wife," Bo said.

"If you'd done that, I wouldn't be out here freezing my ass off for nothing." Reginald stopped to light a cigarette.

"I thought you were quitting those." Bo gave him a disapproving look.

"Now who's bitching?" Reginald blew the smoke in his friend's face.

"When you're on an iron lung, I don't want to hear it."

"And then when you're—"

"Did you hear that?" Bo darted toward the sound.

"Hear what?"

"Something's coming." Bo peeked through the brush to find a silver wolf prancing toward them.

He raised his rifle and fired, hitting the beast in the chest. The animal collapsed.

"Yeah, I got it." He jumped in the air. "And who didn't want to come?"

"It only took ten years." Reginald traipsed through the clearing to get a good look at his friend's catch. "Oh, my God. What have you done?" He hurried over.

"I shot a wolf."

"No, you didn't, you idiot. You shot a woman." Reginald stared down at a naked woman with a platinum blonde hair and a bullet wound to the chest. "Hurry! Call an ambulance."

"I didn't mean to do it. I saw a wolf." Bo was shaking so badly he couldn't dial the numbers. "Dammit, I can't get a signal." He felt dizzy.

"Hurry! Go get the truck. We're running out of time. If we don't get her to the hospital soon, she's gonna die." Reginald took his flannel shirt off and used it to apply pressure to the wound.

"I'm gonna be sick."

"It's going to be all right. Just relax. I can't have you going to pieces, and having to take care of the both of you. Let's just focus on getting her to the hospital."

Bo nodded and took off toward the truck.

The hawk that had been circling earlier landed on a branch nearby and watched as the men place Nola's limp body in the truck.

Back at the house, Toni could no longer sit by and do nothing. She decided she was going to try and find Jenna herself. She went out the front door to get some air, and saw the apparition of Annabelle crying.

"Annabelle, what's the matter?"

"The pain won't go away," the spirit moaned.

"What pain?"

"The pain of being trapped within the walls of this house forever. Many of us have been here since our deaths. We suffered brutal fates, and our souls must be released so we may rest in peace. Toni, you must find my remains and give me a proper burial to end my torment, and also exorcise the lost wing of the mansion so we all can finally be free from the evil forces that are still working against us."

Annabelle vanished, leaving Toni intrigued by the quest ahead of her. She began to look for the long-forgotten wing to banish Annabelle's soul.

After spending an hour trying to get upstairs, Jenna at last found a route through the cobwebs, broken railings, and fallen mortar that took her to the second floor, which looked unscathed. The upstairs rooms were freezing, and the ceiling dripped. All the doors were closed, and an ungodly smell surrounded her. A mouse scurried across her foot, causing her to scream, which triggered more of the ceiling to collapse.

Knowing time was running out, Jenna searched everywhere, but came across nothing of use. She crossed over to the other side of the hall, to a room consisting of a wrought iron bed, a small table, and tiny closet. A Bible lay open on the table, next to a single candle.

Next door were more living quarters, this one by far the most elegant of all. The walls were ivory, and the drapery red velvet. The floor polished hardwood with throw rugs. The bed was fit for a queen, and portraits of more ancestors accented the walls, with a granite fireplace to give the room warmth.

The bright room had many windows. A wall-sized vanity was filled with brushes, combs, cosmetics, powders, and perfumes galore. Many fluffy pillows lay on the bed, with the red bed curtains pulled back. There were no dressers or trunks, and every article of clothing or accessory she owned was in the gigantic closet at the foot of the bed.

A portrait hung above the fireplace mantle. The subject was Landon Rutherford Lord. He was handsome, and unlike some of their other relatives, he was smiling.

Jenna finished and went across the hall to another bedroom, and it was the dreariest of all she had seen thus far. A bearskin rug was sprawled on the floor. Animal heads decorated the walls, from moose to elephant. Pistols and rifles took up two display cases. Had it not been for the broken-down vanity table, you would have never known a woman shared the room.

Jenna rooted through the trunks at the end of the bed and turned up empty-handed. She left the room and passed some more empty ones before finally stumbling upon Annabelle's room. Gazing around, Jenna saw many mirrors, a large crimson settee, and a flowered basin. A pleasant scent of roses still lingered in the air. Velvet crimson blankets and pillows adorned the ivory bed, and a veil-like curtain hung from the canopy.

"At last, you've come to help," the specter of Annabelle cried.

Jenna took one look at the apparition, and fainted.

21

A MOMENT IN TIME

TONI FINALLY GAVE UP ON FINDING THE child, and began the long trek back to the house. Every sound, every movement, gave her the heebie jeebies. She picked up the pace, and in typical klutz fashion, tripped over her own feet and wound up eating grass.

As she got up, she noticed a piece of Jenna's shirt snared in a thorn bush. Toni found the hole when she fell into it. The whole way down, she felt like she was on a water slide as she skidded down the chimney.

Inside, the air was damp and stale. She groped around in darkness for a few seconds, then turned on the tiny light from her keychain, which barely illuminated the room. Toni could still see the grandfather clock in the corner, and a beautiful oil painting of Windwood hanging over the fireplace mantle.

She found some matches and a candle on the mantle. After lighting the wick, she was confronted by eight specters.

"Don't be frightened," an older woman said, with an air of elegance. "We will not harm you. Please sit."

Toni stood frozen.

"I am Katherine Lord. Welcome to my home. Allow me to present to you the remainder of my household. The one seated at the window is my daughter-in-law, Diana. The twin girls playing the clavichord are my great-granddaughters, Lorna and Lana." She slapped her hands together and turned to the young girls to scold them for stopping.

The room was prettier than the drawing room that the family currently used. The parlor was laid out in Georgian fashion, and the lime green curtains hanging in the window were pulled back on both ends.

Katherine had a warm, motherly look about her. Her gray hair, tinted with white, was pinned to a plum satin bonnet. The old woman's skirt was of the same color.

"The rest of my family includes my daughter, Deborah. The men on the circular sofa are Mister Alden Pierce and my son, Nelson. And I presume you already know of our Annabelle."

"How did you all end up here?" Toni said. "The truth about what happened here that night was covered up and forgotten."

"Lana and Lorna were found floating in the Aurora because of Deborah," Katherine said, "who at the time was under the influence of the witch. Deborah even poisoned her own mother with cyanide," she muttered.

"I died by my own hand," Diana said. "One by one, we all succumbed to tragic ends. Once the good Lord called my beloved Annabelle home, I gave up and found myself in the attic. I attached a rope to the rafters and jumped."

"Marshall murdered me in my sleep," Deborah said, in a spine-tingling tone, her eyes filled with fury and pain. "Before Luna tired of my body, she took his. He came to me in the middle of the night and bludgeoned me to death with an ax."

"My wife Olympia and I were sailing on a warm day in late July," Nelson said. "Olympia hated the water and didn't know how to swim. Like a fool, I stood up and began to rock the boat. When I fell in, the mast hit me in the head. Well, I trust you can judge for yourself what happened next."

"My dear, you are now on your own," Katherine said. "If this is to work, you must do it alone. Farewell, Toni. Thank you!"

They all disappeared.

When Jenna came to this time, she noticed the trunks hidden under some clothing that had been strewn about over one hundred years earlier, and still remained there. Jenna shrieked at the discovery of the skeletal remains of Alden and his lady love, Annabelle, in the hope chest.

"Hold on, sweetie," Toni said. "Nonna's coming."

The poor kid tried to grapple with what she saw. She was afraid to reach into the trunk, until she saw the blue diamond necklace sticking out from under it. The girl sat on the floor and used both legs to push the trunk, but the necklace was caught. She yanked it, and when it gave, the bones flew all over the room. Jenna scurried back into the hallway and collided with Toni.

"Am I glad to see you." Toni got down on her knees and took the girl into her arms. "The whole house has been out of their minds with worry." She fought back tears. "Are you all right?"

"I just want to go home." Jenna clutched the necklace in her palm while keeping it in her pocket and out of sight.

"We will. But I have to do something first. Can you do me a favor and just sit here on the steps till I come back?"

Jenna nodded.

"Good. I'll be back in a few minutes."

Toni returned to Annabelle's room to retrieve the remains.

Jenna pulled the clunky silver necklace out of the pocket of her pink shorts, and stared into the deep blue gem until an image appeared inside. She saw a beautiful sorceress lying on a straw mattress, holding a baby girl. A wealthy woman came in and snatched the baby, then set fire to the small shack, trapping the woman inside.

"You will pay for that." Jenna felt an odd rage erupt within.

"Who are you talking to?" Toni came down the hall with the bones wrapped in a blanket.

"Huh? I didn't say anything." Jenna had already forgot what the pendant had showed her.

A loud rumble echoed as the roof gave way. Toni leapt on top of the girl and took the brunt of the trauma.

"Are you okay?" Toni pushed a rafter off herself, and then brushed Jenna off as she turned her around to make sure she wasn't hurt.

"I'm okay. Can we go now?" The girl moved towards the stairs.

A few moments later, they were downstairs. Toni stood in the middle of the foyer and began to dig a hole between the broken floor boards, which was easy since they had been sopping wet underneath for over a century. She gently laid the bones in the hole, then covered them. In a thunderous voice, she chanted a prayer that would expel the spirits from Windwood.

With that, the phantoms of the distant past were laid to rest forever.

A gust of wind blew past Toni's ears, and she swore she heard Annabelle's sweet voice whisper, "Thank you."

"Nonna, look! There's an opening in the wall. It must've happened when the ceiling collapsed. I think we can get out that way." The girl rushed over to what she hoped was their exit.

"Jenna, wait for me. You could get hurt."

"See. It leads right to the basement."

"So it does. I'll go first to make sure it's safe. And once it is, you can follow."

Toni slipped through, found everything in order, and allowed Jenna to enter.

Donna took one look at her daughter and lost it. She sobbed as she held the girl in her arms. Tears even glistened in Joshua's eyes as he stroked his daughter's hair.

"I'm sorry," Jenna whispered, with a shaky voice. "I didn't mean to upset everyone."

"We're just glad to have you home," Donna said. "You've had a long day, so let's get you upstairs into the bath, and then to bed." She scooped Jenna up in her arms and carried her out into the foyer.

"Thanks for bringing her back, Toni. I don't know what we would've done if—"

Toni put her hand to Joshua's mouth. "No what-ifs. She's home, and that's all that matters." She poured herself a brandy and sat on the sofa. "I'm glad I could do it." Grief washed over her as she remembered Carla, and how she could do nothing to save her. "Stop fussing with me, and go spend time with that precious little girl." She took a swig of the brandy.

"You really are wonderful." Joshua kissed her on the cheek before heading upstairs.

"Happy birthday, Carla. Wherever you are." Toni raised her glass in the air.

A few moments later, she nodded off on the couch, with the tumbler still in her hand.

Lila did as Channing had asked, and continued to watch the cottage through the night. Finally, in the early hours of the morning dawn, under the guise of a field mouse, Lila squeezed through an opening underneath the door. Once inside, she saw Gideon fast asleep on the couch, with an old sitcom on TV. She continued down the hall to the bedroom that Georgia and Simon shared, and found them sleeping as well. A wedding photo of the couple sat next to the bed in a sterling silver frame. A woman in the picture's background caught Lila's attention.

This woman had bronze skin, black-as-night hair, and a motherly appearance. For some reason, Lila felt like she knew this woman, and the more she stared at her, the more she felt it to be true.

In a flash, she saw this woman again, sitting at a kitchen table, amongst an array of nail polish. The memory took hold as Lila began to recall something about her past.

Toni had been up all night, taking care of the bar and making sure everything was just right so she could take the day off and attend Simon and Georgia's wedding. She had to make it. Rosa Lord was one of her best friends, and she considered the Lords to be part of her own family. Especially Joshua. Ever since he was a boy, he always went out of his way to help her, whether it be with the trash or sweeping, and sometimes he would come just to listen to her. He even sweet-talked her into closing down the inn so Simon could have his bachelor lunch there.

Toni put her cigarette in the ashtray and got up from the table to check on the cherry cassata torte she'd made especially for Simon. It was his favorite. After pulling the dessert out of the oven and placing it on the counter to cool off, she looked up at the clock over the stove to see that it was already after four o'clock.

She sat back down, poured herself some more red wine, and tried to enjoy the rest of her cigarette. All she had to do now was shower, dress, and finish her hair, then get this dessert over to Windwood before someone else—namely, Carla—ate it.

"Ooh, my favorite." Carla came into the room and tried to touch the torte.

"That's not for you." Toni slapped her hand away. "Wow, you look beautiful!"

Carla was wearing a black mini-dress. Her gold locks were layered around the bangs and face, then curled and teased, giving it lots of volume. Black diamond earrings hung from each lobe, and a necklace of the same caliber brought attention to her plunging neckline.

"I think if I'm not careful," Toni said, "I'm gonna have to beat the men off with a stick."

"Do you really think I look good? Or are you saying that because you're my grandmother?"

"Ah, my little Stellina. You will shine so bright you may eclipse the bride." Toni held up a finger. "You're missing something."

She rummaged through all the cosmetics she had spread out on the table, and reached for a red lipstick.

After applying it, Toni said, "Now you're perfect. Look!" She held up a hand mirror.

"I look like I could be a model." Carla smiled.

"I've always said you had a million-dollar smile," Toni put her hands on her granddaughter's shoulders, and stared into the mirror, too.

"Nonna, I was thinking about maybe going to see Marie." She turned around to face Toni, who seemed upset at the mention of that name.

"If you really want to go see your mother, we can go first thing Saturday morning. If she's still at that address in Florence, we could be there in a matter of hours. But I can't stress enough to you that if she's using again, it may not be a pretty sight."

"I'm well-aware of that and everything else she's done, including swindling you and Nonno's life savings, and trying to sell me to that poor couple who couldn't have kids. Nonetheless, she is my mother and deserves a second chance."

22

IN ANOTHER LIFE

TONI SAW SO MUCH OF HER MARIE IN CARLA that sometimes it was like they were one and the same. They could easily pass for twins instead of mother and daughter.

"You remind me more and more of her every day. I have no problems with you seeing her, or even letting her back into your life. I just don't want you getting hurt again, like the last time. We almost lost you, and I promised myself I'd never let her do that to you again."

"I promised you and Nonno that I'd never try to take my own life again."

"If this is really what you want, then I'm okay with it. Now, I have to go finish getting ready. I should've had this torte over three hours ago." Toni placed the sweet dish into the plastic cake carrier.

"I'll take it over for you. I want to go now and make sure I get a good seat. I still can't believe it—Simon Lord is actually getting married." Carla grinned as she took the cake holder from the counter and clutched her purse in the other hand.

"Save me a seat," Toni called after her.

It was a mild evening, with a breeze blowing. Carla opened the trunk and placed the cake in the back of her Buick LeSabre, jumped in the car, and sped off toward Windwood. She cracked the windows slightly to avoid messing up her hair, then she fiddled around with the radio until she found a suitable song.

Carla continued down Route 7 until she saw a muscular man with a shaved head, standing in the street, trying to flag someone down. She slowed down to pull up beside him, and rolled her window down.

"Are you in some sort of trouble, sir?" She looked up at the giant.

"Damn raccoons. I'm afraid I was flying down the road, not paying attention, when one of them things came out onto the street. I tried to avoid it, and swerved out of the way, just to end up in this ditch. Now I'm stuck and can't get out." He looked down at her.

"If you like, I could give you a ride into town. I'm going that way, anyway." She unlocked the door.

"I'd appreciate it. That would be a big help to me. It's not often you run into decent folk anymore."

"You from around here?" She kept her eyes on the road.

"Nope. Born and raised in West Virginia." He slapped his knee.

"What brings you to Solomon's Wake?"

"You." The man reached into his pocket and pulled out a plastic bag of yellow dust. "I need a witch to help me. You're perfect for the job. The Corsini witches are famous. I've heard all the stories about how you can shapeshift, heal the sick, and even cure a curse." He flashed an impish grin.

"I'd sooner die than help you, wolf," she said, after noticing the canine in his eyes.

A mere mortal would never have been able to see it.

She started to get out of the car.

"Oh, but you will. See this little bag here?" He pointed to the yellow concoction. "It's memory dust. Once I blow this in your face, life as you know it is over, and Carla Romano will be no more."

"Why are you doing this?"

He gripped her thigh. "Because your beloved grand-mother helped keep me trapped in that cavern. She, along with my father, tried to erase me from existence. So I want to hurt them where it counts—family. So I'm gonna give Toni a taste of her own medicine and erase you."

"Fuck you!" Carla slammed her foot on the gas and sped toward the same ditch.

The two bounced around the car like a fish out of water, until the LeSabre slammed into the trench. Carla had a gash on her head, and the man flew out the front seat and through the windshield.

Dazed and not seeing clearly, she fumbled with the lock and managed to open the door. She could see the man lying face down on the hood of the car. Her instincts told her to run and to forget about him, but she wanted to make sure he was dead or unconscious.

Carla stared down at him, and before she knew it, he twisted around to blow the dust right into her face. She choked and coughed as memories of her life began to fade, and the woman who had raised her since she was three, her beloved Nonna, was now just a stranger on the street.

Her vision was blurred. She was unaware that the man had put her back in the car. Her head felt like it was hit by a sledge hammer. Pain radiated from her chest where it had smashed into the steering wheel. As she fought to stay awake, she could hear the footsteps get closer, and a gruff voice called out to her.

"Lila, you okay? Can you hear me?" The broad-shouldered man poked his head into the car.

"What happened?"

"You were following me, when all of a sudden, a raccoon darted out onto the street. I swerved to miss it, and that's when you sideswiped me, and we went off the road. Do you think you can stand?" He opened the door.

"I don't know."

He reached out to help her out of the automobile. She was wobbly at first, but eventually was able to stand without any help.

"You don't remember me, do you?" he said. "I was afraid of this happening. I think you hit your head pretty hard." He looked down at the young woman who sat on the curb, staring blankly.

"I'm afraid I don't. I don't remember anything." She choked up and put her hands on her face.

Her blonde hair was now wet and flat, clinging to the sides of her face. Traces of dry blood were caked above her temple.

"My name is Channing. I've been your boss and friend for the past fifteen years." He slid down next her on the curb.

She gazed at his handsome face, in search of answers, but found none.

"I'm sorry. I have no recollection."

"Don't force yourself. Your memories will come back to you in due time." He put his arm around her neck and drew her close.

"What is it exactly I do for you?"

"You, my dear Lila, are a shapeshifter. The best one I have. You're the only one I can count on to get the job done." He smiled at her.

"And we were going to a job tonight?"

"Yes, we were on our way to cause chaos at a wedding." Channing stood to light a cigarette.

"Why?"

"Let's just say, payback's a bitch."

"Well, if that's what we were going to do, then let's finish the job." She hopped up.

"No, the job can wait. We need to get you to a hospital to get checked out. You've suffered a concussion and memory loss. I think it may be serious."

"I'm fine. I feel much better, honestly. I'm even starting to remember you. So if I said I was going to help you tonight, then I'm going to."

"All right. I'm not going to fight with you. As soon as we get my car out of this ditch, we're on our way."

"And where precisely is that?"

"To a house called Windwood.

As the memories flooded back, Carla fell back with the picture clutched to her chest, and began to weep. She forgot where she was, until Simon stirred in bed. She stopped dead like a statue in a department store window, until it was clear he was still asleep.

"Nonna, I've missed you," she whimpered, as tears hit the glass picture frame. "I don't care how long it takes, I will find my way back to you."

Her head felt like it was going to explode, and blood began to seep out of her nose. She felt like she was going to pass out or die.

Channing made sure the memory dust had a buffer component so that if Lila remembered anything about being Carla Romano, her head would pound and pound until she either passed out or forgot.

She shut her eyes for a minute, and then it all ended.

"Mama, don't shoot!" Simon yelled in his sleep, then rolled over onto his side.

"Get it together, Lila, before one of them wakes up," she said to herself, and set the photo back on the night-stand.

She shifted back into a mouse and scuttled out of the hole she had come in through. Once outside and in human form, she crept over to the garage, which was connected to the small cottage. Inside was a baby-blue 1967 Camaro.

"This is perfect."

The driver side door was unlocked, but the keys were nowhere to be found.

"Guess I have to do this the hard way." She fiddled with the wires underneath the steering wheel, and in minutes, the engine came to life. "Pleasant dreams."

Lila got out of the car and closed the garage door, leaving the carbon monoxide to fill the home.

Donna stayed by her daughter's side the whole night, unable to take her eyes off her. The idea of losing her awakened so many dormant feelings. Feelings that were shut down the minute she became a vampire. Emotions she had hoped to never feel again.

A knock on the door brought her out of her thoughts.

"We're ready whenever you are," Sutton said, from the doorframe.

"All right, let's do it!"

The day had finally come to clean and organize the attic. Since Donna had returned to Windwood, all she wanted to do was restore the majesty of this once-grand mansion, and that's what she was going to do, from top to bottom.

Toni, Brandon, and Sutton stood outside with mops, buckets, and brooms, awaiting their next orders. After they climbed the massive wooden steps, they paused in front of a rusted iron door. The knob squeaked back to life when Donna turned the handle. They poked their heads inside and saw miles of cobwebs, and inch-thick layers of dust on everything. Rodents scampered across the floorboards, and pigeons used the rafters for roosts. The windows were so filthy the sun rays were forever blocked out.

"When was the last time anyone was up here?" Brandon swiped at the cobwebs hidden in the doorway.

"1910," Toni said, sarcastically.

"This is going to take all day," Brandon said.

"Then it's a good thing we all don't have plans," Donna went in first.

Toni and Brandon just stared at each other, while Sutton brought up the rear.

The vast attic was a trove of forgotten treasures. The more they cleaned, the more they found—old clothing, silver, furniture, and just about everything else in between.

"Mom, do you have any idea who this woman could be?" Brandon held out an ancient painting of a woman with piercing green eyes, creamy white skin, and auburn hair, who wore a kind, almost noble, grin.

"Where'd you get that?" Donna said.

"It was next to this diary, on a shelf by the window." He pointed.

"That woman's our ancestor, Flora Lord. She was the grand duchess of the country of Marin, and wife of Solomon Lord, founder of this town. In 1812, she was found near the swamp, ripped apart by alligators, after catching her husband with another woman."

Tears begin to sting Donna's eyes as she remembered the horrible events that led up to her mother's death.

Toni noticed that Donna was about to lose it.

"Can you go see if Aaron needs help moving the trunks?" she said.

"Why's it always me?" Brandon threw up his arms and marched out.

"Are you okay?" Toni placed a reassuring hand on her shoulder.

"This is the first time I've seen her in over two hundred years." Donna choked up as tears flowed down her face. "I almost forgot what she looked like." She continued to stare at the portrait.

"Have you ever read this?" Toni held up the diary.

"No. I didn't know she kept one." Donna took it from her and skimmed the pages.

"Well, maybe, just maybe you can get to know your mother again through her journal."

Toni smiled and walked off, unaware that Sutton had heard the whole exchange.

23

ORIGINS

A FEW HOURS LATER, AFTER THEY'D FIN-
ished with the attic, Donna took the diary up to her room
so she could be alone. She sat at the desk, flipped the lamp
on, and placed a piping-hot cup of coffee in front of her.

She was afraid to open the book, for fear that the pages
would fall apart. With a careful touch, she opened the
diary and saw that it was written in her mother's hand.
She took a sip of coffee, then leaned back into the chair
to learn all she could about the mother she adored.

In 1794, the day began like any other day at Windwood.
The slaves were in the fields, the house slaves were buzzing

about the mansion and Caleb Lord went for his ride at 6:45, as he had every day since he was old enough to ride. A pregnant Flora, and Solomon, as well as his sister Regina, had just sat down to breakfast when one of the field slaves, called Toby, came flying up the front flagstones, all flustered and out of breath, screaming for Solomon.

"Massa Solomon, it's Mister Caleb. He's been hurt real bad." Toby bolted into the dining room.

Solomon pushed out his chair and stormed outside. Flora sobbed in her chair as Nessy and Porter fanned her, while Regina put a cold compress on her head.

"What happened?" Solomon said from the porch, when he saw overseer Burton carrying the limp body of his boy.

Blood poured out of the wound on the side of his head. "I'm not quite sure, sir," Burton replied. "I found him in the field after he had been thrown from his horse. He struck his head on a tree."

Burton was an older man with a large scar down his face, and hands the size of cinder blocks, which he would use from time to time on the slaves. He was tall, dark, mean, and would take a bullet for Solomon.

"Hurry up and get him upstairs and into his bed." Flora came up beside Solomon.

"He's going to be fine, my dear," Solomon said, to convince her, as well as himself.

Flora squeezed Solomon's hand as she followed the men into the house. Then she doubled over and watched as her water broke all over the entrance hall floor.

"Solomon, the baby's coming. Something's wrong. It's too early." Flora wailed as she doubled over again.

This time, blood dripped from between her legs.

"Regina, help Nessy take Flora upstairs."

Solomon took a deep breath and closed his eyes while trying hard to fight back the tears.

Flora's screams echoed from the second-floor bedroom. Outside the master bedroom, Solomon paced as he waited for news on his wife's condition. Regina sat patiently in a chair outside the door.

"Calm yourself, brother. I don't know what's getting to me more—Flora's screaming, or your pacing."

Minutes turned into hours, and by eight o'clock that night, Solomon's grief overwhelmed him. Nessy brought out some jambalaya, cornbread, and mint julep on a tray. Solomon jumped up, yelled, and sent the tray flying into the wall before storming off.

"Parker, fetch Massa Solomon." Sadie came out of the bedroom with blood splattered all over her white apron. "The baby's here. It's a boy."

Tears welled in her eyes, and the normal smile she greeted everyone with was nowhere to be found.

"Aunty, what happened in there?" Nessy said. "What's my sister-in-law's condition? Where's the midwife, and how come I don't hear the baby?"

Nessy and Toby stared at Sadie, who crumbled.

Solomon stopped at the top of the stairs. After seeing Sadie sobbing, he rushed into the master bedroom. Flora lay propped up on large feather pillows, her eyes closed. Lots of blood and afterbirth littered the king-sized bed, and the smell of childbirth hung heavy.

"Where's the child?" Solomon said to the midwife, who had her back to him.

"Right here, Mister Lord." The midwife handed the wrapped-up child to his father. "The boy was stillborn. Missus Lord lost a lot of blood. The strain of the delivery may have weakened her heart. I suggest you have Doctor DuPont examine her when he's done with your son. She's sleeping now, and may sleep for hours." She grabbed her things from the floor and left.

"Flora, I warned you about having another child at your age. You were so adamant, I couldn't refuse. What did it get us—more heartbreak, and you near-death?" Solomon looked down at the angelic face of his son, and cried.

Regina lingered in the doorframe. "Is there anything I can do? Maybe get Nessy or Parker to bring you something else to eat? A breeze is blowing in from the Aurora. Maybe I could open up the windows or the gallery door and let some air in." She moved toward the window.

"I would like to be alone with my wife and son."

Regina nodded and closed the bedroom doors.

Out in the hall, Parker the butler and Nessy were consoling a hysterical Sadie, who seemed to be on the verge of fainting. Nessy fanned her while Parker made her sip from a glass of water.

"You's didn't see it. Poor Miss Flora struggling for breath, and screamin' like I ain't ever heard. The midwife said the baby been dead for weeks inside Miss Flora." Sadie blubbered some more.

A few moments later, Dr. DuPont came out of Caleb's room. The grim news was written across his aging face. He looked at the group with sad eyes, and tried to find the words to say. When he saw the anguish in Solomon's face, he knew this was going to be harder than he thought.

"Sorry, Mister Lord. Your son is dead. The head injury was traumatic. His skull fractured. He slipped into a coma and passed away about five minutes ago. I am truly sorry. I did all I could." He went into Flora's room.

Solomon fell to the floor and sobbed like a baby. Regina tried to comfort him, but he shoved her away. Even Sadie tried, but his heartbreak got the best of him. They left him alone on the floor to deal with the harsh reality that in just one day, he had lost two sons and almost his wife.

Flora might as well have died that day, along with the baby they named Jacob, and her beloved Caleb. Her torment suffocated her, keeping her from the life she once loved. Solomon tried to reach through the barrier his wife had created, only causing her to slip further and further away.

Dr. DuPont suggested that maybe an almshouse would suit her needs better. Solomon responded by punching him in the nose and chasing him off Windwood. Under no circumstances would the former Grand Duchess of Marin be subjected to one of those places.

Regina assumed all of Flora's duties, including hostess. The Lord cotillion—the social event of the season—would be upon them before they knew it, and this year Regina was at the helm. All of Solomon's Wake waited with bated breath to see if Regina had what it took to follow in her sister-in-law's footsteps and make the event a success.

Solomon had no worries about his sister's capabilities. After all, as the crown princess of Marin, she was bred for just this. Even though the monarchy fell, and their royal titles in America couldn't hold water, Solomon still ran his house like their former palace, expecting his wife and sister to act like the princesses they were born to be. Plus, deep down, he believed someday they would return to the throne.

Feeling sorry for himself, Solomon sat in the gallery with a bottle of whiskey in hand, taking in all of the wonderful aromas that made him love South Carolina. Here in the Grand Duke's new domain, Solomon got to live the life he'd grown accustomed to while being a sovereign.

Intoxication got the best of the former monarch, and he began firing his pistol into the night sky, then at the slaves, all the while laughing like a banshee and wearing his military uniform, which he always pulled out of the closet whenever he felt down.

"Massa Solomon, you's gonna fall," Sadie cried, as she watched Solomon teeter on the edge of the balcony.

"Solomon, come down from there this instant," Regina hollered.

She couldn't take her gaze off him standing up there with his red jacket covered with all his war decorations. He looked so refined with his silver hair pulled back into a ponytail.

"Why don't you come up and get me." He bowed, and almost losing his balance.

The crowd gasped.

"Stop fooling around and go back inside before you hurt yourself." Regina stared up at her brother, from the ground.

"If I wanted to go inside, I would," he barked.

"Please, Solomon, get down."

"All right, mother hen. I'll get down." He saluted the air as drops of whiskey landed on his sister's wavy hair.

Once he stepped down, his right foot got caught under the railing, and he fell face first onto the floor, smashing one of the wooden chairs in the process, as well as his ankle.

Regina grabbed her burgundy velvet dress and hurried up the stairs, with Parker and Nessy in tow. The hallway remained dark. The ledges and railings were sticky from the humidity.

Regina opened the door and found Solomon sprawled out on the floor. Blood gushed from his nose, and his ankle was so twisted she thought it was broken.

"Parker, let's get him on the bed," she said.

"Is everything all right in here?" a dazed Flora said from the door, with wild hair, and skin white as snow.

The green robe looked like it had been in a firing squad.

"Everything is under control," Regina said. "Aunty, please take Missus Lord back to her room, and fix her a nice cup of tea while I tend to my brother's wounds." She lifted Solomon's leg onto the bed.

"Yesum." Sadie's heart broke seeing the mistress of the house so devastated.

It brought tears to her quarter-sized brown eyes.

"Let's get you back in bed," she said. "Then I'll brings ya some of that chamomile tea you loves so much." She led Flora toward her bedroom.

"T-there will be n-no more h-happiness in this house." Solomon reached underneath the bed and pulled out a near-empty bottle of bourbon.

He downed it, then threw the tumbler at a portrait of Flora. Shards of glass sprayed the air and the floor, leaving the portrait ruined and discolored. Regina set out to clean the mess up, when her brother seized her wrist.

"Let one of the house slaves clean it up," he growled.

"At least let me see to your wounds. You're bleeding."

He nodded, and Regina sat beside him. Nessy filled the wash basin with water and handed it to Regina. Using a rag, she began cleaning his knuckles. Solomon sat silently, not even looking at her. The devil's brew—as Flora called any alcoholic beverage—had a tendency to give the beneficiary loose lips.

"Flora used to be a good woman. Now she won't even look at me or let me touch her. When we ruled, we ruled together as equals. I always allowed her to speak freely and do whatever she saw fit. From me letting her have a free reign, she thinks she can shut me out. I would give everything I have to see her smile or laugh again. I'd even sell my soul to Satan himself to give her another child if it would make her happy again."

He passed out.

24

THE BEGINNING OF THE END

SOMETIME AFTER TEN THAT MORNING, Solomon began to stir, feeling like someone was bowling inside his head and slamming a spike into his ankle. He shifted his legs over the side of the bed to step down on the other foot, and it felt like every bone in it cracked. He whimpered and sat back down on the bed.

"You're lucky it's not broken," Regina said, from a chair near the side of the bed.

"It feels like it is." He sat hunched over, with his hands on his silver head.

"Maybe next time you'll lay off the booze and not carry on like a commoner." She kept her blue eyes glued to him, all the while crocheting.

"I don't think you have to worry about that for a long while." He leaned over to grab a glass of water from the nightstand. "Have Nessy bring me something to eat. I'm starving."

Regina called out to someone in the hall to have them bring the food.

"What was that all about last night?" Regina shoved the door closed. "It's not like you."

"I really don't know. I see her so despondent and miserable, and it breaks my heart. I've tried everything to reach her. I don't know what else to do. I'm afraid I'll lose her if I don't do something." He looked to his sister with tears welling in his cerulean eyes.

A slight knock on the door, and Nessy entered with a tray of fried chicken, collard greens, and chocolate doughnuts.

"There is something you can do," Regina said. "Go out to the swamp and look for Luna. She can help you."

Nessy dropped the tray, sending the chicken to the floor and collard greens all over the wall.

"I's so sorry." She hurried to clean up the mess. "I'll get Parker to fetch another tray."

"That won't be necessary." Solomon put up his hand. "What is it that's got you so spooked?"

"Nothin', Massa. I's just a klutz." Nessy kept her gaze on the floor and the mess she'd made.

"I don't believe you," he barked.

"Don't be afraid, child," Regina said. "Tell the truth."

"She's wicked, and don't help nobody without a price. Dicey over at the Caulfield plantation tole me that the mistress of Noble Oaks couldn't pay her back, so Luna put something in the water and made all her hair fall out. And she took one of her cherished spaniels and ate it. Worst of all, Dicey say she turned one her daughters into a wolf."

"Thank you, Nessy, for your honesty," Regina said. "We can manage from here. You can come back and clean this up later."

Nessy gathered as much of the broken glass and smashed food as she could in her apron, and slipped out the door.

"And you want me to go see this woman?" Solomon lay back down on the bed in frustration.

"You don't believe all this mumbo-jumbo, do you? It's just slave talk. Nothing more, nothing less."

"Maybe so, Sister. But she was to be executed for witchcraft, in Italy. Rumor has it she is a Zorn by birth, which means she has the powers of darkness on her side."

Regina looked like she was going to faint.

"The vampire family from Germany?" she said. "I thought they died out years ago."

"No one knows for sure what really happened to them. Luna was married off to a duke of Tuscany. Many of the servants claimed she never gave up her evil ways, and continued to practice the black arts. Her husband was found a few years later, drained of blood, and she was put on trial. Another powerful baron fell under her spell and helped her escape to America before she could be hanged. Not to mention her bewitching beauty, which is so renowned that some are calling her the new Helen of Troy."

"So that's it?" Regina said. "You're just going to give up?"

"What choice do I have? I cannot combat such evil." He sat back up in bed.

"Please, Solomon. You must do it for me." Flora stumbled into the bedroom. "If she can give me another child, you have to do it, or I will die. Every day that goes by is harder than the last, and almost unbearable for me to live. I'm empty, and nothing can help me except a new baby. If you don't get me a child, I will take my own life." She fell to her knees and begged some more.

"Flora, you don't know what you're asking." He stared down at the stranger his wife had become. "What you want is sacrilegious. And if we cannot pay her back, then what?" He yanked her up and forced her to look at him. "If we do this, it will bring about our downfall." He stared into her clouded eyes. "I love you, and would move heaven and earth to make you happy. But this I cannot condone."

"No, no, no!" Flora beat Solomon's chest, then ran from his arms over to the window. "I will jump if you don't relent on this. Parker and Nessy will be cleaning me off the flagstones for a week." She threw the windows open and stepped out onto the ledge.

"First, you," Regina said. "And now her. I swear, the two of you are going to be the ruin of me, not a witch. I'm going to have Aunty summon the doctor."

She moved to open the door, but Solomon stopped her. "No, this is a family matter that stays between us. Just leave us alone for a while."

"If you cannot control your wife, then might I suggest you find someone who can." She bustled out into the hall.

"Mind your tongue, woman," he thundered, "or I will put you out of this house. Do I make myself clear?"

"Yes." She bowed and left.

"Flora, please come inside." Solomon whispered, as he straddled the floor and the ledge.

He grasped the crown molding, and reached for her with his free hand. She moved farther away.

"Either you agree, or I jump," Flora wailed.

She lost her balance and wobbled on the edge before falling. Solomon lunged forward and caught her by the wrist, keeping his good ankle locked on the window ledge. Aunty watched everything from below and wept, as it looked like her beloved mistress was about to meet her maker.

"I've got you, Flora. Hold on." Solomon used all his strength to pull her up.

She tried to wriggle out of his grasp.

"Please, Solomon, let me die."

He stared into her tortured jade eyes. "As you wish, my sweet. First thing in the morning, I will look for Luna."

Flora let him pull her to safety. "Thank you! Thank you." She threw up her arms and wrapped them around Solomon's neck while kissing his cheeks and lips.

For the first time in months, Flora almost seemed herself.

"Don't thank me yet. I can't help feeling that this is a mistake, and we're all going to pay for it." He led her back through the window, where Aunty and Nessy awaited—

one with a blanket to wrap her, and the other with a cup of her favorite tea.

"Take Missus Lord back to her room," Solomon said. "I'll be back to talk to you later." He kissed her on the cheek.

"I's got some more piping hot tea for ya in your room." Aunty placed an arm around Flora's waist to help steady her.

Nessy stood behind the duo in case her mistress fell backward.

Solomon sat in the corner chair next to the window, and let out a heavy sigh as he stretched his legs out. With all the excitement today, he had almost forgotten about his foot. He looked down to see that it was still swollen like a balloon, and bruised.

"You should elevate that." Regina entered the room.

"Do you know how to knock?" he growled.

"I want to go with you tomorrow, when you see the witch." She slid a stool under his leg.

"That is out of the question."

"Why?"

"The swamp is no place for a former princess."

"Well, then, at the same time, it isn't a place for a former grand duke, either."

"This discussion is closed. You are not going. Besides, I am going to pay a visit to the Caulfield plantation first to see what I can find out."

"Noble Oaks? There's not much left of it but a few slaves and the loony owner. The mistress ran off after she tried to burn the house down, and most of the slaves ran off that night." Regina stood and lit a few candles.

"I need to know what I'm getting our family into."

"Make sure you take a couple slaves with you. Matthew Caulfield's been known to take out his shotgun and use it on anything that moves." She blew out the match.

"I'm well-aware of that, Sister. And that's exactly what I'm going to do. Is there anything else you'd like to advise me on? Perhaps how to run my house, my marriage, or the family purse strings?"

"I was worried for your wellbeing, that's all."

"Your concern touches me. Now, if you'll excuse me, I have a long day ahead of me, and I need my rest."

Regina curtsied before she left the room, leaving Solomon to stir in his thoughts.

25

NOBLE OAKS

JUST BEFORE COCKCROW, SOLOMON GATH-
ered Toby and Parker in the entry hall, kissed Flora, tipped
his hat and set out for Noble Oaks. As the horses plodded
along the macadam, the men sat silently as trees, houses,
and soon, the Aurora River disappeared. Solomon stopped
to stare at the mansion. It wasn't the palace he grew up in.
Nonetheless, it was magnificent. The two-story clapboard
federal-style house with a low-pitched roof and large Pal-
ladian windows, afforded a view of the palmetto and oak
trees draped in Spanish moss.

About forty-five minutes later, the burnt-out shell that
was Noble Oaks came into view. As the coach progressed
down the shaded path provided by the live oaks, Solomon
could see that this once-great plantation, known for its
fine tobacco, was now nothing but a wasteland. They

continued on through the rusted and fallen-apart gate, to the front porch, where a white-haired, caramel-skinned woman stood sweeping. She looked at them, then back to the floor.

"Is your master home?" Solomon inched toward the front stairs.

"Whatcha want, Lord?" said a gruff voice, hidden in the shadows of the entry hall.

"I would like to have a word with you, if I may?"

"Don't come any farther!" a crazed Matthew Caulfield hollered, as he thrust open the screen door and faced Solomon down with a pistol. "Why? So you can go back into town and tell everyone that you got to see loony Matthew Caulfield? Or maybe you're here to steal whatever little bit I have left." He kept the gun pointed at Solomon, who held his hands up to pacify the insane man.

"Actually, I'd like to talk to you about the witch Luna."

Matthew's face softened, and he lowered the musket.

"You believe me?" He sighed. "Dicey, fetch the horses some water, and see if you can muster up a little grub for me and Mister Lord." He stepped aside and motioned for Solomon to enter the house.

The mansion was bare, apart from a few scattered-about rockers and crates they used as tables. Stray cats littered the winding staircase, and old newspapers were splayed throughout the downstairs. Windows were broken, and the doors were off their hinges.

"I know she's in a sad state—a far cry from the jewel she once was." Matthew scooted an orange tabby cat from one of the rockers. "Please, sit." He motioned as he sat in the other rocker next to Solomon. "What is it you wanna know about the witch?"

"Anything you can tell me. My wife is prostrate with grief, and Luna may be the only one who can help snap her out of it."

"Whatever you do, don't go to her." Matthew's voice trembled.

"I don't know what else to do." Solomon looked over at Matthew, who had his head laid back and eyes shut.

Matthew was about twenty years younger than Solomon, yet he looked thirty years older. His blond hair had turned white. He wore a patch over his left eye ever since he lost it in a duel. And his face was furrowed, worn, and tortured.

One of the many cats that roamed the house jumped up and settled into its owner's lap.

"Isn't she a beauty?" Matthew scratched the calico under the neck.

"You were saying, about Luna..."

"She will promise you the world, and fool you into believing all her assurances. She will ask you to give her something in return for what she offers, and the moment you can't fulfill your obligation, her vile nature will be revealed, and she will destroy your family and take everything that ever meant anything to you. Look around you. Do I look like I have the world at my feet? An adoring wife, or a thriving plantation? All this was her doing," Matthew waved his hand, indicating the dilapidated condition of Noble Oaks.

Dicey edged into the parlor, carrying a tray of two tea cakes and two cups of tea. The old woman placed the tray down in front of them, and almost toppled over in the process. Then, as she turned to leave, she tripped again over one of the felines.

"You be needin' anything else?" she said.

"That will be all!" Matthew yelled, so loud all the cats scattered. "Dicey's hard of hearing." He handed Solomon a cup of tea. "I'm sorry. I don't have much else to offer."

"This is fine. Thank you. I know this is a sore subject, and I don't mean any harm, but I really must find Luna."

"That does it. Get out!" Matthew roared, and jumped up, sending the tea all over his pants, and the cats running for shelter. "Have you not been listening? I will not tell you. In the long run, you will thank me." He stormed off outside.

"Great. Now what?" Solomon put his cup back on the tray and finished his little cake.

"Psst!" Dicey called, from the shadows of the hallway.

He threw his napkin down, looked to make sure Matthew was nowhere in sight, and followed her out into the hallway. Dicey stared at him with bright eyes and a smooth, gentle face. She seemed almost frightened to talk to him.

"I shouldn't be tellin' you none of this." She continued down the hall and stopped in front of a large oak door.

"What really happened here the night of the fire?" He peered down at the tiny woman.

"I tell ya if ya do somethin' for me." She caressed the door.

"What is it you would like?"

"The key for this here door. My baby girl in there, and I wants her out."

"Why is he keeping his daughter in there?"

"Get the key, and I tells ya."

"Where can I find this key?" He watched Dicey continue to stare at the door.

"It's a skeleton key. Massa keeps it around his neck. About now, he should be passed out upstairs, on the bed. Every day, it the same thing with him. He drink too much, then goes to sleep it off."

"I'll do my best to get it. Are you ready to face the consequences for what we're about to do?"

"Yessir. You's tryin' to save your family, and I's trying to save mine. When the girls were born into this world, I's the one that diapered them. When they got sick with the diphtheria, I nursed them back. And after Miss Mae left, poor Miss Pammy was swallowed by darkness. Then her sister, Miss Lizzy, breathed her last breath, and my sweet girl slipped further away. Massa kept her under lock and key out of fear she bring shame to the family. It ain't right keeping that sweet girl in there."

"All right, I'll do my best to get the key and get her out." He patted her shoulder, made a left down a hall, then crept up the wooden stairs.

"Hold on, sugar plum," Dicey yelled through the door. "Help's on the way,"

Upstairs, the fire had ravaged every nook and cranny of the second floor, and it still smelled like the inside of a chimney. Black soot stuck to the walls like gum. The cool winds from the outside chilled the air.

When Solomon got to the end of the hall, he saw Matthew's room and could hear him snoring. Solomon tiptoed toward the room and saw the room where the fire had started, directly across from the master bedroom. The room had been burnt to a crisp, and was nothing more than an eyesore.

He poked his head inside the open doorway and found that this room was barely touched by the flames, and Matthew was sleeping like a baby, on his back, with his mouth wide open. As Solomon drew nearer he noticed the key was not around his neck. He went to run out of the room, when he spotted an open Chippendale desk to the left of the door.

At first look, nothing seemed out of the ordinary. Books were behind the glass, and papers scattered on the desktop. He rummaged through the mess and found the key hidden under a gold locket encrusted with rubies. A beautiful fair-skinned woman with fiery hair occupied the center picture.

He hurried out of the room, down the stairs, and back to the central hallway, where Dicey had fallen asleep on the floor, with her back against the door. As he watched the woman sleep, he began to have doubts about giving her the key. What if everything Matthew had told him was true, and Luna had destroyed his family? Or maybe she did the exact opposite and made them happy again?

"You gots the key." Dicey smiled wide, revealing a set of beautiful white choppers.

She jumped up from the floor as fast as a rabbit, and went for the key.

"You're not getting this until you tell me everything I need to know." Solomon dangled the key in front of her.

"All rights, I tells ya." She sat on the stairwell and sighed. "Miss Mae wanted to give Massa Matthew a male heir, but at her age it was almost impossible for her to bear children. She begs me to talk to the conjurer, and I did. He couldn't help her, but he told me of someone who could—Luna the witch. Luna lived out in the swamp, in a small shack on the river off Huntoon Drive. You needs a rowboat to get there. We defied Massa Matthew's orders and went in the dark of night, with just a whale-oil lamp to guide us. Her little wooden shack emerged, all lit up like a Christmas tree, and she sat with her legs all exposed, playing the violin and singing some song in another language. I covered Miss Mae's eyes 'cause it ain't fittin' for a woman of Miss Mae's breedin' to see that kind of trash on display. I cleared my throat to let her know we was there, and the most beautiful woman I ever seen in my life looked down on us."

"I did not realize Luna lived that close by." He sat beside her.

"Luna invited us up and offered us some kind of concoction she had brewing in a cauldron. Right aways, she knew we wanted something. Miss Mae told her what she wanted, and Luna agreed, as long as she gots a child in return. We went home, and Miss Mae simmered over it. When she approached Massa with it, he went mad and left the house for days. At last, when he returned, he told Miss Mae to do it, and everything was fine. Miss Mae delivered a beautiful baby named Bronson. Then the unthinkable happened—the child Luna had, died.

"Is she the reason the house burned down?"

"No, that was all Miss Mae. Luna demanded she be paid back, and Massa Matthew said no. That's when things began to get crazy around here. It began when Miss Mae's hair began to fall out, and her beloved spaniels was found ate out in the stable. And then baby Bronson was found dead. And later, Miss Lizzy and Miss Pammy were found in the woods. Poor Miss Lizzie was cold as a wagon tire, and Miss Pammy was cut so bad I thought she would die."

"I thought Lizzie died from a fever?"

"Nuh-uh. She was killed by a wild animal. Miss Mae says it was part of Luna's revenge. And later, she began to believe her own daughter was a wolf. So much, in fact, she set fire to Noble Oaks in hopes of killing her and prit'near everybody else." Dicey choked up at the memory.

"Why is she still in there?" Solomon said.

"You have to the count of three to give me back my key and get out of here." Matthew crept up behind them and pointed the gun at the back of the former grand duke's head.

"I just wanted—"

"Get out of my house, and don't ever think of coming back." Matthew motioned for his visitor to leave, while keeping the gun aimed at him.

Solomon left Dicey sitting on the stairs. He stopped and turned back, and Matthew cocked the trigger.

"I's sorry, Massa," Dicey wailed.

"You're gonna be."

26

LUNA

HUNTOON DRIVE WAS SHADOWY AND DES-
olate when they finally got there. Solomon dismantled his
steed and ordered Toby and Parker to stay, and if he was
not back in an hour, to return to Windwood and let Flora
know what happened.

A wooden rowboat was moored in the swamp. It had
been years since he'd used one, but he believed he could
still maneuver it.

The dark waters of the swamp were still as he glided
toward Luna's shack. There was no wind, no moon, or
even signs of wildlife. Surreal.

At last, the wooden structure appeared in the middle
of nowhere, lit up by candles and a large fire with a cauldron atop it, just like Dicey had described.

After Solomon secured the boat and begun to ascend the ladder, a woman poked her head down. It was as if she had expected him.

Solomon froze and just eyed the beauty before him. Never in all his years had he seen a woman so perfect. Her hair dark as night. Thin, dark eyes. And skin so soft and tan he wanted to run his hands across it.

"Are you going to admire me from down there all night, or are you going to come up?" she said, in a heavy foreign accent.

"I'm sorry. I did not mean to offend." He continued up the ladder.

"The only time anyone comes out here to see me is when they want something from me."

She blew on the fire that had fizzled, and in an instant, she had it roaring.

"Yes, I am afraid I need your help."

"My help is not cheap, and its cost will depend on what it is." She sat on a rocking chair in front of the fire.

"I am well-aware of that." He focused on her bare leg.

"They've been talking about me in town again. I'm glad they are afraid of me, as they should be." She pulled out what looked like a pipe, and began to smoke it. "What is it you want from Luna?" She blew out a plume of smoke.

"I want you to help my wife conceive a child."

She stared at him from a few feet away, in the rocker.

"The price for that will be your seed." She continued to puff on her pipe. "If you refuse, I will not give you what you need for your wife."

"I need to discuss this further with her. I cannot just—"

"Mister Lord, this is the only opportunity you have. If you walk away now, there will not be another chance." Luna stood from the chair to face the night sky, and began to cry out in Latin.

"I should not have come. This was a mistake." Solomon was about to leave, when the image of a broken Flora invaded his thoughts.

"Are you sure you want to leave?" Luna said, in a familiar voice.

He turned to find his wife standing in the moonlight, looking as she did when he first courted her over thirty years ago. Solomon made the sign of the cross and inched away from her.

"What kind of devilry is this?" he hollered, as Luna continued to pursue him.

"I'm just giving you what you want. There's nothing evil about it. You may do with me what you want."

Not knowing what came over him, Solomon ripped the front of Luna's dress completely off, exposing her bronzed bosom.

"Take me. I'm yours," Luna said, in a sultry voice, as she slipped off the rest of her dress.

Then she led the grand duke onto the bed.

True to her word, Luna had given him Flora's favorite lavender bath oil. Once she soaked in it, it would only be a matter of time before the rest happened.

As Solomon galloped back to Windwood, he felt guilty and ashamed for what he had done to his wife. He should have been stronger in his faith and his love to resist the ways of the enchantress.

As they took the usual bend, Solomon could see Flora, Regina, and Aunty through the trees, waiting patiently for their beloved patriarch to return.

"Welcome home, Husband," Flora chirped. "You must be famished after such a long journey. Parker, take Mister Lord's belongings back to his room. And Aunty, go into the kitchen and see if you can rustle up some dinner for Mister Lord. And, my dear, sweet sister-in-law, could you pour us a couple of brandys please?" She took his hat and placed it on the entry hall table.

"Certainly," Regina replied.

"Is that for me?" Flora squealed, when she saw the bath oil.

"Before you get too excited, I need to talk you about something." Solomon took her hands into his.

But Flora was not hearing anything he said.

"Nessy," she called out into the hall. "Draw me a bath and put lots of this in it."

She handed Nessy the bottle, then ripped her clothes off in the middle of the entry hall.

"Flora, I must speak with you," he said.

"Can we discuss it later? I want to start this right away." She scooted toward the stairs, with Nessy in tow.

"Nessy, can you give Mistress and me a moment?" Solomon said.

Without looking up, Nessy slipped out from behind Flora and scuttled off to the bedroom, with the oil in hand.

"Really, Solomon, whatever you must tell me could have waited a little while longer." Flora continued up the wooden stairs, to the second floor.

"Would you please stop walking?" he said, as she neared the bedroom.

Flora acted like she hadn't heard him. Solomon grabbed her and spun her around.

"I don't want to know." She turned back to the door.

"You must." He seized her wrist and made her face him.

The look in her eyes said it all, and Solomon realized he had made a grave mistake.

"I had to bed the witch in order to deliver the bath oil."

Flora continued to stare at him as though he were a stranger.

"Are you hearing me?" He shook her.

"I told you to do whatever you saw fit." She opened the bedroom door, peeled her clothes off, and slipped into the water, letting out such a sigh that Solomon blushed.

He could not take his eyes off her. At her age, her skin was still flawless and smooth as silk. Her hair was full, and shone a bright auburn. Her breasts were voluptuous.

While he gazed upon her, he felt like the happiest man in the world, and decided not to say anything about the other baby.

A WOMAN SCORNED

LUNA'S POTION WORKED, AND FLORA became pregnant. After an easy pregnancy, she gave birth to a healthy baby girl—HRH Princess Martha Jeanette Amelia, heiress to the Grand Ducal throne of Marin. Solomon was so ecstatic that not only did he change the laws of succession to allow Martha to ascend the throne after his passing, he also led a grand parade through town, riding his stallion in full military regalia, while Flora, Regina, and the new princess rode in a new ivory carriage with gold trim.

When darkness fell, the sky lit up in green, red, blue, and gold as fireworks were set off in honor of the birth, followed by cannon fire across the Aurora to let the town and the world know that an heir had finally come.

The family had been the happiest it had been in years. Even Regina, who was naturally standoffish, fell in love with the new addition and offered many a night to watch her while husband and wife enjoyed some alone time.

On this particular night, as they strolled along the river, Solomon's lies caught up to him, and his one night of passion set off a wicked curse that knew no bounds, whose fury reached out from beyond the grave to seek out and destroy anyone with the last name Lord.

"It's such a beautiful night out, my dear," Solomon said, as they walked arm-in-arm along the river, with a lantern and a few slaves behind them.

"Even the air smells sweet." Flora drew in a deep breath. "I love the scent of Carolina jessamine." She brushed her fingers across the yellow flower.

"It's so good to see you smile again." He squeezed her hand and gently kissed it.

"I have a lot more reasons to these days. I was watching Martha the other day, and I swear I saw her follow Aunty all over the room with her eyes. And every time she came back into the room, Martha would smile."

"Already dazzling the masses, and she's not even one." The proud father beamed.

"Solomon," a voice called out, from the darkness.

Flora almost jumped out of her skin, and Solomon stood in front of his wife to protect her.

"Who's there?" He tried to see through the obscurity.

"Something's wrong with the baby." A disheveled, weak, and perspiring Luna came out from behind a live oak.

Solomon blanched and felt his face heat.

"Who is this woman?" Flora stared her down from head to toe.

"I am the mother of his other daughter." Luna returned Flora's glare.

The witch reveled in Flora's pain, as it clearly stung her heart and cut her worse than Luna ever could.

"Solomon, is this true?"

When he didn't look her in the eyes, Flora had her answer. She snatched the child from her mother and charged through the woods. Luna screamed like a wild woman as she raced after her, into the night, every now and then clawing at Flora in an attempt to reach the baby.

"Have you lost your mind, woman?" Solomon stepped in front of his wife to stop her from walking.

"Solomon, this child is another heir, and a living, breathing person. What kind of Christian woman would I be if I didn't try to help?"

She stepped around Solomon as she set out to find Luna's shack.

"Why not return to Windwood?" he said. "I don't see the point in going to that awful shack."

"Time is of the essence, and this child will die if we don't do something soon."

"Do whatever you must to save my baby," a weakened Luna said, as she trudged up the rear.

"Is it much farther?" Flora panted, holding the girl to her bosom.

"Just about another half-mile through the woods." Luna stopped to lean against a tree.

The moonlight radiated off her like a beacon, and Solomon took notice, much to Flora's chagrin. To get through this ordeal, Flora just prayed and left it in God's hands. That alone was enough to give her strength.

"Solomon, go back to Windwood and bring the carriage to the swamp, so when the baby is strong enough, we can leave right away."

"I can't just leave you in the middle of nowhere."

"For once, Husband, just do what I ask. I will be fine. Unlike the child if we don't get back to that shack."

"There it is!" Luna said.

"I will be home in a matter of days. Promise." Flora pecked his cheek and hurried over to the row boat.

Once the women were inside, Solomon pushed the wooden boat and watched them until he could no longer see them.

The women sat in silence the entire ride to the shack. The little one remained still as well.

Luna tied the boat, took the baby, and flew up the ladder before Flora was even out of the boat. The whole structure looked like it would tumble into the swamp at any given second. Flora was a woman who did not frighten, but this was enough to shake her.

"Are you going to stay down there?" Luna called down.

"Just a moment." With a deep breath, Flora began to ascend the ladder.

The Southern air was stifling, and the swamp surrounding them was eerily quiet and obscure. Even the crickets were silent.

Luna continued to keep the fire under her cauldron going.

"When did you notice the child wasn't herself?" Flora ripped a piece of her dress off and soaked it in the water from under the hut.

"This morning. She wouldn't eat, and became very ornery. When she wouldn't stop crying, I picked her up and noticed she was burning up."

"Is that when you decided to bring her ashore?"

"I didn't know what else to do. I've already lost a child, and I can't bear to lose another. You of all people should know how that feels."

"I do. I lost both my boys on the same day. If it wasn't for Martha coming along, I would be lying in the mausoleum with them." Flora sighed as she took the baby back from Luna. "Why don't you go get some rest while I stay with the baby? You look exhausted. And quite frankly, you will not be any good to her in this state."

"I could use some rest. Thank you."

Luna scuttled off toward the back of the shack, while Flora sat in the rocker and sang a lullaby to the baby, who seemed to be resting comfortably. She was so tiny and angelic she stole Flora's heart.

She continued to look down at the baby. "I don't even know your name."

Flora heard something splash in the water below, and realized where she was. She concluded that a shack in the swamp was no place for the decedent of a former monarch to live. Getting the child away from

Luna wouldn't be easy, and could end up being Flora's death, but she had to try.

Looking around, all she saw was open space and the radiance of the flame that kept her cauldron warm and supplied the ignition source for Luna's pipe. Keeping the child close to her bosom, Flora crept over to the ladder and was about to climb down, when Luna came back out.

"Going somewhere?"

"I-I was just—"

"Give me back my daughter." Luna's face became dark, she pursed her lips, and her eyes blazed red as she staggered toward Flora. "I'm afraid, my lady, you've toyed with the wrong woman."

A dense black smoke began to envelope the shack as Luna cried out some Italian words and changed into a giant cobra. Frozen, the grand duchess watched as the witch grew bigger and bigger. The baby wailed, bringing Flora back to reality. Her gaze then fell on the cauldron and the fire a few feet from her.

"Go back to the depths of hell, where you belong, witch." Flora kicked the cauldron over.

The boiling brew burned Luna, transforming her back into a woman. She screamed in agony as the brew seared her skin, and fire began to claim the shack. The fire spread rapidly, trapping Luna behind a wall of flames, and allowing Flora to take leave with the baby. Luna's screams trickled out as the shack burned, and soon the roof collapsed on the witch. And then the flames devoured the rest of the shack.

Flora and the baby just made it away in time, for the foundation gave way and crashed into the muddy swamp water, causing a surge that nearly flipped the little boat and propelled them back to land in seconds.

A worried Solomon waited on the banks of the shore.

"What have you done?"

She didn't answer him.

"Flora?"

28

WHAT'S DONE IS DONE

SHE LOOKED AT HIM WITH A STONE-COLD glare and pursed lips.

"What I had to. Why are you still here?" Her tone was chilling, and took Solomon by surprise.

"I waited a few minutes, and as I was leaving, I saw the fire."

She continued to leer at him.

"You did not answer my question." He found his spine and asked her again.

Only, this time he was more resolute.

"What have I done? This is your daughter, Husband. Your child that you were going to let be raised in the swamp by a witch whose own lineage dates back to Satan himself. How would that look to our subjects? Or what could it do to our chances of reclaiming the throne? Do you think Marin would welcome us back with open arms, knowing that the second-in-line to succeed you is a product of your affair with a condemned witch? Not just any witch, but a Zorn. That name alone is enough to strike fear in the hearts of the most valiant of men." Flora made a few silly faces at the baby to make her laugh.

"That's just hearsay." Solomon knew she spoke the truth, but hoped his reply would be enough to stifle his wife's tirade.

"Perhaps. Then answer me true. Why was Zorn Castle almost burned to the ground? And that captain also said he staked them all while they slept in their tombs? I'm sure if we went to Munich, we could find more information about them in the imperial library."

A red-faced Solomon said, "What do you want me to say, Flora? It's not true? Or tell you that it's all in your head? I told you this was a bad idea, yet you insisted. As you so eloquently put it, it was a *Zorn* you set on fire. Did you ever think there would be reprisals for killing her and taking her baby? When I went to Noble Oaks, I found out that the fire, the death of the Caulfield girl, and the reason Mae ran off was because of Luna. They neglected to pay her back, and as a result, paid the price. And now, my dear, so will we."

The baby began to cry.

"It's okay, Princess. Papa's here." He took the girl and rocked her in his arms.

"Oh, Solomon, I didn't..." Flora slipped down to sit on the ground.

She continued to look out at the remnants of the shack. The logs that were its foundation now floated on the water, giving them the appearance of alligators under the light of the full moon.

"What's done is done," Solomon whispered. "I think we should be on our way." He offered his hand to Flora. and she accepted it. "I think when we get back to the house, we need to come up with a name for her."

"I would like to call her Eleanor, after my mother," Flora said, as they ambled toward the road.

"Eleanor, it is." He helped Flora over a fallen tree.

The forest was dense, and treacherous at night, and there was no telling what animals lurked in the dark.

"How far is the carriage?" Flora said.

"It's just through that clearing."

A howl filled the air. Followed by another, and then another.

"Solomon, what was that?" Flora gripped his hand tighter.

"I don't know. Let's not wait around and find out."

"I'm scared."

"Look. You can see the carriage from here," Solomon said, after they cleared another ditch.

Flora saw the white doors and the lanterns ablaze. "Thank the good Lord!"

Another howl filled the night air, spooking the horses, and they kicked and neighed until they broke free from the carriage. Parker and Toby chased after them, trying to get hold of the reins.

Toby got his hands on Trigger, a beautiful white American Quarter Horse, the older of the steeds. It had a wild streak, and only Toby seemed to be able to control him. The other, a female of the same breed, named Lace, was nowhere to be found.

Toby let out a sigh of relief. "All right, boy. Take it easy." He gripped the leather bridle. "Everything gonna be jist fine."

Trigger nuzzled his head into Toby's hand.

No sooner had the stallion calmed, when an eruption about an acre away created a crimson hue that lit up the sky for miles. Plumes of gray and white smoke drifted up toward the heavens and engulfed the area with the smell of burnt oak.

Flora gasped. "Solomon, what was that?"

Trigger broke free again, but this time he came down on Toby's foot. Toby screamed in agony as his bones crushed underneath Trigger's hoof, and he dropped to the ground like a sack of rice. Trigger galloped down the path at lightning speed just as Parker came out of the clearing. The horse rammed into him, sending him flying into the air, and rendering him unconscious in the brush.

"I think we need to move." Solomon took Eleanor from Flora.

The baby cried in his arms as they hurried down the path that was now fully lit from the fire.

"What could cause such a pyre?" Flora said.

Her auburn hair broke free and cascaded down her back.

"I think it's Noble Oaks," Solomon replied. "Has to be. It's the only thing big enough to cause such an inferno."

Another howl tore through the woods, a lot closer this time.

"Did you hear that?" Flora whispered.

The two froze in their tracks as they saw the bushes up ahead moving. A fawn trotted out, and they both giggled and breathed a sigh of relief, until a huge red wolf bolted out from behind the smaller animal, taking the fawn in its steel-like jaws, and mashing it like its teeth were a food processor.

The wolf stopped and stared at them. It snarled and growled, and as it advanced toward the hapless family, Solomon set Eleanor behind a large rock. Flora screamed as the beast inched closer to her. Solomon tried to intervene, but with a flip of the paw, the beast sent him into the carriage door.

It was so close to her face that she could see right into its nostrils, and even saw the fawn's fur still in its teeth. Flora thought she was a goner. She closed her eyes and made the sign of the cross.

A shot rang out, and the wolf yelped as a bullet pierced its ribcage. The beast collapsed in a heap, revealing Mae Caulfield standing behind it, looking stone cold and about as friendly as a viper.

"Silver gets them every time," she said, with an air of regality as she stepped over the carcass.

Her blonde hair was brushed back from her oval face, and her small green eyes glistened with tears yet to flow.

"What was that thing?" Flora tended to the baby, who was still behind the large rock.

"You're looking at what remains of my little girl, Pamela." Mae continued to fight back tears. "I warned Matthew that we had to destroy her, but he could not be reasoned with. He locked her in a room downstairs, and used silver shackles to keep her there. He kept the only key. With no choice, I—"

"Set fire to Noble Oaks," Flora said.

"I did what I felt was best. I could not let that thing get out and spread this disease. I failed the last time, but tonight I succeeded. I returned home to find Pamela had escaped, killed Matthew, and severely injured Dicey. This time, I made sure the house—"

The wolf sprang up to clamp its mouth down on Mae's neck, and dug its claws into her shoulders.

"Shoot me." Mae grimaced as Pamela continued to gnaw on her throat. "Don't let me become one of them."

Pamela threw her aside like a frisbee, and then set her sights on Flora. The beast rushed at her like a freight train, with the speed of a cheetah and the stealth of a leopard. Flora froze as the wolf leapt into the air to pounce on her, when another bullet was fired.

Solomon had fired from the rifle that Mae dropped, and shot Pamela in the head. When she crashed to the ground, a beautiful young blonde woman had replaced the wicked beast. She lay a few feet from Eleanor.

"Flora, are you hurt?" Solomon ran up to her and wrapped her in his arms while kissing her on the head. "Let me see." He took her hands and looked over them.

"I'm fine. Just a little shaken." Her voice was shaky as she looked down at the body of the Caulfield girl.

"Let's get Eleanor home." He put his arm about her waist, and they plodded toward the baby, who was still behind the rock.

Toby and Parker, though banged up and defeated, ambled along the path back toward their master.

"Kill me," muttered a barely conscious Mae, as she lay dying on the ground a few feet from her daughter.

Blood trickled down the corner of her mouth, and her neck continued to bleed out.

"Do not let me become one of them." She kept her gaze on Solomon.

"Flora, don't look," he said.

The moment she turned around, he fired at Mae, hitting her right between the eyes.

Flora reached down to pick up Eleanor, and noticed a little scratch on her cheek.

"Solomon, look!" She pointed to a tiny mark that barely broke the skin.

"I'm sure it's nothing. We can have the doctor examine her when we get back to Windwood."

Donna pushed away the journal and let out a huge sigh before slamming her fist down on the desk.

"All these years ... it was you who started all this!" She looked at the portrait of her mother that rested against the wall in front of her. "I will never forgive you for this."

She took the little bit of coffee she had left and threw it on the painting.

29

DANGEROUS TIMES

AFTER A LONG DAY AT THE HOSPITAL, BO and Reginald left around nine o'clock. The doctor said there was nothing else they could do for the woman they brought in earlier. Bo continued to beat himself up for shooting her in the first place.

"I'm telling you, Reg, it was a wolf." He pressed the button with the G on it as the elevator doors closed.

"I think you need to go have your eyes checked. That was clearly a woman."

"I know what I saw. I don't need glasses." Bo frowned.

"Just make sure that next time we go hunting, you don't mistake me for a wild turkey or a cougar." Reginald patted Bo on the back.

"I'm not going hunting again. I almost murdered someone tonight, and you're going to joke?"

The doors opened, and they entered the garage.

"Look, I didn't mean—" Reginald's phone vibrated. "It's the wife. I gotta take it." He put the phone to his ear and walked over to the soda machine.

Bo got in the truck door and turned the key in the ignition. Nothing. He tried again. Nothing. He flung open the door and kicked the side of the truck.

"Now? Of all times?"

"Maybe I can help." Channing approached.

"Yeah, you got a new starter?"

"Where's the woman?" Channing said.

Bo hit him square in the face and almost broke his hand. Channing caught him by the throat and squeezed until the poor guy began to turn blue.

"What the hell are you doing?" Reginald yelled, and approached the car.

"I want the girl your friend shot earlier." Channing growled, and discarded Bo as if he was a piece of trash, sending him flying into a Mazda five cars over.

"What the hell are you?" Reginald stared at him, wide-eyed, as Channing changed into a large brown and tan wolf.

He pounced on Reginald until he was pinned against a wall.

"I will ask you one more time." The wolf blew his hot breath all over Reg's face.

His white fangs were exposed and glistening under the overhead lights of the garage.

"She's upstairs, on the third floor. Three doors down from reception." Reginald grimaced as Channing inched his face closer.

"That wasn't so hard, was it?" He patted the top of Reginald's head, then turned and trotted away.

Reginald breathed a sigh of relief and hurried over to Bo, who was lying on the ground, bleeding from his ears, nose, and mouth. He felt for a pulse, and found none. He reached into his pocket for his phone and started to call the police, when Channing appeared and smacked the phone out of his hand.

"I can't let you go." The beast struck Reginald in the face.

Blood gushed out from the gashes. He was dead before he hit the ground.

Channing changed back to human form and put on Reginald's clothes, then headed for the elevator.

The trio watched from the top of the hill as the house exploded, shaking the foundation of the town, and leveling anything nearby. Gideon was so overcome with emotion he could barely talk. That cabin was the place he and his late wife use to go to escape the real world. And it was the home they'd first brought Georgia to. Upstairs was where Ginny was conceived.

"Thank God you smelled the exhaust, or we'd all be hot dogs," Georgia said to Simon.

"Not funny." Gideon kept his gaze fixed on the inferno below.

"It's not, Daddy. It's actually sad. But what else do we have? If I can't laugh, I'm gonna cry. We've lost everything, and that's about all I have left."

"Maybe we should get moving," Simon said, coming back from the embankment. "Whoever did this may still be down there."

"Channing will not get away with this." Gideon stared down at what was once his home. "I will end this once and for all, before anyone else gets hurt."

"Let's get going," Simon yelled, from the car.

"He's right, Dad. We can discuss it in the car."

"All your Mom's things were in there."

"C'mon!" Simon yelled.

"Dad, we have to go." She pulled on his arm.

Gideon didn't put up a fight, but he continued to stare at the ruins.

Being in the house again was beginning to get to Andrea. Every time she turned around, she saw something that reminded her of Calvin, whether it be a photograph, his favorite chair or TV show, which was Dallas. A few times, she had gone into his room just to smell the half-empty bottle of Aramis that sat on the dresser next to a framed photo of a much younger-looking Rosalie. Andrea found it hard to sleep this night, and after making some warm milk, she returned to Calvin's room just to be near him.

She opened the closet door and took his robe from the hook to wrap herself in it. To her pleasant surprise, she found a re-run of Dallas on TV. In this episode, the Ewing's were attending the Oil Barons' Ball, which was almost identical to the Lords' Tuggy awards. On more than one occasion, the cops were called to break up a fight, women were known to end up in the pool after one accused the other of flirting with their man, and Andrea was pretty sure more than a child or two was conceived on this night.

"Those were the—" She heard sirens and commotion going on downstairs.

The widow Lord opened the bedroom door, stepped out into the hallway, and saw in the mirror that she was wearing the green sequin gown she'd worn to Simon's wedding. Even her hair was the same.

"What in the world?" She rubbed her hands down her dress and through her hair.

"Look at you standing there, admiring yourself, when your husband and sons are God knows where," Rosa barked, slithering out from the upstairs parlor.

Her hair was down. Her eyes were puffy, and she wore no makeup.

"Not now, Rosa." Andrea went to the attic, with the gun still tucked underneath her dress.

"Don't you walk away from me when I'm talking to you!" Rosa followed her into the vestibule, and up the long, narrow staircase.

"Blow it out your ass, crone." Andrea was surprised at how easily the words rolled off her tongue, and the relief she felt in saying them.

"How dare you!"

Andrea spun around to glare at the old lady.

"You snide bitch, do you ever shut up?" she spewed, through clenched teeth.

For the first time, Rosa was scared of her.

"Because of you, my daughter has completely lost her mind," Rosa said. "I will never forgive you for this. And once things calm down, I will tell Calvin exactly what type of woman you really are. My poor Helena has to spend her life in a padded cell, while you roam free. It's not right. It should've been you in that room."

"Let me tell you something, Rosalie Giovanni Lord. You're not gonna get a chance to say anything."

"I beg your pardon?" Rosa stood there, stunned.

Andrea shoved her down the stairs, and Rosa broke her neck and died before reaching the bottom of the steps, where Sutton would later find her. Her death would be ruled a heart attack brought on from the stress of the night's events.

Andrea smiled as she looked down at Rosa, who lay on her back, and whose eyes were blank and wide open.

"My, how the mighty have fallen."

Andrea bolted up in bed after the shriek she let out woke her up. She was relieved to find herself in her own bed. She dropped her legs over the side and stared at the window and the shadows that danced across her ceiling.

"Mama, are you all right?" Joshua barged in and flicked on the light.

He eased down beside her on the four-poster bed.

"I'm sorry, Son," she said, in a shaky voice. "I just experienced one of my nightmares. Didn't intend to wake anyone."

"No need to be sorry. I'm glad it was nothing serious." He put his hand over his hers.

Andrea thought her heart would burst through her chest. Had Joshua finally forgiven her?

"Can I bring you anything? Water, tea, or a wet rag?"

"I'm fine. Honest. You go on back to bed."

He got up and headed toward the door.

"Before I forget, the sheriff was out here again, looking for Loretta. Her family is starting to worry. Are you sure she didn't mention where she was going?"

"I'm positive. All she said was that she had to go into town. And that was it."

"Okay, Mama. Good night. Get some rest. I'm glad you're okay."

She feigned a smile as he shut the door.

"So the cracks in the dam begin to break," said a familiar voice.

Andrea hopped out of bed to find Rosa, who goaded her from in front of the fireplace.

"It's only a matter of time before your son and the whole town finds out you killed me and that poor helpless nurse."

"Go to hell." Andrea closed her eyes, picked up a vase from her nightstand, full of purple and white hyacinths, and hurled it at the fireplace.

When she opened her eyes, Rosa was gone.

It was just your imagination, Andrea. Pull yourself together. No one could possibly know you killed the old lady or the nurse.

30

CAT AND MOUSE

AFTER STOPPING OFF IN THE MEN'S ROOM on the way up to the third floor, Channing cleaned himself up and donned the white lab coat he stole from the guy in the stall next to him after he snapped his neck and propped him up against the stall's metal frame. He looked at himself one more time in the mirror and chuckled when he realized that once he put the lab coat on, he really did look like Mr. Clean. Or better yet, his more handsome brother. Channing made sure his buttons were correct and everything was tucked in before reaching for the door. Happy with what he saw, he winked at himself and then entered the hallway.

All kinds of machines, gurneys, and wheelchairs lined both sides of the brightly lit corridor. Channing walked by the waiting room and saw it was filled to capacity.

People had to stand outside. A young woman in her twenties had more kids with her than the old woman who lived in the shoe. Instead of watching them, she was on the phone talking about her husband jumping bail and getting shot, and how she had to spend the next umpteen hours here waiting.

Her youngest, a boy of about five, was running up and down the corridor, hollering, running into people, and then playing with the TV. He threw the magazines on the floor, along with the pillows, then kicked a lady's purse on the floor. The little brat came flying out of the waiting room, laughing and making flying motions, and collided with Channing, who gripped him by the arm and stared at him until his eyes began to glow, growling from his very bowels. The boy froze and almost burst into tears before bolting over to the nearest chair, where he sat without moving a muscle.

"No wonder we eat our young." Channing approached the boy's mother, snatched her cell phone, and crumbled it to dust. "How 'bout instead of spending your time on the phone, you watch your kid and stop letting him run amok and cause problems for everyone else." He strutted down the corridor, like a boss.

Channing knew he was getting closer to her. He could smell her scent everywhere. The closer he got to the end of the hall, the stronger it became. He took a left and then advanced a couple feet, until he was in front of her door, where he gently opened it and found Nola in a medication-induced sleep. Seeing her like that almost tugged at his heart. But then he realized it was just gas.

A flashlight-bulb-sized light illuminated Nola's small face. Channing took the lab coat off and threw it in the dirty linen basket.

"Did you really think I'd be stupid enough to use the virus on one of my own pack members? Tsk-tsk." He shook his head and made a pouty face. "You know me better than that. Well, I thought you did, anyway." He stared down at her virtuous face and stroked her cheek.

"I'm sorry. I didn't mean to intrude." A middle-aged male nurse entered to check the IVs and Nola's blood pressure.

He smiled at Channing and left.

"Now, where were we? Oh, yeah, right. I let you get away. I wanted you to believe I wanted to kill you, because I knew you'd lead me right to dear old Dad. And then you go and get yourself shot." He bent down to take off his shoe, pulled back the sole and took out a vial of clear liquid.

"She's still sleeping?" A young black man said, carrying her dinner tray.

Channing nodded.

"All right. I'll leave it right here so she can have it when she awakes. I'll also leave the menu so she can pick her breakfast." The orderly left.

"Once I put this in your IV, I'll be able to track your every move. And when you reach Gideon, I'll be waiting."

Channing found a bunch of wrapped syringes near the sink, next to some latex gloves. He unwrapped a syringe and filled it. As soon as he injected the IV tube, alarms went off throughout the hospital.

"That's my cue to leave."

He strode over to the window, forced it open and jumped out, transforming into a wolf in midair.

Sutton was more determined than ever to find out what Donna was hiding. After hearing her exchange with Toni in the attic, he knew there was more to Donna Lord than met the eye. He had come up empty-handed at the library, and now he was going to see what he could dig up at the Solomon's Wake Historical Society.

The building was an old red-brick structure with a high-pitched slate roof and large windows. It was probably a school at one time, and built when Solomon founded the town. The wooden porch creaked as he climbed the stairs to the front door, which had an OPEN sign hanging on the glass. A bell chimed when he opened the door, signaling to a woman behind a large redwood desk that she had company.

"I would like to see anything you have on the Lord family," he said. "from about 1780 to 1830."

"Everything is on the microfilm rolls in date order, in large metal drawers down in the basement."

She was an elderly woman with white-as-snow hair, a small frame, and old-fashioned cat-eye glasses that rested on the bridge of her nose. She wore a white blouse with a cameo brooch at her neck, and a pencil above her ear.

"Follow me," she said.

Sutton followed her to the back and down a flight of stairs. Dust covered everything. Cobwebs shrouded furniture, windows, and the ceiling. A dim light flickered. Row upon row of bookshelves were piled high with mismatched encyclopedias, magazines, books, and old newspapers.

"The last aisle on the left should be where you'll find it. The instructions for the microfilm machine are written and taped to the side of the machine. If you don't mind my asking, why are you so interested in the Lord family? There are a lot of other well-to-do families here in Solomon's Wake."

"I am a novelist hired by one Joshua Lord, to do a biography of the family."

"I see. Well, I hope you find what you need. If I can be of further assistance, I am at the top of the steps."

Sutton nodded his thanks and began to scroll through piles of microfiche, one by one. A half-hour went by, and he was still empty-handed.

Finally, he struck gold.

54-Year-Old Flora Lord Gives Birth to 7-Pound-6-Ounce Baby Girl.

After reading the article, he came across a few others on Martha, and then they stopped.

The title of the next article he picked up said, *Eleanor Rose Lord Ties the Knot at 18.*

As he read on, he learned that Eleanor had married her cousin Richard, in 1813, and gave birth to Benjamin Phillip Lord a year later. Eleanor was one of the first women in South Carolina to open a finishing school. Most of the articles were about her sister or her father. Then Sutton read about what had led to the family's downfall.

Animal Attacks Continue Across Solomon's Wake.

The town had been placed under a curfew until further notice once the body count reached twenty-five.

Alligators Take the Life of Grand Duchess Flora.

Flora's mangled body was found out near the swamp, by her daughter, Martha.

Eleanor Lord Dies at 22, Leaving Martha Sole Heir.

A year later, Eleanor lost her life in a tragic accident. Martha Lord shot her sister, believing her to be a werewolf. During Luna's trial, it came out that she was Eleanor's birth mother. Before the noose broke her neck, she called on her Zorn ancestors to curse Martha.

23-Year-Old Martha Lord Dies.

Martha was found in her bedroom, drained of all blood and white as a sheet. Her beloved Aunty had said a vampire did it. Shortly after Martha was found, her body disappeared. And contrary to popular belief, it was not buried in the Lord mausoleum.

"I'm not sure if you are interested in these paintings I have back here." The old woman came up behind Sutton. "Rosa Lord donated them to the society back in the '80s, but we never did anything with them."

He followed her to the far end of the room, to a wall that had tons of sleeves that contained hundreds of paintings the society had collected over the years.

"I have to go back upstairs, but you are more than welcome to take a look." She pulled a portrait out from the first pocket. "Here you go."

Sutton watched her walk away before he removed it.

"What do we have here?" He held it up to get a better look at it.

The inscription read, *Marshall Lord, painted in* 1910. Sutton took out another, of Theodore Lord, followed by Iris Lord, and then a picture with no date or information. He had to reach all the way back to get the last painting, and almost fell over when he saw the portrait of Martha Lord, from 1812, and the uncanny resemblance to Donna.

"I knew it. You're the same person, and it's only a matter of time before I expose you to the world."

He fished into his pocket for his cell, and took a picture of the painting before shoving it back into the sleeve.

31

THE RAGING STORM

THE BLACK SEDAN GLIDED ALONG THE DARK stretch of I-95, with Georgia at the wheel, Gideon asleep in the back, and Simon zonked out in the passenger seat. It had been hours since anyone had spoken, and they hadn't made a pit stop since Virginia.

In sleep, she came to him dressed in Edwardian fashion. He reached for her, and she moved farther away. He tried again, but she slipped through his grasp once more. After finally finding his voice, he called to her.

"Ginny, don't go!" He searched for her through the fog that enveloped them.

"Help me, Daddy, please," the young woman cried. "I'm scared, and it's dark."

"I don't know what to do. Tell me what to do!" Gideon reached for her hand.

"You must come back. You must come back," she said, in a distant tone, right before being sucked up into the air.

"Ginny!"

He woke up and squinted at the morning sun radiating onto his face.

"Bad dream?" Georgia looked at him through the rearview mirror.

"I'll be fine. What time is it?"

"Ten-thirty. You've slept through Virginia and North Carolina. You had me worried there, Daddy." She switched lanes and passed a furniture truck.

"Where are we?" He rolled down the window to light up a smoke, and the fresh air hit him.

"We're about three hours or so from Windwood. Want to talk about the dream you were having?" She looked at him the way a nun did right before she cracked you on the knuckles with a ruler.

"It was Ginny. She was trying to tell me something. I just don't know what she means by it." He tossed the butt and rolled up the windows, then folded his arms and settled back into the seat.

"What did she say?"

"You must come back."

"That's easy. She's telling you to go to Windwood, just like Simon said." Georgia swerved back into the right lane to go around an elderly man doing thirty-five in a fifty-mile-per-hour zone.

"How do you know?"

"Woman's intuition. You hungry? We can stop at Denny's." She slowed up to make the exit to the rest stop.

"Sure. I need to stretch my legs."

Toni was awakened by a soft tap on her door. She rolled over and saw by the clock on the nightstand that it was about a quarter after two, and her room was dark aside from the night light plugged in by the bathroom so she could see where she was going and not break her neck. When she had lived in Venice, she got out of bed late one night and tripped over a pair of shoes. She broke her wrist and sprained her neck, resulting in her wearing a brace and a cast for a few weeks.

"I'm coming." She reached for her yellow robe before flicking on the light.

She cracked open the door to see a Donna's tear-streaked faced.

"What's the matter?" Toni opened the door all the way and ushered her in.

"It's all her fault. Everything that has happened to this family is a direct result of my mother and what she did to Luna." Donna threw herself down on Toni's bed.

Toni moved to comfort her. "What did she do?"

"She stole Eleanor from Luna, and burned Luna's hut down, causing her to be disfigured. If she hadn't done that, none of this would've happened. There'd be no curse, and

I wouldn't be a vampire. And I just took the last of my pills." Donna wailed in Toni's arms.

"I am going to try to enter the mine to get the blood-root as soon as I can. Until then, I'll set up a room in the basement that you can use to rest during the day. We'll tell Joshua that you're helping me look for a new house, and then we'll take a few days and go to Myrtle Beach for a woman's getaway."

"I don't want to become that woman again. I am a danger to you, my children, and my husband." Donna got up from the bed and trudged over to the window to stare at the moon. "I need to get used to seeing that again."

"It will not come to that. I promise. It'll be a couple days at the most. I want you to go out tonight and celebrate your anniversary."

Donna looked at her with wide eyes.

"Yes, I remembered. And I'll watch the kids so you two can have some fun for a change. And you can say your goodbyes till we can figure something out."

Sutton went into the parlor to tidy it up, and saw Jenna staring out the window. He went about his business—polishing, arranging the magazines on the table, picking the dead flowers out of the vase, and fluffing the pillows on the sofa.

"I saw Nonna and Mommy move a coffin into the basement," the girl said, from behind the crimson curtain.

The butler looked at her with his mouth agape and his head cocked.

"I think someone's been watching too much Vampire Diaries," he said.

Jenna came out from behind the curtain with her hair pulled back into a ponytail. Her Nikes were so white they put his polished kitchen floor to shame. And the light from the window reflected against the blue diamond necklace she wore, making it gleam and dance across the walls.

"I'd put that back before your mother knows you have it. You know she doesn't like you rummaging through her jewelry box." Sutton began to wipe down the mirrors in the room.

"Oh, no." Jenna broke the clasp to the necklace and let it fall to the ground.

"What?" He put down the paper towels and glass cleaner.

Jenna cried, looking down at the floor where the necklace lay.

"The necklace broke," she said.

"The clasp's just loose, see?" He picked it up and used his forefinger and thumb to lock it back in place, then handed it back to Jenna.

"Uh-oh. I think I chipped it. Mommy's gonna kill me."

"I'm sure it's fine, honey." Sutton took it back and strode over to the window to get a better look at it. "I don't see anything wrong." He continued to examine the gem.

"Look deeper," Jenna said, in Luna's voice. "You are now in my control, and you will serve me until death. Do I make myself clear?"

Sutton nodded.

"I need you to go down into the basement and find a coffin hidden long ago. Once you locate it, come back and see me."

"Jenna, go put this back before your mother notices it's gone, and you really do break it." He handed the necklace back, with no recollection of the conversation.

"I will. Thanks, Sutton." She strolled off into the foyer.

The old man sat in one of the chairs, feeling woozy and tired, with a sudden urge to roam about the basement.

Andrea sat on a white lounge chair in front of the Olympic-size swimming pool, with an iced tea in her hand and a romance novel in her lap. Her sunglasses kept the bright sun out of her eyes, and an oversized sun hat protected her fair skin, along with sun block she'd loaded up on.

She had forgotten how beautiful and tranquil the estate was, and all the good times they used to have. For a moment, she could smell the burgers and dogs Calvin insisted on cooking himself with his top-of-the-line grill. Then he would grab her and pull her in to dance to their song, "Can't Help Falling in Love," by the King. Joshua would be splashing around on the steps with his colorful inner tube, and Simon would be doing laps in the pool.

The sound of the gate opening brought her back from her memories.

"I'm sorry. I didn't know you were here." Toni closed the gate and stopped to stare at Andrea. "I'll come back later." She threw the red towel with *Myrtle Beach* scrawled across it in blue letters, over her shoulder.

"You don't have to leave on my account." Andrea sipped some tea and motioned for Toni to sit in the empty recliner next to her.

"That's okay. You looked like you were in your own little world." Toni turned back to the gate and put her hand on the latch.

"You don't like me much, do you?" Andrea said.

"No, I don't." Toni turned back to face her. "You single-handedly destroyed this family in one night. You shot and killed one son, while the other one watched him fall out a window. My best friend, Rosa, died due to the stress your actions caused. So excuse me if I don't welcome you home with open arms." She was so hot the pool couldn't even cool her off.

"Rosa was a bitch who had it in for me since day one. As for Simon, I made my peace with that." Andrea picked up her novel.

"You may have made peace with what you did to him, but I haven't. Simon was a fun-loving, handsome man who had the world at his feet. I would've traded places with you and been his mom in a heartbeat. I would've loved him unconditionally, werewolf or not."

Brandon came up to the gate with his headphones on and an inner tube around his waist.

"Nonna, you coming in, too?" he yelled at the top of his lungs.

The two women continued to glower at each other.

Then Toni pulled one of Brandon's earbuds out.

"No, sweetheart. I've had enough sun. I'll see you later." She kissed him on the top of his head and left through the gate.

"Mom and Dad are going out tonight for their anniversary. You think we could rent some movies and stay up all night?"

"I think we'll be able to come up with something." Andrea grinned.

The wheels in her mind began to turn. With everyone being out of the house tonight, she was presented the perfect opportunity to kill Brandon.

Sutton still didn't know why he was crawling all over the cellar and ripping everything apart. The old man knew every inch on the floor, ceiling, and walls. There wasn't anything he didn't know about Windwood.

Frustrated, he leaned against the wall, shut his eyes and tried to think. There were so many hidden tunnels under the house it was like trying to find Waldo. Not helping matters was that he didn't know exactly what he was looking for.

Something big rubbed up against his leg. His heart beat so fast he thought he was going to pass out. He was afraid to look at what it was, until he heard the *meow*.

Sutton looked down to see Hank, the gray tomcat with black stripes, who had made the estate his home about five years ago.

"I thought you ran away."

He picked the cat up, and it purred and rubbed up against his cheek.

A black mouse scurried across Sutton's foot. Hank dug his claws into Sutton's shoulder and sprang off his chest like a diving board, doing a twist in the air, and landed on all fours, licking his chops.

"I would've gotten you something to eat in a minute." Sutton rubbed his shoulder.

The mouse was too fast, and shot off down the corridor. Hank gave chase, and Sutton followed.

"I can't run that fast," he said, trying to catch up.

Down the endless dark passageway, he always seemed to fall a few feet behind Hank. The butler finally ended up in front of a door hidden behind a metal rack.

"I'll be damned."

Poor Hank lost his prey when it slipped through a crack under the door. Now he just stared at the door.

Sutton slid the rack away from the door, and found that to be the only easy thing. The door was locked and appeared to be nailed shut.

"I don't suppose you have a key?" he said to Hank, who kept his gaze on the door. "Let's go upstairs and find you something to eat, and something to open this door."

32

THE FAÇADE CRUMBLES

DONNA LOOKED HERSELF OVER IN THE mirror and began to have reservations about going out. She sat on her vanity chair and started to take her shoes off, when Joshua came out of the bathroom, all freshly shaven.

"No way," he moaned. "I have been looking forward to this all day. We barely ever have time to ourselves, and I'm not gonna let you bail on me now." He sat on the bed to put his sneakers on.

"I just have a bad feeling."

"Everything is gonna be fine. Sutton, Mom, and Toni are here. I'm sure Brandon will be glued to his video game, and won't ever come out of his room. Jenna will be out like a light by eight." He got up from the bed and moved over to the vanity to massage his wife's shoulders.

"How about we stay in and you do that all night?" She sighed.

"Meet me downstairs in five." He kissed the top of her head and went out into the hall.

Jenna spied him from the keyhole and smiled, knowing they would be out soon, and Sutton would at last get the door open to the hidden room.

Andrea listened as Joshua went over the rules with Toni. He told her what time Jenna needed to be in bed, no drinks after a certain time, and to make sure Brandon took a break from his game to give his eyes a rest. Once she knew Toni wasn't looking, she dropped two Ambiens into the witch's tea.

"We have it under control. Don't we, Andrea?" Toni looked over shoulder, at Andrea, who sat in a chair by the fireplace.

"Yes. Now you kids go and have a good time."

Toni waved from the door as the couple left. She returned to the parlor and sat across from Andrea, on the new baby-blue loveseat Donna had ordered with the same-color sofa, curtains, and end tables. She even got

the new rugs to match the curtains to a T, as well as a
giant flat screen TV.

Sutton took a crowbar from the garage and returned to
the basement to have at the door again. He tried multiple
times to open it, but it wouldn't budge. He threw his arms
up and dropped the crowbar, then started back upstairs,
but Jenna blocked him.

"Jenna, what are you doing down here? If your grand-
mothers find you down here, it'll be my hide." He grabbed
her arm and directed her toward the steps, when he
noticed the necklace.

He became transfixed and under its control once more.

"The both of us should be able to get a rotting, splintering door open," Jenna barked, as she reached for the
crowbar.

"What's so important about this door?"

"Never you mind. Just help me get it opened."

Toni fell asleep in a matter of minutes, with her needle-
point still in hand.

Andrea began the trek up the stairs, toward Brandon's
room. From the doorway, she could see that he had passed

out on the floor with the video controller in one hand, and a gamer magazine in the other.

She placed two Ambien in the half-drunk bottle of soda in front of him.

"I am so sorry." She took a pillow from the bed and stood over Brandon.

The decaying door was no match for them, and gave in with little effort. A rush of dank air escaped and caught in their throats. A putrid odor burned their eyes. It was dark and near impossible to see what was inside.

"What is that smell?" Sutton said.

"Quit being a sissy, and get inside." Jenna gave him a shove.

"Is someone there?" a woman's voice called out.

"My God! Someone's in there." Sutton hurried through the open door and crashed into a something in the center of the room.

With a flick of Jenna's wrist, the room illuminated to reveal what Sutton had crashed into—a chained coffin.

"T-that's a c-coffin," he said.

"Why, yes, it is." Jenna got closer to it. With a wave of her hand, the chains dropped to the floor, the lid popped open, and the woman inside was on Sutton like bees to honey.

"Hello, Kara." Jenna said, after the vampire finished with Sutton and let him fall to the floor.

They arrived at Anthony's shortly before ten, smiling, laughing, and feeling like school kids again, both grateful to Toni and Andrea for offering to watch Jenna so they could celebrate their anniversary.

Donna looked amazing. Her hair was wavy and down. She had on the right amount of makeup, and a dab of Obsession. A simple choker graced her neck, and the mauve summer dress hugged her nicely.

Joshua, on the other hand, felt underdressed in his Nikes, jeans, and T-shirt. However, he had gotten a haircut and shaved for the occasion. And when they got into the car, he gave her a dozen roses and the emerald earrings she wanted.

The small bar and grill was filled, as young and old crammed in to watch the Phillies and Braves go head-to-head, while enjoying a beer or two. Others were enjoying karaoke out at the bar. It was eighties night, and such hits as, "Video Killed the Radio Star" and "Take Me Home Tonight," filled the room.

"You look beautiful." Joshua reached for her hand after they sat down. "I feel kind of naked." He smirked.

"I knew I married you for a reason." Donna winked at him. "You're still the sexiest, most dashing man I ever met."

She watched a group of college girls doing Blow Job Shots at the bar while being cheered on by their beaus.

"Not so long ago, we would've been able to drink them under the table," he said, with a hint of jealousy.

"Those were the good old days. Remember when you used to run up to the stage, grab the mic and sing to me?" Donna was still looking at the girls while taking a trip down memory lane. "The one time, you were so drunk you fell asleep mid-song." She bellowed out a laugh.

"Wasn't that the same night you saw Sheila Gilroy making eyes at me? Later, when we were all skinny dipping at the lake, you hid her clothes."

"I don't know if she ever found them."

They both laughed.

"I'm going to get a beer. You want anything?" Joshua got up.

"A glass of Moscato would be nice. It's such a beautiful night, I think I want to sit on the deck."

"Your wish is my command. I'll meet you out there." He disappeared into the crowd.

She strode toward the exit that led to the patio. Joshua soon followed, and nearly got his ear clipped by a dart when he cut right through two drunk guys in the middle of a match. The song, "Nothing's Gonna Stop Us Now," played.

He watched his wife sway to the music, looking like a vison under the glow of the moon. He came up behind her, placed his arm around her chest, and began to move with her while grazing her ear with his lips.

"I love this song," she whispered, and relaxed into her husband's embrace.

"I remember. You used to blare it every time it came on the radio or TV, and you were just as bad with the movie."

"What can I say. I like the classics." She giggled. "I don't want this night to end."

"You ready to go back in and sit?"

"Yes, I'm feeling a bit woozy from the wine. I'm not used to it anymore."

Joshua led her back inside to a small table for two, at the back of the room. It was still loud, but at least the music wasn't on top of them and they could hear each other. When the waitress came by, he ordered a shot of vodka with a Bud chaser, and despite feeling buzzed, Donna ordered another Moscato.

"Do you remember what our friends used to call us?" Joshua said.

She looked up at him. "Paul and Linda, because we were always together." She gazed deep into his eyes.

Joshua jumped up from the table and went up front to the Karaoke machine, whispered something to the DJ, and then took the microphone.

"This is for the lovely Donna Lord." He pointed the mic at her.

The music played, and he sang the lyrics to Paul McCartney and Wings' "Silly Love Songs." Soon everyone was on their feet, singing along with him, clapping and shouting, even lighting their lighters and waving them in the air. It wasn't an '80s song, but when you're Joshua Lord, you can sing anything you want.

"You are one lucky lady," some young girl with a pierced nose and pink hair whispered in Donna's ear.

"Yes, I am."

When he finished, the patrons were congratulating him and patting him on the back. Donna headed to the bar to get her man another drink. She noticed the TV above the bar was tuned to Fox News, and the scroll across the bottom said that the people of the village of Zorn in Germany had voted unanimously to change their name to Stroudsburg.

"It's a step in the right direction if you ask me." The older bartender handed her a beer. "Maybe now they can put all this vampire talk behind them."

Tears welled up in Donna's eyes when it dawned on her that by this time tomorrow, she'd be a vampire once more, and didn't know when she'd see Joshua again.

"You ready to get out of here?" Joshua said, when he made it back.

"Yeah, give me a sec to freshen up." She kept her back to him.

Wiping the tears out of her eyes, Donna pushed through the throngs of drunkards, toward the woman's bathroom, which was next to the jukebox and coat rack. As she put her hand on the door, she looked back at Joshua, who was talking to the bartender, and she felt a blunt object dig into her side.

Donna was shocked to find a detached Sutton was the culprit.

"Don't say a word, or I will pull the trigger and splatter you all over the wall. Make your way outside without turning back or bringing attention to us. Move." He jabbed the gun into her back and ushered her out into the night.

Everything was quiet except for the music coming from inside the bar. There were no cars on the road, no people anywhere, and the lamp posts had broken bulbs, rendering them useless.

"I know what you are," he sneered.

Sutton led her farther and farther away from the bar, to an open field and a waiting truck.

"For some reason, the men in this family are blinded by beauty and don't see the evil that lurks on the inside of that prettiness. Joshua, Calvin, and to an extent, Simon, all paid the price for loving the wrong woman. Andrea is just crazy. Georgia is a werewolf, and you're a vampire. I am tired of being the one to clean up the mess you broads leave behind. Nothing good could ever come from loving you women."

"I think you're as crazy as Andrea if you believe any of what you're saying." Donna stopped when she saw the coffin in the back of the truck.

"The look on your face says it all, Martha."

"Please don't make me get in there." The fear of being locked inside began to cripple her.

"I'm sorry. I can't allow you to roam about. I heard you tell Toni that your pills were about to run out, and when they did, you would be a vampire again. I admire

Joshua too much to let you hurt him. He deserves better." Sutton seethed as he opened the lid.

"Oh, my God. I never saw it until now. You're in love with my husband, and that's why you want me out of the way."

He shepherded her into the coffin.

"I'll die in there. I'm not a vampire yet. Please, Sutton, think this through."

"I have." He slammed the lid shut. "This is something I should have done a long time ago."

He could her screams as he climbed into the front seat and started the truck.

33

TRAPPED

NOLA COULD HEAR THE VOICES AS SHE came to, but was unable to open her eyes. Their hands were cold as they changed her gown and checked her vitals. One nurse changed her IV, while the other typed the info into the computer.

"You were so lucky you weren't here yesterday, Margo." The younger brunette kept her gaze on the info she typed.

"I heard. It was all over the news, the Internet, and the papers." Margo took off her gloves and tossing them in the trash.

"They found the poor guy crumpled in a stall in the men's bathroom. You know, the one on the first floor, around the corner from Emergency. The body was so mutilated they said it looked like a wild animal could've done it. What makes it even scarier is they saw him enter this room and never come out." She looked at Margo, who stared at her wide-eyed.

"Get out."

"I swear to God it's true, or my name ain't Tiffany Marie Baker."

"Wow. How did it get out of this room if the hospital was on lockdown?" Margo played with her stethoscope. "I am beyond creeped out now."

"It seemed to vanish into thin air," Tiffany said.

"How about the patient. Were there any marks or anything on her?"

"Not even a scratch, which makes it even odder." Tiffany began to wheel the computer out onto the floor.

"What if it comes back?" Margo followed.

"I heard through the grapevine that corporate's going to post a guard outside, starting tonight."

The two stepped out in the hallway, when Tiffany realized she had left her badge by the bedside. She turned to go back inside, only to find the patient gone. She rushed to the bathroom and pulled the shower curtain back. Looked under the bed and in the closet. Nothing.

"What's the holdup?" Margo bounced back into the room and noticed the empty bed. "Where did she go?" She threw her hands up.

"How does a whole body disappear?" Tiffany sat on the bed.

"This happens in the movies, not in small towns in the middle of nowhere." Margo reached for the phone. "I have to call this in."

Donna opened her eyes to see the purple satin lining of her coffin, and noticed a silver crucifix strapped to the inside of the lid. She reached a hand up to push open the lid, only to find it had been chained. She screamed, cried, and howled while she fought to raise the coffin lid. Her fingertips bled, and her eyes clouded over in a dazed frenzy at the thought of being trapped again.

"Don't try to fight it, dear creator. It's no use."

A woman sat on top of the coffin, cackling, while Sutton stood behind her, ever the obedient servant.

Donna knew that was the voice of Kara, someone she thought she'd never see again. She tried to claw at Kara's legs, but couldn't get her arm out far enough to do so.

"When I get out of this—which, I will—you'd better hope I don't find you. For when I do, I'll drain every last ounce of blood from your body. Then I'll bury you from the neck down 'til the sun ravages your face beyond recognition. I won't have to scatter your ashes, because a youngling like you can't survive direct sunlight, so there's no need for me to worry about you coming back to haunt me. I promise you, Kara, let me out, and I'll teach you all I know."

Kara continued to sit on the casket, pretending to examine her nails.

"Sorry. No can do. I have orders from Luna herself that if I lift a finger to help you, I'll wander the underworld forever. And we both know she has the power to do it." Kara slid down. "Why would I help you after you left me to die in that room for decades?"

"You threatened to attack my family. You would've done the same if the shoe was on the other foot. Now it all makes sense. Sutton is under your control. You're feeding him your blood. That's why he's suddenly so strong. Up until the other day, he couldn't walk up the stairs without being out of breath."

"Enough chatter!" Luna's voice said.

Donna could see Luna in the guise of Jenna. Her heart broke, knowing her daughter was under the witch's spell.

"Jenna, I know you can hear me. I need you to be strong for me, so you must fight Luna with all you have. Listen to my voice and find your way back."

Donna watched as her little girl's eyes closed and fluttered.

"Mommy?" Jenna's sweet face stared back at her.

A few moments later, she erupted in a fit of laughter.

"Did you honestly think I would let you run around the estate? I told you, over two hundred years ago, that I'd take my revenge. And tonight, I shall. You're going back into the ground, and this time it will be for good. Get her out of here!" Luna threw her arms up.

Donna's muffled cries echoed as they carried her out of the truck and into the dark.

Nola sprinted from the hospital. Knowing Channing was in her room, standing over her, made her skin crawl and her stomach turn. What was he up to? Why was he there? All this raced through her mind as she bolted down the street. The bullet wound was still sore, and she felt feverish, but all she could think about was getting back to Gideon.

She found the nearest bus station and lumbered over to the ticket counter to purchase a one-way ticket to Solomon's Wake, in hopes he'd be there. Unfortunately, the bus wasn't leaving for another six hours. And since the town was about the size of a small boat, all she could do was wait.

Nola had snatched one of the nurse's purse, and with it, her American Express, so she could at least get something to eat and buy some new clothes. The blue scrubs she wore made her skin itch and felt like sandpaper, given that she didn't have any undergarments on.

The only thing open at this hour was a small twenty-four-hour gift shop-restaurant in the deserted terminal. Her stomach won out, and she decided to eat first.

Every trucker this side of Dixie was inside, along with a few drunks who seemed to think the party was still going on.

"Table or booth?" said Wanda, a blue-haired woman in her mid-sixties.

Her pink and white checkered uniform was too big for her, and her soda-bottle lenses made her eyes look too big for her face.

"A booth is fine," Nola said.

Wanda led her over to a booth by the door. She threw the menu down and was about to go over the specials, when one of the drunks vomited all over the floor.

"I just mopped that floor." She charged over to the table of college kids.

Nola shook her head and picked up the menu to scroll through it, oblivious to Channing watching her from the plate-glass storefront.

Joshua realized something was amiss when, after twenty minutes, Donna didn't return. He asked one of the waitresses to check the woman's room for her.

When the waitress returned and delivered the news that Donna wasn't in there, Joshua knew something must've happened, because there was no way she would've just left.

The bar had now emptied out, and last call would soon be announced.

Joshua checked his cell again—no calls or texts. He grabbed his keys and decided to go back to Windwood, hoping she'd be there.

34

FULL CIRCLE

THE TRIO PULLED INTO WINDWOOD'S LONG drive. The sky was clear as hundreds of stars pranced and twinkled across the stratosphere. A gentle wind rustled through the trees and carried with it the scent of Southern magnolia. Simon was transported back to his childhood.

He got out of the car first and stared at the house. Still an imposing monument. He scanned the front porch, and from there, followed the white pillars up to the second floor, around the side of the house, to the balcony that had been Rosa's room.

The red pyracantha still clung to the west-side wall, and seemed to completely overtake the trellis as it rose toward the third floor. From the balcony, he followed the pyracantha to the attic, and then the cupola.

Georgia put a hand on his shoulder. "We don't have to do this right now. We can come back in the morning."

She took him by the sleeve while he stared up at the cupola.

"For years, my mother has gotten away with what she did. It's time she pays." He charged toward the front door.

"Simon, you don't even know if she's in there," Georgia hollered, trying to catch up with him.

Gideon too had a tough time going inside. His mind kept returning to Ginny and the night she disappeared. So many lives were destroyed because of this house and the secrets it contained. He couldn't help but wonder if the same was going to ring true tonight.

With a deep breath, he followed suit, and stood with Simon and Georgia in the foyer.

"Where is everybody?" Georgia looked down the long hall that led to the kitchen and the servants' quarters.

"S-something's not right." Gideon opened the double doors to the parlor. "Can I get some help in here?" he called, after finding Toni slumped over.

"Georgia, call the police." Simon started upstairs.

"Wait for the police to get here." Georgia grabbed his arm and stopped him on the third step. "Simon, I'm not going to let you make me a widow again. Please let the police handle this." She sniffled.

Simon pulled her into a kiss.

"This time, I'm coming back. I promise." He flashed his pearly whites, then bolted up the stairs.

She reached for her cell and dialed 911 as her gaze settled on the portrait of Andrea across from her, in the parlor.

Andrea stood over Brandon and didn't feel at all triumphant, but instead found herself second-guessing her decision. At least with Simon she knew without a shadow of a doubt that he was a werewolf. She couldn't say the same about Brandon.

As she looked down at his face, a lone tear fell from her eye and landed on his lips. Then the tears began to flow.

"I'm so sorry. But I have to make sure, for all our sakes, that this plague that's infected our family forever is finally snuffed out."

She wiped her eyes with her sleeve and reached for the pillow she'd dropped earlier. Drew a deep breath and pressed the pillow over his face, determined to make sure the job was done.

"What are you doing, Mama?" Simon hollered, as he entered the bedroom.

Andrea's blood ran cold, and she stopped dead, unable to turn around to face her greatest fear. She squeezed her eyes closed, just like the doctor told her to do whenever she was having one of her delusions.

"This is not real. It's all in your head." She breathed in and out like she was in labor. "When you open your eyes, he will be gone."

Simon reached out and touched his mother on the shoulder.

"I assure you, I am real."

Andrea shuddered and scrambled to her feet, then darted to the doorway. Simon was too quick, and stepped right in front of her. Their gazes locked. The fear dripped off her like beads at Mardi Gras. Simon could hear her heart pounding. Then he moved closer, and Andrea gasped as she lost control of her bodily fluids, leaving a puddle by her feet.

"They make adult underwear for that problem." He laughed.

"I killed you," she murmured.

Her mind was swimming as memories of the asylum took over, triggering her body to twitch. Then her eyes rolled into the back of her head.

"Mama, I have waited a long time for this," Simon snarled. "I will not let you zone out on me now." He scurried over, grabbed and shook her.

"Get your fucking filthy wolf hands off me!" she screeched, and shrugged him off.

The expression she gave him was the same calculating, insane look that had haunted him for over two decades. Five seconds ago, she peed her pants at the sight of him. Now she was ready to slit his throat.

"I was left to rot behind the walls of that sanitarium for murdering my son," Andrea seethed. "Your father locked me up and threw away the key. I watched as he remarried, had another child, and I lost my Joshy. What was it for? Nothing!" she squealed, slamming her fists into her sides, and kept her piercing gaze on Simon.

Tears welled up in his eyes. He fought back the nausea creeping up into his throat. He had hoped that after all these years, she would've been happy to see him, or shown some remorse. They were so close at one time. How could she just turn her emotions off like a switch and forget that she was the one person who should love him unconditionally?

Andrea continued to glare at him like a serpent ready to strike.

"I never realized how much you look like that bitch Rosa."

Something snapped inside Simon, and before he knew it, he had his mother by the throat.

"Don't you ever talk about my Nana like that again. Rosa Lord was ten times the woman you'll ever be, and she had more class in her pinky than you have in your whole body. I loved that woman with all my heart, and if you ever disrespect her again, I'll snap your neck."

Andrea stared at him with such hatred he released her.

"She was a bully who controlled everyone and everything. When I killed her, I did the world a favor."

"What?"

Simon felt like he was in a bad dream. Everything was moving in slow motion, and Andrea's voice sounded like a slowed-down cassette tape.

"That's right. Your precious cow of a grandmother pushed me a little too hard. And I, in turn, pushed her down the steps."

Andrea giggled as she picked up the glass Brandon drank from and smashed it on the TV cart. With a bloody hand, she lunged for Simon, with a giant shard poised to slice his jugular.

"Aargh!"

Simon cold-cocked her with a right hook. She went down fast and didn't move a muscle. He stared down at her and felt nothing but pity.

Simon stepped over her and moved to the door.

"Wait," she called, as he was about to step into the corridor.

"I'm done waiting for you. Save whatever you have to say for your lawyer!"

"Please." She tried to crawl over to him.

Her cheek was swollen and beginning to bruise where he had struck her.

Simon hesitated at the door and watched as she struggled to inch over to him. She was still beautiful for her age, and for a fleeting moment he saw the woman he once adored, and despite all she'd done, still did.

Against his better judgment, he reached down to help her up.

"Simon, the police are on the way," Georgia said.

Andrea, who still had the large piece of glass in her hand, shoved Simon and slashed Georgia across the arm. Georgia kicked at her, but Andrea was relentless and pinned her against the wall.

"I will never go back to that place," Andrea said, through clenched teeth.

Georgia closed her eyes as Andrea prepared to stab her again.

Simon charged his mother, and her eyes widened as he smashed his head into her gut. She fell back, hitting her head on the wall, and slipped down to the floor. The piece of glass flew across the room.

Georgia got to her feet and covered the gash inflicted by Andrea.

"You okay?" Simon rushed over to his wife. "Let me see." He looked over the wound. "You might need stitches."

He felt a sharp pain as his mother repeatedly drove a fork into his back. The burning sensation traveled up his spine, and he flailed his arms to get the fork, but couldn't reach it.

Simon's vision began to blur as he toppled over. The last thing he saw was a demented Andrea springing at him with the shard of glass again. Seconds later, he lost consciousness.

"Leave him alone!" Georgia tried to wrestle the glass out of Andrea's hand.

Andrea kicked her in the shin. Georgia kicked her back, harder.

With one shove, Georgia stumbled back and watched as her mother-in-law was about to cut into Simon like a turkey.

"Are you deaf? I said leave him the fuck alone."

Like a Brahma bull, Georgia rushed at Andrea and only stopped when she heard her screaming as the older woman plunged out the bedroom window.

The whole way home, Joshua kept trying Donna's cell, Andrea's and Toni's. No one was answering.

Now, he knew something was wrong as he turned onto the drive. The red and blue lights from the ambulance and paddy wagons lit up the white stucco of Windwood. There were cops and paramedics all over the porch. He was so worked up he almost jumped out of the car before putting it in park.

Broken glass sprayed across the front lawn as Andrea Lord crash-landed on the hood of Joshua's car.

"Hi, Mommy," said a little girl in a white dress with pink flowers.

"Melanie?" Andrea felt a happiness unlike any other.

She saw her own mangled body, and the paramedics placing a sheet over it.

"It's time to go," Melanie said.

Andrea gladly took the child's hand and drifted toward the fog. For the first time in years, she felt peace.

35

PICKING UP THE PIECES

KARA AND SUTTON BURIED DONNA AS FAR down as they could, in the middle of nowhere, far from Windwood. Donna pleaded while they dug. And even after the two covered her coffin with dirt, she implored them one last time to let her out. Both ignored her and continued to bury the casket.

Kara patted the dirt with the shovel one last time, then jumped into the waiting pickup with Sutton, and they sped off.

As Donna lay in the darkness of her tomb, it dawned on her that the one person who could save her was Julian. She called to him, in hopes that he'd save her again.

"Hear my voice, Julian, through the void of time, which separates us, and by the bonds of our devotion, which carries on, return to me, my love. Return to me."

Now, all she could do was wait. Toni's words still worried her, but she had no choice. If Julian didn't come, she would die. Or if the others found out, she could die. A catch-22 either way, and somebody was gonna get hurt.

Andrea literally broke when she slammed into the hood. She hit it with such force the engine fell out of the bottom and all the windows blew out. The sight of his mother lying across the front of the car, with blood leaking out of every orifice, including her eyes, was too much for Joshua and he vomited all over the driveway.

He bawled like he had the night of Simon and Georgia's wedding, when Andrea shot Simon and Calvin. His world was thrown into a tailspin that night. Had it not been for the love of Donna and the kids, he would be a much different man today.

Once again, he felt alone. And when they brought the gurney though the front door and down the steps, with the white sheet covering the corpse, he let out a wail so tragic Donna heard it in the ground.

"Who is it?" He reached to pull the sheet off.

The coroner and a deputy tried to stop him, but Joshua persisted until he succeeded in yanking it off. To his surprise, it was Loretta Thornton. He couldn't help but smile and giggle as his defense mechanism kicked in, thankful it wasn't his family.

"Are you all right?" the young deputy said.

Joshua just shooed him away with his hands.

"No, no. My baby boy!" a familiar voice shrieked, as another victim was brought out of the house.

Recognizing Toni's voice, Joshua leapt out from behind the car to see his son being wheeled out next. Brandon was being fed oxygen as they hurried him into the ambulance.

"Brandon, what did they do to you?" He stroked his son's head and clung to his clammy hand as the tears stung his eyes, and for a moment he couldn't find his voice.

"Mister Lord, we have to get him to the hospital," said the middle-aged paramedic. "Your son has lost a tremendous amount of oxygen to his brain. We must find out exactly what's wrong, and time is crucial."

He and a younger woman loaded the boy into the back.

"May I ride with him?" Joshua asked the girl.

"Of course." She motioned for him to climb in.

"Brother." Simon placed his hand on Joshua's shoulder.

Joshua turned to see his older brother alive and in the flesh. The younger squeezed his eyes closed, since insanity ran in the family, and right now he felt he was on the cusp of losing it, too.

"Mister Lord, we have to go," the man said, about to close the back.

"Josh, go," Georgia put a hand on his face. "We'll be here when you get back."

Joshua's eyes rolled into the back of his head as he fell back. Simon tried to catch him, but wasn't fast enough. Joshua hit his head on the bumper, and was knocked unconscious.

"Take care of your brother." Toni came out of nowhere. "I'll go with Brandon," she said, her voice hoarse, as she climbed into the back.

"I'll go, too," Gideon said. "When he comes to, you guys are going to have a lot to explain. It'll be better if I'm not here. He's already had enough excitement for one day." He kissed Georgia on the cheek and hopped into the ambulance.

Joshua awoke in his four-poster king bed, with his sister-in-law at the foot, and his brother beside him, holding his hand. Joshua rubbed his eyes, shook his head, and even pinched himself when he saw Simon.

"Is that really you?" He used his elbows to sit up, all the while keeping his gaze locked on his brother.

"I'll give you guys a few moments." Georgia stepped into the hallway.

"Yes, yes, it is." Simon moved closer to the head of the bed.

He knelt close to Joshua's face to give him a better look.

"God, you sure are ugly."

They both laughed. It hurt Joshua's head, but he didn't care.

"I ought to knock your block off for that," Simon said.

"I don't understand. Where have you been all this time?" Joshua said.

"Get some rest. You had quite a shock." Simon guided his head down on the pillow. "I promise I'll be back to see you."

"Simon," Joshua called, as his brother opened the bedroom door.

Simon closed the door and moved back to his brother's bedside.

"What is it now? You're like a little kid stalling on Christmas Eve."

"I missed you, man." Joshua still had enough strength to pull Simon into a bear hug, bringing tears to both their eyes.

"Stop being mushy and get some sleep," he said, when Joshua let him go. "I'm home for good," he whispered, before closing the door.

Simon looked up and thanked God that the bond he had with Joshua wasn't broken.

Toni was still sitting Indian style on the beige sofa, with her eyes closed, in the waiting room of Wake General. Gideon stood in front of her with a white Styrofoam cup in one hand, and a few-year-old magazine in the other. He watched, amazed by how she could sit so still and quiet. Five minutes like that would buckle his legs when he got up, and she'd been like that almost an hour.

"Take a picture," she said. "It'll last longer."

"Ah, there she is. I knew I'd find the real Toni in there." He plopped down beside her. "I was beginning to think you'd gone soft."

"Don't you have anything to do besides bug me? How long's it been since we saw the doctor?" She stood, and started to wear a hole in the floor.

"About twenty minutes since the last time you asked." He sipped from his cup.

"I should've known better than to let that woman any-where near them." Toni ran her hands through her dark tresses. "What kind of woman smothers her own grand-child? What if he doesn't make it?"

Her tough exterior began to crumble as she feared the worst.

"Let the doctors do their job." Gideon took her into his arms.

Toni relaxed in his embrace and let it all out.

Once she was finished, they remained silent.

"Thanks for what you did for me tonight." She gave him a nudge. "If you hadn't come along, who knows how much worse it could've been."

"If I didn't know better, I'd think you were beginning to like me." He said closed an eye closed and cocked his head to the side.

"Nah, I still hate you. But I'm glad you're home."

"I'm happy to be back, even if I have to look at a crone like you." He winked. "As much as I hated this place, it is home, and I could never stay away long. Besides, you'd be lost without me."

"I'm already regretting saying anything."

"Missus Corsini?" The doctor came out of the large double doors.

Toni squeezed Gideon's hand so tight he winced.

36

AWAKENINGS

JOSHUA LAY ON HIS BACK IN A DEEP SLEEP—
thanks to the drugs and the knot on the back of his head—
as fog seeped in from under the bedroom door, and a
specter hovered above him, within an inch of his face.
He let out a deep breath as he rolled over onto his side,
allowing the being to enter his body through his mouth.

He opened his eyes and sat up slowly as his vision
adjusted to the darkness that surrounded him. He stuck
out his arms to make sure they were there, then dropped
his legs over the side of the bed, slowly getting to his feet.

He opened the bedroom door and staggered from being
momentarily blinded by the overhead lights. Using a small
oak table for balance, he caught a glimpse of himself in
the mirror hanging above the table.

"Julian's on the way." He turned and headed down
the stairs.

Halfway down, he heard voices.

"Are you sure you weren't followed?" Luna said, through Jenna.

Her little head bobbed as she stood with her hands on her hips.

"Positive," Sutton replied. "I buried her in a part of town that's been abandoned since the Second World War."

His hair was mussed, and his flannel shirt was soiled and muddy from the dirt.

"Why don't you go clean up before everyone gets back? I'm gonna go check on Joshua." She started to go upstairs, and turned back. "Where's Kara?"

"I don't know. She was right behind me."

"Go find her before she ruins everything," the girl barked at Sutton, who raced off like a dog with his tail between his legs.

Julian waited by the stairs, and as Jenna rounded the corner to ascend the steps, he jumped out, startling her. She tripped up the stairs, falling on her face, which knocked her out. Julian grabbed the duct tape that he took from the junk drawer in the kitchen earlier, and bound her legs and hands. Jenna's eyes opened as he finished taping her mouth.

"Hello, Luna. We're going for a walk."

He threw Jenna over his shoulders and carried her wiggling body down the front steps and out the door.

Julian had been digging for hours. His arms ached and his fingers cramped, but he had to keep going. She needed him.

"See, Luna. Not even you could stop us this time."

He climbed out of the hole to fetch the wire cutters in the satchel next to her bound body, grabbed the wire cutters, then jumped back down into the hole, where he began to carve through the chains that held her prisoner.

Finally, he got the links off and pulled back the lid to find a wild Donna. The vampire's eyes were glazed over. Her fangs were out, and her fingernails were broken and bloody from trying to escape.

"Martha." Julian reached in to touch her face.

She shot up and bore down on his neck and fed until she nearly sucked him dry.

Jenna cackled, snapping Donna out of her bloodlust. Realizing she'd almost killed Joshua, she shrieked as tears of blood trickled down her cheeks.

Wiping the red from her lips with the back of her hand, she whirled around, her eyes black as she glowered the possessed child.

"This ends tonight. I will not let you take him from me again, Luna. I will finish you off once and for all, even if it kills me in the process."

She gazed down at Joshua, who was so pale he made a vampire look tan.

Luna glared up at her, unable to speak because of the tape over her mouth.

"I'm so cold," Joshua said, in a weak voice.

He soon blacked out, and Donna knew if she didn't do something now, she would lose him. His chestnut hair appeared red in contrast to his colorless skin. His breathing was labored. She could feel his life force slipping away.

"You'll pay for this!" She turned back to Luna. "I promise." She plopped down on the grass and slid over to Joshua to pull him into her lap. "Hold on, babe." She bit down on her wrist till the blood flowed, then placed the opened wound over his mouth and let the blood work its magic. "Please work."

Then the ghost of Julian appeared to her, wearing a large grin. With tears in her eyes, she looked at the spirit as he began to fade.

"I will always be by your side and forever in your heart." His voice echoed in her head.

"Goodbye, my love. Thank you."

Donna heard footsteps, and turned in time to see Sutton running off with Jenna. She hoisted Joshua over her left shoulder and set out for Windwood, intent on stopping the witch, once and for all.

Simon sat in Calvin's office chair just staring at a photo of Rosa sitting on the desk, while nursing a tumbler of his grandfather Teddy's favorite bourbon. He hadn't been home a whole twenty-four hours, and already Windwood had claimed his mother, and it looked like his nephew, too. He wasn't sure if it was the booze, or if he was just tired, but he thought he saw a woman run by the window, with Joshua over her shoulder.

"Help!" Donna screamed, as she rushed through the front door.

"What happened to my brother?" Simon choked.

"S-simon?"

"I can't leave you guys alone for five minutes," a worn Toni said, from the front door as she returned from the hospital with Gideon.

"Let's get him upstairs." Simon took him from Donna. "Gideon, could you help me?"

Gideon picked up his legs and started up the stairs.

Donna ran right into Toni's arms and sobbed.

"Jenna's been possessed by Luna, and she put Sutton under her spell. Sutton, with the help of a woman I turned, buried me. I summoned Julian, who possessed Joshua long enough to save me and reveal that Jenna is the culprit. In my madness, I attacked Josh." She continued to sob, staining Toni's sky-blue shirt with the blood of her tears.

"I need you to listen to me." Toni wept as she took Donna's hands and sat on the sofa. "While you were gone, something happened to Brandon." She broke down and couldn't finish.

"An accident? What happened to my boy? I knew it. When I was in the coffin, I heard Joshua's cries." Donna crumpled to the floor and wailed so loud the transom above the door cracked, as did a vase on the parlor table, and the overhead light bulbs in the chandelier broke.

"I need you to be strong and return to your coffin," Toni said. "There is nothing you can do for Josh, Brandon, or Jenna until tomorrow night."

The sky began to explode in orange and blue.

"Please watch over and protect them," Donna said. "And whatever you do, do not let Sutton back in this house."

She trudged to the basement door, down the steps, and to the room that housed her coffin.

Kara knew she had a few more minutes at most to find shelter, or the rays of the sun would finish her off. But she pressed on, knowing what was in there was worth a thousand burns. She knew the hidden cavern was close, and she could get rest there.

Out of nowhere appeared a large circular cement wall with a steel grate that emerged a few yards away, with a ladder going up the side.

"That has to be it!" She made a dash for it, just as the sun began to rise.

Her skin began to burn and smoke as the sun set her insides on fire. It was becoming harder for her to walk as the flames engulfed her body.

She collapsed in front of the ladder. A figure covered her with a blanket and herded her into an awaiting van. When she pulled the blanket back, she was greeted by

Channing, Lila, and a scrawnier man who looked like a mouse. Surrounded by two werewolves and a shape-shifter, Kara bared her fangs.

"Ooh, we got a wild one here," the mousy guy said.

"I don't believe it," Lila said. "I thought the last vampire died at the turn of the century."

Kara continued to hiss, and pinned the scrawny guy against the van wall, where she ripped open his collar and almost bit him. Channing injected her with silver, and she collapsed.

"That was close." The guy rubbed his throat.

Channing snapped his neck.

"Whatcha do that for?" Lila moaned, staring at the body.

"He was weak and could've gotten us all killed. I don't have patience for fuck-ups."

"That was just wrong."

"You could always join him." Channing opened the door and tossed the body out. "Everyone is expendable, including you." His bald head was glistening from sweat, which rolled down his neck to his back, creating a smiley face on his shirt.

"What about her?" She pointed to Kara, who was still unconscious and face down on the van floor.

"We are going to drain her. Do you know how much vampire blood goes for? Ten million for just an ounce. It's also the only cure for the virus. And if one of us is bitten, it could save our lives."

With that, he began to cut Kara open with a butterfly knife he kept in his back pocket. Lila turned away in disgust, kicked open the van doors, and exited the vehicle, stepping over the carcass of her comrade. She felt bad that she didn't know his name, or where he came from, or why it affected her so much that she was crying.

"Where are you going?" Channing barked.

"I need to get some air." She wiped away the tears with the back of her hand.

"Here. Take this." He handed her a wooden stake tipped with silver. "There could be more."

She hesitated, then took it and walked away.

Lila didn't know where she was going, and didn't care. All she knew was that she had to get away from him for a while.

37

LETTING GO

LATER THAT DAY, A BROKEN SIMON returned from the morgue, where he had to identify Andrea's body. He went to her room and sat at her desk. On top was a photo album opened to a picture of him and Andrea, taken at his wedding while they were dancing.

Simon hated her, yet his heart was being torn to pieces at seeing the two of them so happy. The tears hit the plastic-covered pages as he flipped through the images of his life. The past he wanted to forget was being revealed through these pictures.

"There you are," Georgia said, from the door frame. "I was looking all over for you. Thought maybe we could go catch a movie."

With tears dripping down his face, Simon looked up at his wife, no longer able to contain his emotions. She moved to the desk and stroked his head as he sobbed, his hands hooked around her waist.

"I'm good now." He let go of her.

"Is this you?" She handed him a few tissues that were by the desk lamp, then picked up the book and pointed to the top picture.

"Let me see." He turned in the swivel chair and knocked the book out of her hands and on to the floor.

The clasp broke, and the pictures went everywhere.

Georgia began to pick up the prints, and in the mess, found the unopened letter Calvin had left Andrea.

"Can I see that?" Simon tore into it.

My dearest Andrea,

It's been a long time, and if you're reading this, I've passed. It's been over thirty years since we spoke, and I wanted you to know that I've forgiven you, and in all our years apart, you remained the great love of my life, which is why I must tell you that Simon is still alive.

Sutton and I, with the help of Georgia, kept him from you for your protection, and his. I'm telling you this now so you may let go of the past. He was always your favorite, and it showed in the way you doted on him.

Andrea, I never got to see my boys again. Don't make the same mistake I did. Forgive yourself, and Simon, and be a family.

Love always,
Cal

The tears began to flow again, only this time they were happy tears. Simon folded the letter and smiled.

"What'd it say?" Georgia was looking over his shoulder.

Simon sighed, "That I wasn't forgotten. I really had a family. They were here the whole time." Simon sniffed loudly, clearing his nose. "You still wanna catch that movie?"

Joshua continued to sleep upstairs. It had been over twenty-four hours, but Toni thought it best he remain out of it until she figured out what to do about Donna, Sutton, and Jenna. As of today, there was no change in Brandon's condition, either. Fortunately, while she was in the boy's hospital room, she was able to slip some silver in his IV, or she'd have another werewolf added to the mix.

"How long have you known Martha?" Gideon entered the parlor.

Toni looked puzzled as he poured himself a drink and sat beside her on the sofa.

"We know each other quite well." He took a sip of bourbon.

Toni groaned. "I don't understand."

"I am over three hundred years old. I was here at Windwood in 1912, when Martha was released the first time. I knew what she was, and vice versa. I needed an ally, so I would protect her during the day, and she would look after me when I changed. If it wasn't for her, I'd be trapped with the others in that underground prison."

"And you are just telling me this now?" Toni said.

"Hey, it's not like you mentioned to me that you were protecting a vampire, either."

"The fewer people who knew about her, the better. Let's just call it even, and I'll forget about you not telling me that Channing got out." She smirked as he glared at her.

"Here we go again. Thirty years pass, and you still can't let that go? I'm not apologizing again."

A sound out in the foyer stopped them.

"What was that?" Toni whispered.

Gideon placed a finger over his mouth to keep her quiet. He thrust open the door to see that Joshua had fallen down the stairs.

"I must find Martha." Joshua tried to pull himself up by the banister, but he was still too weak, and collapsed again.

"He's starting to remember." Toni frowned.

"Remember what?" Gideon said.

"Just help me get him back upstairs, and I'll explain later."

Sutton and Jenna were holed-up in the lower level of the Lord mausoleum. No way Sutton could return to his job, now that they knew what he and Jenna had been up to.

After sleeping in the park, the mausoleum was the Ritz.

"We need to figure out what to do next." Sutton sat on one of the marble slabs. "This is no place for a little girl."

"You know better than that." Jenna closed her eyes and rested her head against a statue of some Lord ancestor.

"I just meant—"

"The only way this stops is if Martha and the rest of that family are wiped from this planet. You want to end this sooner, I suggest you get busy and figure out a way to eliminate them."

"This has gone way too far. I never wanted any of this. I'm done, and I'm gonna turn myself in, in hopes that they'll go easy on me." He jumped up and stormed over toward the exit.

"No, you're not. You are going to do exactly what I tell you, or I'll make sure your fate is worse than anything you can imagine."

"I don't care." He continued to the stairs.

Jenna fixed her gaze on him. Sutton heard buzzing in his head as it began to throb, and he fell to his knees as blood trickled from his nose. He cried out in pain as blood spilled out of his ears.

"All right! Enough. I'll help."

In a matter of seconds, the pain she had inflicted was over.

"I knew you'd see it my way. Now let's get some rest."

38

FRIENDS AND LOVERS

WHEN SIMON AND GEORGIA RETURNED TO Windwood, a letter was delivered from Andrea's attorney, with handwritten instructions stating that Andrea wanted to be cremated, and for half her ashes to be placed in the Lord mausoleum, and the other half to be scattered in the Aegean Sea, off the Greek coast, where Calvin and she had honeymooned.

"What are we going to do?" Georgia said.

"I want to see what Joshua thinks," Simon replied, "as well as Toni. I'd rather flush her down the toilet, but she was also Joshua's mother. I hated her, but he didn't. With everything else being taken from him, I don't want to take this from him, too."

Georgia kissed his cheek. "You're such a good man. After everything she did, I don't know if I could be so calm. I would rip up that letter, dump her in the trash, and call it a day." She headed into the parlor.

"I don't want to do anything for her. And if I could, I'd skip the funeral. But it's not about me or my feelings, remember?" He followed her into the room.

Toni and Gideon got Joshua back in bed and resting comfortably. The sun was setting, and soon Donna would be up and about.

Gideon sat in a chair next to the bed.

"Are you going to tell me what's going on?" He sat back, with his arms folded.

"The night of the wedding, I came back to the inn to host an after-party. I found Martha, who I renamed Donna, in the basement, where I went to get champagne. I had her wait there until the party was over. Joshua had been drunk, and was in no position to drive home. I had him stay with me, in hopes of sobering him up. Martha and Joshua took one look at each other and ... well, you can figure out the rest."

"What does any of this have to do with Joshua?"

"He is the reincarnation of Julian Lord, the man Martha ran off with in 1853, and ended up alongside at the bottom of the Aurora. If he were to remember, and panics or starts running his mouth, it puts them both in danger. If any of the other leaders or the Monarchs discovered that one of the last vampires was here in Solomon's Wake, and no one told them, we would have another Crimson Rising on our hands, and none of us could survive another war."

"The Weres would hunt her," Gideon said, "harvest her blood to cure those of their ilk that still have the virus, and the Monarchs would use her blood to create more vampires, forcing the witches, changers, and others to pick sides." He exhaled and looked down at Joshua, who let out a gurgling sound as he rolled over.

"With that in mind, I used an old Zorn remedy of bloodroot and other herbs to create a pill that made Martha human, avoiding another conflict altogether." Toni sat on the edge of the bed after she covered Joshua with a blanket from the closet.

"You do realize The Order, or the Monarchs, could hang or behead you for this. It's an act of treason."

"I know. But I love them both. And to protect my family, I would walk through fire and face the worst the Monarchs, or The Order, could throw at me."

"Did you hear that?" Gideon placed a hand up to his ear.

"Really? I'm in the middle of spilling my guts out, and you let your imagination run wild. If you didn't want to hear it, you could've just said so."

"There it is again."

Loud knocking, followed by what sounded like someone kicking the front door in, downstairs. It continued for a few minutes, and when the banging stopped, a woman shrieked.

Gideon darted over to the window, pulled the lace curtains back, and saw Nola standing in the middle of the lawn, yelling, arms flailing, and face red as the sun.

"Nola." His heart burst as he dashed out of the room.

He hurried down the staircase, hitting only a few of the steps on the way down. Thrusted open the door, sprinted down the cement porch steps, and stood a foot away from her.

"It's about time," she said. "I thought I was gonna lose my voice, or break my hand."

She was about to say something else, when he planted one right on her.

After years of beating around the bush and denying their real feelings, they threw caution to the wind and lived in the moment. Nola circled her arms around Gideon's neck and relaxed into his embrace as the two kissed under the stars and moonlight, with a graceful Windwood watching in the background.

While Nola and Gideon were getting reacquainted, the tracker Channing had placed inside her began to go off on the monitor inside the van where Lila and Channing were sleeping. A vampire had also swooped into the van and stolen the vile of Kara's blood.

They slept like logs, and were asleep a good twenty minutes before Lila heard it. Groggily, she rolled over on her side and saw the red-light blinking and heard the continuous beeping from the beacon. She looked over at Channing, who was sitting up in front of the monitor, knocked out.

"Channing." She hit him on the shoulder.

When he didn't budge, she struck him again, this time waking him up.

"What?" His eyes were still half-shut as he cracked his neck and stretched his arms.

"The beacon is going off." She tapped on the screen with her red nail.

"I'll be. I knew she would come here. And my guess is, she went right to Daddy. Okay, Lila, fasten your seatbelt. Things are about to get bumpy."

Back at Windwood, Nola was basking in the warmth of the shower, giddy with happiness. The water was warm and refreshing as it hit the nape of her neck. She closed her eyes, tilted her head back and lathered up her hair, letting the water cascade down her face. Steam filled the bathroom and fogged up the mirrors.

A cold hand pulled her into a kiss. Nola jumped, and the suds from her hair got into her eyes, causing them to burn. When the soap washed away, Gideon was before her, naked and staring at her with sheer lust.

"I thought you might need some help." Gideon moved in for another kiss.

"Gideon Blake, you scared the hell out of me!"

He massaged her shoulders and breathed down her neck. Nola cooed and giggled as he began to kiss her all over.

"I'll get out if you want."

He turned to leave, but Nola pulled him back in.

"Don't you dare. I have waited way too long for this." She kissed him again.

Gideon pressed her against the wall and ran his hands over her breasts. She moaned as he fulfilled her wish.

39

ASHES TO ASHES

TONI WAS IN HER ROOM, SITTING ON HER bed, looking over old journals, pictures, property lines, and some maps, trying to figure out exactly where the mine entrance would be. In the '80s, it had been filled in to build a mall. And about ten years ago, Calvin sold the land to South Carolina, who designated it federal land. In doing so, the exact location of the entrance was now lost.

Toni heard the hallway floorboards, creaking and knew someone was coming. She gathered all the paperwork and pulled back her comforter to conceal the stuff. Grabbed the remote and put on a cooking show, then sat in the mauve recliner in front of the TV, just as there was a knock on the door.

"Toni, you got a minute?" Simon cleared his throat.

"Since it's you, I'll give you five. Come on in."

Simon looked like he was carrying the world on his shoulders as he sat at the foot of the bed. His hair was all over the place, and he looked like hadn't slept in days. Gone were the smiles and the confidence he'd exuded a few days ago.

"I got a letter from Mama's attorney. It says she wanted some of her ashes placed in the mausoleum, and the rest scattered off the coast where she and Dad honeymooned." He sighed staring at his feet. "I don't know what I should do. I know she was Josh's mother, too, but I want to feed what's left of her to the catfish in the bayou." He sobbed. "After everything she's done, I'm still over here crying over her."

"You listen to me, Simon Lord. You are a good, decent man. Your mother was a fool, and just plain batty for not seeing what everybody else does." Toni sat next to him, with her arm around his shoulder. "I don't care if you're a werewolf, or were-bear, or whatever other Were ... I missed you. You are a kind-hearted soul. I can see it in how you look at your wife, and most recently, in the way you've taken care of your brother. That, my dear boy, is something that's in you and cannot be faked." She kissed him on the cheek. "And I love you, and that's a miracle in its own right because I don't like anybody."

They both broke out in a fit of laughter.

"Thank you." He took her hand and kissed it.

"Now, what is it you wanted to talk to me about?" She reached back for the tissues on the nightstand.

"Should I tell Joshua?"

"What would your mother have done if the shoe was on the other foot?"

"She probably would've fed my ashes to everyone in nightcaps, or spread my remains in the horse stable."

"Then there's your answer."

Joshua screamed and woke himself up. He'd had another dream about the *Mary Agnes* sinking, with him on it. After sitting up, he found the sheets drenched, and then noticed a fresh rope burn on his hand.

"I'm losing my mind." He stared at the burn, which suddenly disappeared.

Joshua hopped out of bed, scuttled over to the bathroom, flicked on the light, and upon further examination, found nothing wrong with his hand.

"You should not be out of bed," Simon said. "I leave you alone for five minutes, and you—"

"Are you real?" Joshua reached out and touched the stubble on Simon's face.

He then crumpled to the floor and sobbed as he beat his hands on the marble floor.

"I'm becoming Mama, Simon. I'm seeing shit that's not there, hearing voices calling me by a different name. I even dreamed I tried to kill my own daughter."

With his hands on his face, he continued to bawl as he drew his knees up to his chest.

"I promise, you are not becoming her." Simon slid down next to him and put his left arm around him.

He hid his face from Joshua so his brother wouldn't see the tears in his eyes. Truth is, he was worried about his brother. Lunacy ran in the family, and struck any gender or age without warning. To this day, Helena was rotting away behind the walls of an asylum because she saw a werewolf, and Andrea suffered a similar fate after learning the truth.

Simon blamed himself for both, and as he stared down at his defeated baby brother, vowed he would lose no one else. He stayed with Joshua until the younger Lord fell asleep, then lifted him and carried him to the bed.

"I will not let you down. And I will do whatever it takes to protect you. I wasn't here to help you when Dad died, or when they carted Mama away. Until now, you had the burden of this house and our secrets. But I'm here now, and I will be the big brother I was intended to be." Simon patted him on the shoulder and left.

A few moments later, Donna came through the bedroom window. Joshua looked so serene in his slumber, but she could feel his torment bubbling below the surface, and it was only a matter of time before the dam broke.

"I am so sorry you are going through this." She fought back tears. "You are not crazy, nor are you becoming your mother. You are just remembering something from another life that you're not supposed to. I will make it all go away. And in doing so, you will not remember me biting you, or what happened to Jenna. After you wake up, you will tell everyone that you got a call from me, and after talking it over, we decided to move Brandon to a special clinic in New York. Jenna and I went with him because we needed to get away from all the ugliness of the last few weeks, and you will follow us after you settle your mother's estate."

She touched his leg, and with her hip, hit the side of his bed until he opened his eyes. He stared blankly at her. Then his eyes widened with elation when he realized his wife was there.

"Donna?" He tried to get out of bed.

"Look deep into my eyes. I want you to stare until you feel like you can float into the sky. Everything that has happened will be a distant memory, and you will be good as new."

She pushed him back down on the bed, kissed him on the lips, and leapt out the window.

Donna was able to see Brandon after visiting hours were over, in part due to her donating a million dollars to the new wing of the hospital. She held his hand for hours and read him stories as she moved his arms and legs.

"Has there been any change?" Toni came in from the hallway.

Donna shook her head. "Still the same as yesterday and the day before. What brings you here at this hour?" She wiped her son's face with a wet wash rag.

"We need to get Joshua and the others out of here. We cannot have them here while we go into the mine. It's too dangerous." Toni kissed Brandon on the forehead.

"I've taken care of it. I could not watch the love of my life descend into madness like so many before him. Especially when I'm the one who caused it." Donna wrung the rag out in the basin next to her.

"I don't think you'll be able to hypnotize everyone." Toni sat in a chair to the left of Brandon.

"Didn't you tell me that Andrea left specific instructions that she wanted to be buried off the coast of Greece?" Donna placed the rag in the basin, and put the basin on the table next to the bed.

"That woman doesn't deserve a funeral, or any type of service. Just a one-way ticket to hell." Toni grimaced.

"Don't you get it? Joshua and the others can carry her ashes to Greece while you, Gideon, and I go into the mines."

"That just might work. I know Simon doesn't want any part of dealing with Andrea's last wishes, but maybe Joshua can work on him and get him to see things differently."

"He's got to. Time is running out, and if we don't get into the mines soon, I will be a vampire again, and Jenna will be lost forever."

40

BROTHERS

FIRST THING IN THE MORNING, THE DOCTOR arrived to examine Joshua. He and Simon were alarmed when they got to his room and he wasn't there. They took off down the hall and came down the front steps just as he was coming in from an apparent jog.

"What's the doc doing here?" Joshua closed the front door and ambled toward the dining room.

"I was worried about you after last night," Simon said. "I wanted to make sure you were okay."

He and the doctor followed Joshua.

"Last night?" He sat, grabbed a glass of orange juice, and threw his sweaty towel on the floor beside him.

"You told me you weren't feeling yourself." Simon was becoming more concerned as Joshua continued to act as if nothing had happened.

"I'm fine, really. I talked to Donna this morning. She had Brandon moved to a special clinic in New York. One that specializes in brain trauma. She and Jenna will be staying for a few days to recharge. I'll join them in a few days, after we deal with Mama's wishes."

"He looks perfectly fine," the doctor said. "If you need me, you know where to find me." He nodded and left, leaving Simon with more questions than answers.

"Have you tried this?" Joshua heaved a large spoonful of breakfast parfait into his mouth. "It's delicious," he said, through a full mouth.

"Josh ... about last night—"

"Look, I appreciate the brotherly concern, but I'm good. I'm sorry if I scared you." He scooped every last bit of parfait out of the container. "If I so much as cough, I give you permission to get the doctor back here. Deal?"

"You win. I won't push the issue."

"Just like that, you're gonna let me win?" Joshua pushed his chair out and stood.

"Yup. Been doing it since you were five."

Simon pushed his chair out, and the two stared at each other across the table, like lions watching an antelope.

"I bet I could beat you now," Joshua said.

"I really don't want to do this now."

Josh flung the parfait on his spoon, across the table, and hit Simon on the nose.

"How 'bout now?"

Simon wiped the mess off with his hand.

"You are so dead!" He chased his younger brother out of the dining room and toward the front door, almost knocking Nola and Georgia over on the way out.

"I love that Simon is so happy," Georgia said, as the two women entered the dining room. "The one thing that he clung to was his relationship with his brother. Seeing them running and laughing makes my heart sing. This house poisons everything, sooner or later. But those two have a bond most people dream of."

"I feel that way about your father," Nola said, as one of the new maids poured her a cup of coffee.

"I know. I've seen how different he's been since you came back. My father never gave up on you. He believed you were out there, and that one day you'd return. I see that you make him happy—something I never thought could happen after my mother."

Nola smiled. "I love him. I guess I always did."

"You have my blessing." Georgia smiled.

"That means a lot." Nola beamed as she grabbed a plate from the buffet and sat down to breakfast.

With the barriers removed, she now felt like she and Georgia could be friends, and that she and Gideon were one step closer to being a couple, now that Georgia had given her approval.

Gideon bounded down the stairs while trying to fix the top button of his maroon polo shirt, when Toni caught him by the arm before he joined the others for breakfast. He looked puzzled as she led him from the dining room, down the long hall, and into the office.

"I was hungry." He sat down on the edge of the desk. "You could've at least let me get a sip of coffee, or a bite of a bagel."

"I need your help. Donna and I need to get into the mine for the bloodroot. But before we do, we must get everyone out of the house. Georgia and Nola will be safer if they aren't here. Donna was able to wipe Joshua's memory, for now. I also discovered this while going over the security cameras I had installed around the area." Toni handed him a photo of Channing near the entrance.

Gideon looked down at the photo and felt his blood run cold.

"He's here. What do you suggest we do?"

"Do you still have that yacht?" Toni said.

"Yeah, she's docked in Miami."

"We send them on a cruise. Andrea wanted her ashes scattered off the coast of Greece, and your boat can take them there."

Gideon nodded and smiled.

After Joshua and Simon came back from their jaunt to the stable, Simon was once again the victor, and taunted his little brother into another race, which ended with them in the pool.

"Face it, Josh. I will always win."

"I let you." He splashed his older brother.

Simon dunked him underwater.

"Remember when Dad would pretend he was drowning," Simon said, "and the moment we got near him, he'd reach up and pull us both in?" He chuckled, and for a moment, saw his dad laughing and tickling them.

Andrea was standing near the edge, in a black swimsuit, with her blonde hair loose and flowing, laughing so hard you could see the tears in her eyes.

"Hard to believe that at one point we were the picture-perfect family," Joshua said, bringing his brother back to reality.

"In the blink of an eye, it all came crashing down." Simon tilted his head back and set his sights on the window he'd fallen out of.

"Like it or not, she was our mother, and we need to figure out what we're going to do with her ashes."

"I don't care what happens to them." Simon scoffed, and slipped under the water.

"I would like to fulfill her wishes and go to Greece. Simon, I hate her for what she's done to all of us. Dad was never the same. He became a drunk, womanizing recluse who stood trial for murdering his second wife. Out of that union, a girl was born, named Peyton, who couldn't handle the loss of her mother. She took off, and we never heard from her again. Aunt Helena lost her mind and continues to wilt away behind the sanitarium walls. Poor Nana lost her hearing and suffered a massive stroke, and was found at the bottom of the steps. Gideon's daughter Ginny vanished into thin air upstairs. And I haven't set foot in Windwood in years. I blame her for all of it, Simon. However, I want to do it for the woman she was."

"If you insist on doing this, you have my support. But I still don't think she deserves it."

"She doesn't. But we're better than her."

Joshua pushed his brother under the water again, but Simon grabbed his leg and pulled him down, too. Both came up laughing, and splashed one another until they had no strength left.

"Can you tell me about Peyton?" Simon said, as the two stared up at the blue sky.

"I really can't. I haven't seen her in a long time. If she were to walk up to me on the street, I wouldn't know her. I've tried to find her. I even hired private investigators to track her down. It's like she never existed."

"If she wants to be found, she'll come out when she's ready." Simon climbed out. "I don't know about you, but I'm starving. Race ya." He darted toward the house before Joshua could even get out.

"Good times." The younger brother giggled as he got out of the pool, and hurried back before Simon could eat his lunch, too.

41

SAILING DAY

GEORGIA, GIDEON, AND TONI WERE already seated, and had nearly finished the entire course by the time the boys showed up. Simon kissed Georgia and sat beside her at the table. Joshua took his place at the head of the table, feeling down as the couples whispered amongst themselves. He couldn't help but miss Donna, and it showed.

"I heard from Donna while you and Simon were in the pool," Toni said. "She sends her love, and wanted you to know that Brandon is making progress, and even moved his foot. Jenna has been asking for her daddy, demanding you come see her." She sipped on a glass of sherry.

"Jenna will have to wait a little longer. Simon and I have decided to honor Mama's wishes and scatter her ashes in Greece."

Georgia shifted her gaze to Simon, who crammed so much pasta in his mouth he looked like a puffer fish.

"I would like to lend you my boat," Gideon said, "the *Lady Tara*, so long as you take Georgia and Nola with you."

If looks could kill, he would be lying on the floor from the daggers Nola was giving him.

"I'd love to go," Georgia said. "It would be the honeymoon we never got to have." She squeezed Simon's arm while he demolished his third helping of pasta.

"How soon can you have her ready?" Joshua said to Gideon.

"I'll call my people now, and you can be ready to go by tomorrow morning."

"I better get packing." Georgia sprang up and hurried up the stairs.

"If I don't stop her, she'll take everything but the kitchen sink." Simon took a gulp of red wine, and went after his wife.

"If you'll excuse me, I'm going to give my wife a call." Joshua slipped out.

"Do I not have a say in this?" Nola barked, as she threw her napkin down and shoved her chair out. "I just got back, and I really don't want to go." She stormed out of the room.

Gideon followed her.

Toni looked around the empty room, shrugged and poured herself a stronger drink from the flask she kept hidden under her seat.

"What did I do to anger you?" Nola said. "Please don't make me go." She moved into Gideon's arms, tears streaming down her face.

"You did nothing wrong." He held her tight to his chest as he kissed the top of her head.

Nola could hear his heart beating as she clung to him.

"Channing is in Solomon's Wake, and I can't allow him to hurt you or Georgia. It's for your own protection. When you get back, I want you to be my wife. That's, of course, if you want to be. I love you and can't imagine spending the rest of my life without you."

She was on top of him before he could say another word, and the two made love more than once that night.

In the morning, Gideon and Toni drove them to the airport and stayed until their plane left.

"We've got a lot of work to do." Toni got back into the car.

The family crowded into the trucks that awaited them when they got off the plane. When they reached Miami, the two Hummers rounded the bend, to where *Lady Tara* was visible.

"It's absolutely stunning." Georgia gasped as she gazed at her father's 340-foot, seven-thousand-ton masterpiece.

When they got out of the vehicles, one of the stewards began loading their luggage onto a gold cart. The family climbed the gangplank with much anticipation. In the main salon aboard the yacht, the crew was standing everywhere, talking and moving about.

A stately woman approached Georgia. "Hello, Missus Lord. My name's Madison Taylor, and I am the chief stewardess on *Lady Tara*. I have a list of the staterooms you will be staying in. You and Mister Lord have the master cabin, located aft of the ship. Your brother-in-law is in the twin cabin, directly below yours. And Miss O'Grady is across from him. If you have any questions, please ask me."

The ship left port with three loud whistles as people cheered and waved goodbye to their loved ones, from the dock. Joshua saw the specter of Annabelle in the crowd, mouthing, *Don't go.* Joshua became frantic, afraid that maybe something dreadful would happen on this voyage.

Simon and Georgia's room was flawless. It had a balcony, and beige and white decor. A queen-sized bed with a cream bedspread draped over it sat in the center of the room. Tan velvet curtains hung on the balcony doors. The bathroom was accented with remarkable gold fixtures, and the suite's furniture had the same appointments.

Joshua's room was just as elegant. He had twin beds and a beautiful sitting room. The furniture was black, and the cushions covered in light gray. The rest of the room echoed the same shades.

Nola's room mirrored Joshua's.

The next morning, when Georgia sat down to brunch on deck, a seagull flew right past her head, causing her to almost drop her coffee. A tired Joshua trudged up to the sun deck, exhausted from being up all night, thanks to the bad dreams, and noticed a seagull had been wounded after it slammed into a porthole. He picked up the gull and carried it back to the table.

"Aww, poor thing." Georgia looked up through her sunglasses.

She wore a large sun hat to protect her fair skin, plus tons of sunscreen.

"It clipped its wing," Joshua said. "When I walked by, I heard it squawking, and I didn't have the heart to leave it there. Where is everybody?" He plucked up a napkin and placed it on his lap before laying the bird on the empty chair next to him. "I'm starving."

A young man in his early twenties, of Filipino descent, poured him some coffee.

"Simon's probably grilling the captain," Georgia said. "You know how much he loves the sea, and how ships work, and the knots it moves, and blah-blah-blah. And Nola went for a jog." She grabbed the sunblock from the bag by Joshua's feet, and put some more on. "I'm gonna go lay out for a little bit. You wanna join me?"

"Maybe later. Right now, I need more of this." He raised his mug. "And food."

"I'll leave you to it." She smiled and headed farther out into the sun.

Joshua headed back to his cabin, still holding the wounded bird, which began to fidget as he got closer to the passageway. Then it leapt out of his hands and flew away.

"How do you like that?" Joshua shrugged as he continued on his way.

The bird flew a few miles out to sea and circled another vessel close by. It screeched as it landed on the deck. A few seconds later, a naked Lila was standing in the bird's place.

"Did you set the bomb? And was she there?" Channing sat on a deck chair, petting Ming.

He threw Lila the white robe he had folded in his lap, and she hurried to cover herself.

"Yes, it's been taken care of. She was there, as well as her husband, brother-in-law, and Nola."

"Was my father there?" He put Ming down in front of a bowl of milk beside his chair.

"I only saw them. Doesn't mean he isn't there."

"I'm sure he's not. He's still in Solomon's Wake. He thought he was doing Georgia a favor by sending her away. He has no idea of what's to come."

Channing moved over to the railing and stared across the sea, toward the *Lady Tara*.

42

RENDEZVOUS WITH DISASTER

A FEW HOURS LATER, AN EXPLOSION rocked the ship and threw them all to the floor. The sound of shattered glass echoed, followed by the agonizing screams of the cook being burned alive. The galley caught fire and couldn't be contained. It soon spread to the rest of the yacht. The foursome watched in horror as a wall of flames separated them from the exits.

Simon got Georgia, while Joshua and Nola herded the crew and trekked to a different exit.

Everyone was thrown to the floor again as the ship rocked.

"Dear God, what's happening?" Georgia said.

The captain ordered everyone to gather on the sun deck and wait for help, assuring them an SOS had been sent.

"Let's get to the lifeboat, quickly!" Simon said.

When they reached the staircase that led outside, another explosion ripped a huge gash on the starboard side of *Lady Tara*, mortally wounding her. The group knew the ship would soon founder, and they had to flee the dying liner before she took them all to the bottom of the Atlantic.

After a long struggle up the staircase, they emerged outside.

"Mister Lord, please get your family into the lifeboat," Madison said.

Lady Tara began to slowly turn over onto her starboard side, and people began screaming in panic.

"Madison, you have done your job," Simon said. "Now get into the lifeboat."

"Not until all the passengers have gone." She was in her early twenties, with auburn hair and brown eyes.

"As owner of this liner," Georgia said, "I command you to get in."

Madison hesitated. "Yes, ma'am." She eased into the tiny boat.

"It's for your own good." Simon watched her sit.

The sea crept up the deck, spilling into open portholes and doorways. The water continued to rise, and fear of the *Lady Tara* capsizing became a reality as the starboard side of the doomed yacht leaned closer and closer to the sea. People had to hold on to the banisters, tables—anything to keep them grounded. The incline became too treacherous and slippery for them.

"Georgia, honey!" Simon said. "You and Nola go next."

Georgia stepped up, and another explosion shook the boat, causing the railing to snap. Joshua and Simon watched, wide-eyed, as Georgia and Nola were sent screaming into the roaring waves below, and vanished from sight. The emergency breakers gave out, and the lights shut off forever.

Bawling, Simon called out his wife's name over and over as he looked for her in the murky waters.

"Simon, we have to go." Joshua tried to pull him into the lifeboat.

"I can't go without out her." Simon continued to sob.

At 11:30 that evening, just an hour and ten minutes after the explosion, the *Lady Tara* capsized and sank in a whirlpool of debris, taking at least five souls to a watery grave. The survivors, overwhelmed by grief, sat in silence and waited for the help they prayed was on its way. Now, all that remained of this elegant yacht were a few things bobbing here and there on top of the watery surface. An unconscious Nola was fished out of the sea and pulled back into the lifeboat by a crew member.

Channing's ship was close by the scene, and had rescued Georgia. She had suffered a concussion in the fall and was slipping in and out of consciousness.

Finally, she awakened, and began shouting weakly.

"Where am I?" Georgia cried out of an opened porthole, when she realized she was handcuffed to the bed.

Booming footsteps were coming her way.

Channing entered the small cabin. He was six-feet tall, handsome, with broad shoulders and high cheekbones. Right away, she knew it was her brother.

"We meet at last, sister." He looked her over.

And when she turned away, he pulled her hair to make her look at him.

Georgia whimpered.

"You will not rob me of this moment." He sneered as he relaxed his grip. "I lived in your shadow long enough, and you are going to suffer every bit as I did. Gideon wants to ignore me and act like I don't exist. Well, maybe now that I have you, he'll listen." He sat down at the foot of her bed.

"Spare me the sob story," Georgia said. "You murdered my mother, and you want me to feel sorry for you? You got the wrong girl." She fidgeted on the bed to get comfortable.

"I don't need you to feel sorry for me. I just need you to get me into that tomb. Our father won't open it for me. But now that I have you, I'm sure he will."

Channing twisted her big toe, and she screamed.

"You're in fantasy land if you think your mother is alive after all this time," Georgia said. "If she is—"

Channing jumped up and punched Georgia in the face, knocking her out again.

"That's better. You were giving me a headache."

"Was that necessary?" Lila entered the cabin.

"Was what necessary?"

"Putting your hands on her." Lila grimaced as she stared at the bruise on Georgia's cheek.

"I don't know what you're talking about. See to it that the captain increases our speed. I'd like to be back in Solomon's Wake in two days."

"That's a day before schedule."

"I am aware."

"Why?"

"I am really tired of your questioning me. Last time I checked, you worked for me. And if you want to continue in my employment, you'll keep that in mind next time you wanna play Twenty Questions."

He left Lila standing by Georgia's bedside.

43

THE FORGOTTEN

OVER THE NEXT FEW DAYS, WORD OF THE *Lady Tara* sinking had reached every news outlet in the country. The phones at Windwood were ringing off the hook, but no one was there to answer them. Joshua had given the staff the week off since most of the household would be away. And Gideon, Toni, and Donna were busy trying to get into the mine.

Last time either of them were at the mine, a three-story mall was above it. Now it was gone, and the lake was restored.

"According to the map, it's here," Toni said. "Put your hand in the water. It's colder here than any other spot in the lake, which leads me to believe that this was where the quarry was."

She yanked her hand back and went over to a large duffel bag that seemed to have an endless amount of room.

Gideon followed her lead.

"I'll be damned," he said. "It is."

"What's that?" Donna said, when she saw Toni pluck out what looked like a synthetic fish wrapped in a plastic dome from a bubble gum machine.

"Watch and learn." Toni dropped the fish into the water.

It grew into a large, pigmented cavefish, which began to leave a trail of light under the water as it sped off toward the cavern.

"My friend here will lead us right to them," Toni said.

"What else you got in there?" Gideon tried to peek inside, but Toni pulled the bag away and closed it.

"That light won't last long," she said. "So if I were you, I'd get down there while you can."

"I'll go," Donna said. "I'm a better swimmer than you." She took her *Twilight* shirt off to reveal a skimpy red string bikini, then grabbed a black ponytail holder from her pocket and tied her hair back. "You two try to play nicely while I'm gone." She waved, then vanished beneath the water.

"What exactly is the plan?" Gideon eased back into his seat.

Toni continued to stand still as a tree, her gaze locked on the lake.

"There should be another mark on the map," she said. "leading us to a drainage system. Once we find that, we'll be able to open the entrance long enough to get the blood-root and get out."

"And how long's that, exactly?"

"When the Monarchs built this prison, they installed a safety mechanism that will flood the cavern again in twenty minutes. Your friends were never supposed to get out of there alive." She looked back down at the map.

"Wow. That's not a lot of time."

Splash!

Gideon turned the lantern on the murky water, and an alligator that had grazed their boat.

"No, it's not," Toni replied. "And if we're not quick, we may not get out."

Donna broke the surface and climbed back into the boat. Her blonde hair clung to her cheeks, and the T-shirt she pulled back over her head stuck to her like a magnet.

"I heard them down there," she said. "Some are still alive. I heard them begging to be killed, or pleading to be let out." Red tears streamed down her cheeks. "It broke my heart to hear them so defeated." She held on to Gideon's arm to sit.

"On the other side of the lake is the entrance and the hidden door." Toni was still staring at the map.

"What are we waiting for? Let's go." Donna took the oars and steered toward the other side of Lake Katherine.

When they reached the other side of the lake, a few feet away was the mine shaft. Toni was shocked to find that the mine door was open, because only a Corsini could open it. She looked across the water, up into the trees, and even down into the shaft.

"I don't understand."

She was so perplexed that the bats began to stir, and the tide churned as the elements sensed the witch's trouble.

"I'll explain." Channing came through a clearing behind them.

He had Georgia with him, and a gun with silver bullets, aimed at her back.

"How?" Gideon shook his head. "I made sure to get them away from you."

"I placed a tracking device in Nola before I let her go, which led me right to you. After you put them on your yacht, I sank it. You follow? It's really quite simple."

Gideon rushed toward Channing, but Toni stopped him.

"I swear, Channing, if you do anything—"

"You'll do what? Disown me? Imprison me? Or better yet, let me be raised by the biggest scumbag on the planet? You've already done that, so what more can you do to hurt me? Hmm? I am going to make you suffer and hurt like I did." Channing's temper boiled over as he watched his father gaze lovingly at his sister. "You are going in there with me to find Mom, or so help me, I will inject Georgia with the virus."

"I will go down with you. There is no need to involve your sister."

"Good. We have twenty minutes to get in and out. Remember to stay as far away from the infected as you can. And whatever you do, don't get bitten."

"The water's still there," Georgia moaned.

"It'll be gone in a minute," Channing said.

The water receded, revealing a winding staircase that went all the way down, out of their sight.

"Told ya." He grabbed his sister so hard he popped a vessel on her arm. "You're damn right you're going down there, Dad. Because you don't have a choice." He pushed Georgia into the shaft.

In a flash, Gideon was down at the bottom, and caught his daughter. They could hear the others trying to get out.

Channing soon followed.

"Are you okay?" Gideon held Georgia tight.

"I'm fine. Just a little sore, but I'll live. Listen to them."

The moaning and crying was deafening.

"I hate to break up the lovefest, but once this door opens we need to hurry, find Mom, and get the hell out of here." Channing opened the door. "Let's not waste any more time."

He yanked on the handle, and the door flew open. The smell of decay, feces, and stagnant water overpowered them. After they regained their senses, they proceeded through the entrance. They could hear water dripping from the rocks, and off in the distance, bats flying around.

"I can't take that smell." Georgia held her nose.

"Try not to focus on it." Gideon kept moving through the dark cavern.

"That's like asking me not to—" She screamed when one of the infected grabbed her foot. "Daddy, get it off me!" she shrieked, while trying to kick it off her foot.

The poor thing had become a withered bag of bones who'd kept her werewolf form. It looked like a giant sphinx.

"Kill me, please," she said, in a raspy voice.

"Daddy, she's blind." Georgia looked down into what looked like clouds in place of the woman's once proud, smiling Irish eyes.

"We're running out of time," Channing barked. "C'mon." He moved on through the dark prison.

"We can't just leave her." Georgia stared down at the tortured creature.

"You better decide soon, before we all drown," Gideon said. "She can't hurt a fly. Look at her. She can't even get up."

Georgia followed, looking back, and left the woman on the ground, weakened and near death.

"You two are gonna get us killed," Channing said. "Our smells are all over the place. In a matter of minutes, they'll be all over us because of you slowpokes. Well, I'm sorry. I don't want to die tonight." He turned and stared at both of them. "If I miss my chance to free my mother, I will leave you both down here to die."

"By what?" Gideon said. "More like her?"

"Trust me. The others are ten times stronger, more intelligent, and more bloodthirsty than that pathetic creature on the floor. You don't want to be here when they find us."

44

BENEATH THE SURFACE

THE HOWLS AND MOANS OF THE OTHERS were getting closer, and from the sounds of it, they were not coming to make chit-chat. Georgia clutched onto her dad's arm when she tripped over something, and again screamed so loud the others would be sure to find them.

"What the hell's wrong with you?" Channing shook her.

"I-I'm sorry. I t-tripped."

Channing shoved her and Gideon out of the way, only to trip as well, falling flat on his face. He pulled himself up using a stalagmite, then saw the body Georgia had tripped over.

It was his mother. A stalactite had fallen on her.

"No, it's not her! It can't be." Channing sobbed like a three-year-old. "I'm so sorry, Mama! I tried."

The body was decomposed, and if it weren't for the necklace around her neck—which he had given her for Mother's Day—it would have been impossible to identify.

"Son, we have to go."

Channing continued to try to pull the heavy column off of his mother's body. Again, Gideon tried to drag him away, but he latched onto his dead mother like a vise.

"Today," Georgia whined.

Soon, what looked like dozens of glowing orbs came toward them.

"They're coming!" she yelled.

"Channing, please come on. We have to go." Gideon yanked his arm.

"I can't leave my mother." He bawled as he sat beside her body, holding her skeletal hand.

"Son, I'm not leaving without you. Either you will come with me, or so help me, I'll throw you over my shoulder or drag you by the hair. Your choice." Gideon yanked him up.

"Dad, look out!" Georgia screamed, as one of the infected lunged for him, and in the process, bit her on her arm. "I've been bitten!"

Gideon looked at her and then pummeled the creature until he knocked it to the ground. The rushing water began to flood the chamber, sweeping away some of the other infected before they reached them.

"Daddy, please don't hurt me." The beast pounced on Gideon again.

"Ginny? Oh, my God! How..." He stood still until Georgia knocked him out of the way.

"Get out!" She hit Ginny on top of the head with the flashlight.

Gideon continued to stare at what had become of his daughter.

"Listen to her, you stupid canine." Channing waded toward the entrance.

The water was rising quickly, and it was only a matter of minutes before it flooded the cavern. Many of the infected were left clinging to whatever they could.

"All right, let's go." Gideon reached for Channing's arm.

"Please don't leave me again." Ginny held onto a stalactite as the current continued to churn past them. "I can't hold on much longer."

Gideon let go of Channing's arm and lunged to reach for his other daughter.

"She's not your daughter," Channing said.

Just as Ginny went to bite, Georgia came out of nowhere and slammed into her before she could infect him. Gideon watched as they were carried away.

"C'mon!" Channing roared. "There's nothing we can do now."

Gideon stared after them.

Donna and Toni waited for the trio to return. Every now and then, Toni would peer down to see if anyone was coming. Donna was getting antsy, and worried that they were blowing any chance of getting to the bloodroot.

"I'm going down there." Donna transformed into a bat and nose-dived into the shaft.

"Just great." Toni said.

She descended the rungs, and stopped when she heard the cock of a gun. She looked up to see Sutton holding a pistol, and Jenna, still under Luna's influence, standing above her.

"You might want to get back up here," Sutton said.

Toni climbed to the top and was confronted by Luna.

"Did you really think I would let you have the bloodroot? No, no, no." The girl shook her head. "My curse is binding, and there is no way anyone can undo it. Sutton, give me the gun so you can close the door."

He handed over the firearm and struggled with the lid.

"You, my ungrateful spawn, shall watch as the House of Lord crumbles once and for all. Seal them in!" Luna began to chant a spell that would lock them in the cave forever.

The wind churned, stirring up debris and wildlife.

"I don't think so." Lila strode out of a clearing in the woods, wiping away the hair blowing in her face.

She picked up a stone and threw it at Luna's head. It did nothing but piss her off more.

Luna continued, undeterred. Sutton threw up his hands and scampered off like the coward he was.

"Oh, my God." Toni fell to her knees, and tears of joy streamed down her face as she looked at Lila and realized she was her lost Carla.

A power unlike anything she'd ever felt took over and she rushed toward her beloved granddaughter.

"I thought you were dead." She pulled the girl into an embrace.

"Lady, I've never seen you before in my life," Lila said.

"You are Carla Romano, and I've been looking for you for a long time."

Lila looked at her as if she were a stranger.

Toni projected herself into Carla's mind and saw the steel door that blocked her memories. Toni focused on the bar that kept the door from opening, and a few times she almost had it up, but didn't have the strength to do it.

A familiar voice called out to her, and she turned to see her beloved Gianni.

"Let me help."

Toni smiled, and the two lifted the bar, and the door opened. She stared as her husband became smaller and smaller, and then vanished. She felt a heavy tightness in her chest, and collapsed as she was thrust back to reality.

Carla was paralyzed as the erased memories flooded back.

"Nonna." She dropped to the ground and cradled Toni in her arms. "I remember everything. I missed you so much." She looked down at Toni's worn face. "I will never leave you again."

"We have plenty of time to catch up." Toni struggled to catch her breath. "Right now, you must stop Luna and rip that necklace from her."

Carla went to help her up.

"Don't worry about me. Just go get her."

After transforming into a nighthawk, Carla swooped down on Luna and ripped the necklace off, then soared a few feet away and dropped it into some brush. An ear-piercing hiss came out of Jenna as Luna was forced to depart the girl's body, freeing Jenna of her spell.

Toni moved to get the necklace, and a sharp pain rushed up her arm as she picked it up. She remained crouched over for a few moments, afraid that if she moved it would get worse.

"Nonna, I want to go home." A groggy Jenna tugged on Toni's shirt.

"We will, soon, my little munchkin."

Ignoring the pain, she swooped Jenna up in her arms.

45

AFTERMATH

saved the passengers. The *Minerva* combed the area four times, and there was still no sign of any other survivors, until one of the crew spotted a body two miles from where *Lady Tara* had gone down. Simon prayed it wasn't Georgia.

He gasped when they hauled a charred body from the Atlantic.

"Mister Lord, I'm sorry," said the captain of the vessel, "but we have found no trace of your wife or anyone else. Poor guy. His body got caught in the current, forcing him farther out to sea."

"Could you please look around once more?" said a heartbroken Simon.

"I'll do my best, sir. But I don't think we'll find anymore survivors."

He left Simon on a deck chair, with a wool blanket wrapped about him.

"Simon, are you all right?" Joshua stepped out onto the deck.

"How can I be all right when so much has gone wrong?" Simon gazed out at the ocean. "She was my world. Gideon is going to lose it when he finds out. He already lost one daughter." He stared down at his feet.

"We'll manage and go on with our lives, because we're Lords." Joshua put a hand on his brother's back, fighting back tears.

"Is Nola gonna be okay?" Simon said.

"She's sleeping now. It's just a nasty bump on the head. The doc says she'll be fine."

"Thank God. I couldn't imagine having to tell Gideon that his girlfriend's dead, too. For the first time in my life, I'm afraid. It's always been me and Georgia against the world. And with her gone, I don't know how to be me. She's always been the strong one."

Simon was unable to talk anymore, so the brothers sat in silence as the boat headed back to Miami.

With the loss of Ginny, Gideon's grief overwhelmed him. After years of searching, he had found her, only to lose her for good.

"She's been down there the whole time. My Ginny was right under my nose." Gideon plodded out of the mine.

Donna flew out shortly after, and Channing brought up the rear.

A black cat sauntered down the path to perch atop one of the rock formations along the trail. The feline had the greenest eyes and a coat darker than the deepest fathoms of space. But when the cat went to meow, Marshall's thunderous voice arose.

"An eye for an eye, Gideon. You took my daughter, so I returned the favor. That night, when you conducted the séance summoning me, I used this opportunity to send your daughter back to 1912. Instead of Iris going into the cave, Ginny went instead. At long last, vengeance is finally mine." The cat tilted its head back and roared.

Gideon leapt to strike the cat, which meowed, jumped down, and took off.

"Look out!" Donna hissed.

With her fangs bared, she lunged forward, pushing Gideon out of the way. She tore into the neck of one of the rabid who'd managed to escape before the door closed, and almost sucked them dry. Weakened, and with her head spinning, Donna fell back, unable to move or speak, as was the case whenever a vampire sucked that poison out.

"Georgia?" Gideon reached for the creature that had fallen face first at his feet, and turned it over onto its back.

She had changed back into her old self, and was worn out and battered, but surviving. Gideon sobbed tears of joy, until he looked back toward the cavern and realized his other daughter was gone forever. He dropped to his knees, blaming himself for not knowing she was there, for being unable to save her, and for causing her disappearance in the first place.

"Why!" he screamed, beating the ground with his fists. "Why!"

He felt a hand on his shoulder, which startled him out of his misery.

"Dad, I don't want to make this any harder on you than it already is," Channing said, "but we have another problem." He pulled out another revolver that he kept hidden under his shirt, behind his back.

"How can it get any worse? For Christ's sake, Channing, what else do you want from me?" Gideon scowled when he saw the gun.

"If Ginny was in the cave, then where is my mother, and what happened to her? We are going back in to find out." Channing kept his aim locked on Gideon.

Donna was too weak to help, and Georgia was in no position to do anything either as the vampire bite continued to counter the poison.

Gideon attacked Channing. The gun fired a few times as both battled for control. Soon they were rolling on the ground, punching and biting each other, until the gun went off again, hitting Gideon.

After Luna departed, and Jenna was sleeping in Toni's silver Lincoln Continental, Carla began to fill Toni in on what Channing had done. The more Toni found out, the angrier she became, and the more of a toll it took on her.

"You okay?" Carla said, when Toni stumble back. "Want me to take you home?"

"I'm fine. We can't go anywhere until we finish this." Toni opened the passenger door and pulled out her favorite flask from under the backseat. "A toast to family, and to reconnecting." She took a sip and then passed it to Carla.

"To family," Carla said.

Bang!

"Stay here with Jenna." Toni took off down the path, fighting off the pain in her chest.

The pain was excruciating where the bullet entered his shoulder. Channing jerked him up by the collar and pushed his finger into his dad's wound. Gideon let out a muffled cry as Channing pushed him toward the entrance.

"I don't want to kill you, but I will if you don't move." Channing hit him in the back with the gun.

Gideon began to climb back down, when Toni came out of the clearing.

"Stop!" She lifted her hands and used the last bit of magic she could muster to send Channing tumbling down into the mine.

She struggled with shutting the heavy door, until Carla helped her with it.

"Lock it," Toni said.

46

THE JAWS OF DEFEAT

USING THE SAME SPELL TONI HAD UTTERED decades ago, Carla put a stop to Channing's reign of terror.

Gideon hobbled over and kissed Toni on her cheek.

"I think you like me a little more then you let on," he said.

"Maybe. And if you tell anyone, I'll stick you in there with Channing."

"Mommy!" Jenna yelled, from the backseat when she saw a beat-up Donna stagger down the path.

"Jenna!" Donna ran to her daughter, who had hopped out of the car.

The two sobbed in each other's arms, and Donna cradled the girl. She looked at Toni and mouthed, *Thank you.*

"Can we go home now?" Jenna said, through a yawn.

"Give Mommy and Nonna a few minutes. For now, why don't you climb into the backseat and close your eyes until we're ready to go?" Donna kissed her daughter on the forehead as she nodded, and then the girl got into the car. "I'll be right here," she said, when she heard the door close.

"Donna, there is someone I'd like you to meet. My granddaughter, Carla."

Carla came around from the back of the car.

"Carla, this is Donna. She is family, and I would like you both to treat each other as such." Toni tried to smile through the pain, but it was getting harder.

"I have heard so much about you, Carla. I feel like I already know you." Donna smiled.

"I look forward to getting to know you. Any family of my Nonna's is family of mine."

Carla's blonde hair shined under the moonlight, and her smile was still golden as Toni watched her favorite girls hit it off.

"I almost forgot. I found this." Donna pulled the bloodroot from her pocket. "I got a few more, too."

"It is a happy day." Toni squealed as the three hugged.

The forest was still and dark. The vast number of trees seemed to block the moon from penetrating their leafy boughs. Lake Katherine was black as tar, and calm. The lights from Solomon's Wake were like the little white lights you press in a picture you'd buy at a department store or through catalogs.

Gideon sat by Georgia in hopes that she would come to. He looked over at Toni and her brood, and was happy she'd got both her granddaughters back. But he knew their story was far from happily ever after.

Knowing Ginny was the one that went into the mine meant Iris wasn't in there. And if she wasn't, where was she? Gideon was in Solomon's Wake in 1912, and now, because of the switcheroo, the time band was changed, and Iris was now on the loose, and a danger to them all. And there was no telling what else had been changed.

"Daddy?" Georgia used her elbows to sit up. "I want to go home, in case Simon and the others are waiting."

Gideon stood and offered her his hand, which she took. "Okay, Georgey."

They started over to the group, when the ghost of Ginny appeared before them.

"You must stop her before it's too late. Don't let Iris—"

"Daddy, wake up. It's time to go." Georgia shook him.

He had fallen asleep, leaning up against one of the pine trees scattered along the path.

"Where'd she go?" He jumped up and looked for Ginny.

"Who?" Georgia said.

"Ginny. She was right there." He pointed to the spot where she had appeared.

"It was just a dream. There's nobody here but us."

"I'm telling you, she was right here."

"Let's get you home and looked at by the doctor. I think the gunshot wound is playing with your head."

"I know what I saw."

"Okay, Daddy. It's still time to go. Simon and the others are waiting back at the house."

As Georgia got him into the backseat, Toni started the car. The specter of Ginny watched as the car drove away.

Back at the house, Simon reunited with Georgia. Joshua, Donna, and Jenna shared a bittersweet reunion. Now that Donna possessed the bloodroot, she had to use mind control one more time, and took both Joshua and Jenna back to the night Brandon was hospitalized.

Carla settled into her new digs at Windwood. Toni was helping her turn down the bed, when she collapsed. The doctor, who had been examining Gideon, called an ambulance for Toni. She had suffered a heart attack.

Gideon had been sedated, and woke up to Nola sitting by his bed, holding his hand.

"Look who decided to join us." She looked at him with puffy eyes, and leaned down to kiss his warm lips.

"If I knew I'd get a reception like that, I would've gotten shot much sooner."

"This is no time to joke, Gideon." Nola scoffed.

"Okay, I'm sorry." He got up out of bed and opened his nightstand drawer.

"You shouldn't be out of bed yet." Nola groaned as she came up behind him.

"Will this make up for it?' He held his hand out, revealing a black box with a diamond ring in it. "I want you to be Missus Gideon Blake." It hurt, but he got down on one knee.

Nola was speechless, and just stared at it.

"I could always give it to Toni."

"Oh, Gideon! She had a heart attack. She's on her way to the hospital."

He sat back to take it in.

"Of course I'll marry you. I've wanted to for a long time now." Nola climbed into his lap and kissed him long and deep. "Are you gonna slip it on my finger to make it official?"

And with that, Nola and Gideon were engaged.

47

JUDGMENT DAY

GIDEON AND NOLA'S WEDDING DAY HAD arrived, and the mansion came alive as the caterers, orchestra, and gardeners arrived to make sure everything was picture perfect for the social event of the year. Senator Turner, Mayor Williams and his wife, and a few of Hollywood's elite were on the guest list. Big white tents had been erected in the back of the house to accommodate at least five hundred people. Ponies and clowns were brought in for the children, and champagne crates arrived by the dozens for the adults.

Georgia made sure Nola had everything she wanted. Her wedding gift to the couple was an all-expense-paid trip to the French Riviera. She was elated for her dad.

Georgia was looking over the cake, with her back to the patio door, and her arms crossed, when she felt a man's strong arms envelop her. She turned to see Simon smiling at her.

"What were you just thinking about?" He rested his chin on her shoulder.

"Our wedding day. It was in this house, on a day just like this. I can't help but worry. Nothing ever goes off without a hitch with our families. Those two remind me of us. They had to overcome many obstacles to get where they are now, as we did. But in the end, their love prevailed, and I'm sure they will be very happy together. The curse on the Lord family may have been lifted."

"No talk of curses or ghosts, or anything. Let's just enjoy the day." Simon kissed her on the cheek. "I'm going to check on your dad."

Nola looked gorgeous in the cream wedding gown Gideon had imported from Milan. She admired herself in an oblong mirror, thrilled that it made her look so slender.

Gideon paused at the bedroom door, and Nola noticed the giant smile he wore.

"Can you zip this for me?" she said.

"It looks beautiful on you." He kissed her on the neck and then moved toward her ear.

Donna, Georgia, Simon, and Toni entered the room.

"Save that for later." Donna separated the two.

"Don't you know it's bad luck to see the bride before the wedding?" Toni said. "We've all enough bad luck to last two lifetimes, so I have no choice but to kick you out." She pointed toward the door.

Gideon dragged his feet, but eventually gave in, only to poke his head back in.

"I love you," he said, and then Simon caught him by the collar and tugged him down the hall.

"I owe you an apology," Simon said, as the two meandered outside. "Carla told me it was she who told my mother of the curse and caused that night's events. Channing was responsible for it, not you. So I'm sorry, Gideon." He put his hand out to his father-in-law.

Gideon shook it. "Call me Dad." He pulled his son-in-law into a hug. "I have misjudged you as well, and I can't imagine anyone else for my Georgey."

"You already have something old, so I'm giving you something blue." Donna handed Nola a handkerchief.

"I'll give you something borrowed." Toni gave Nola her pearl earrings.

"I am so glad you're back on your feet." She hugged Toni.

"If you'll excuse me, I want to go check on the guys." Donna said. "Will you help me, Toni?" She rushed down the hall.

"Nola, I am so happy for you." Georgia bent down and looked into the mirror in front of the bride. "You make him so happy—something I never thought could happen after my mother died. Yet you pulled off the impossible. I will be glad to have you in the family, and to also have you as a friend." She squeezed the bride's hand.

There was a knock on the door, and Carla entered with a large blue box with a white ribbon tied around it.

"Since it's your special day, I wanted to make it even more beautiful so the groom can't keep his hands off you tonight."

Nola opened the box to find a green lace teddy and a robe.

"Carla!" she squealed, and threw her hands over her mouth.

The men were all ready to go when Donna and Toni found them outside. They were sitting under the tents, smoking cigars and playing cards. They all looked stunning as they stood there, resembling proud penguins with their tails, top hats, and white gloves. The orchestra began to play, signaling that the time was almost upon them.

"I feel it's time for a toast," Simon announced. "Gideon, when the world gets dark and casts you aside, and you feel like it's too much, always come back to this day and remember how happy you were. And always remember to put your wife first, and you'll do just fine. To Gideon and Nola!"

Everyone clinked their glasses and drank to the happy couple.

The wedding march began with Jenna, followed by Georgia, looking exquisite in their matching lavender dresses. Simon then hooked his arm in Nola's and escorted her down the aisle as all gazes rested on her. Everyone smiled, and some winked, as the bride continued down the aisle. She took one look at her tall, handsome groom and felt like she could burst.

Reverend Shelley presided over the ceremony, as he had done for every Lord couple since Calvin and Andrea. Gideon gave his arm to Nola, and Simon stepped back.

"Who gives this woman away?" the reverend said.

"I do!" Simon then took a seat next to Georgia.

Nola teared up as she realized the happiest day of her life had finally arrived.

The bride and groom had chosen to write their own vows. They were spoken with such love, there wasn't a dry eye in the place. Reverend Shelly barely got *husband and wife* out before Nola kissed her man. The crowd cheered, and then the reception began.

Nola and Gideon chose The Pretenders' "I'll Stand by You" as their song, and invited everyone to dance to it.

Jenna, bored and annoyed that no one had asked her to dance, decided to go wander around the mansion. The little girl loved strolling around Windwood's long corridors, large rooms, and winding staircases. Her favorite part of the mansion was the cupola and the attic. She could play for hours up there, and no one would know.

When Jenna reached the attic door, she heard a noise from behind the entrance. A familiar face waited on the other side.

"What are you doing here?"

A few hours later, and after the dinner of rack of lamb and salmon was served, Donna noticed Jenna wasn't in her seat.

"Where's Jenna?" she whispered to Joshua, and glanced around the giant tent, but couldn't find her.

He scanned over the crowd as well, and saw no trace of his daughter. Donna called out her name a dozen times, but received no answer. She began to panic. They searched the basement, while Simon and Georgia searched the old stable, and Nola and Gideon looked under tables and around the nearby grounds.

For hours, they searched, but came up emptyhanded. The sky had begun to change colors, and the longer Jenna was gone, the sicker Donna felt. All kinds of things were running through her head, each thought worse than the other.

It can't be happening again.

All they could do was pray, wait, and hope that someone would find the little girl.

It was now half-past nine, five hours since Jenna's disappearance. Joshua noticed something he hadn't seen before—a flickering light emanating from the cupola. He couldn't believe he hadn't realized sooner that that was most likely where Jenna would be.

When Joshua reached his destination, he saw the faint light seeping out from under the door.

"Jenna, are you there?" He waited for a response. "It's Daddy."

The door opened, and all he could see was darkness as he stepped into the room. The door slammed shut. Joshua whirled around to see Sutton step into the light.

"She's gone, and you're never going to see her again."

"Don't even think about laying a hand on my daughter." He moved closer to Sutton.

"I wouldn't dream of it. You're the one I've come for."

"What do you want from me? I'll give you anything."

"I gave this family the best years of my life. I lied, murdered, and covered up more lies than Watergate, and he tossed me out like I was trash," Sutton spat, his voice rising with his temper. "I loved your father so much I would've died for him. And when I tried to show him how I felt, he laughed in my face. When I told him I got rid of his wife so we could be together, he hit me and went to call the police. I lost my temper, and the next thing I knew, the gun went off and he was dead." He glared at Calvin Lord's son.

"You killed my father?" Joshua bowled over. "I don't understand. Why?"

"Vivian caught me whacking off to your naked father, in the pool house. I couldn't have her tell him what I'd done before I got to tell him how I felt, could I? So I slit her throat and left her there bleeding all over the flagstones."

"You say you loved my father, yet you let him take the fall for a murder he didn't commit? God, man, you destroyed his life and ruined a whole family. My poor sister hasn't been right since."

"I did love him."

"No, you didn't. If you did, you have a funny way of showing it."

"I would've loved you, too, if only your wife hadn't returned." He moved toward Joshua.

"You're a sick, twisted man. I don't want you here anymore. I want you out of this house for good. And when I get downstairs, I'm calling the police to take you away and put you behind bars where you belong."

"Don't walk away from me, Calvin." Sutton picked up the oil lamp and hurled it at Joshua's feet.

The flames began to rise, separating the two men.

"Where's my daughter, you evil bastard?"

Sutton glowered at him through the fire.

Higher and higher, the flames rose as the oil burned the hardwood and spread to the walls. A huge hole burned into the floor.

Sutton looked back at Joshua. "If I can't have you, no one can!"

He jumped through the floor, to his death.

Joshua fell to the ground in anguish. He repeatedly screamed out his daughter's name before passing out from the smoke inhalation.

The partygoers screamed and gasped as the mighty House of Lord burned. Swarms of drunk and confused guests began to run amok, and Nola clutched to Gideon as they watched the demise of Windwood.

Donna stared wide-eyed. "Oh, my God! Joshua and Jenna are still in there," she screamed, and fell back into Simon's arms.

"Don't worry, Don," he said. "We'll get them out!"

He grabbed Gideon, and they dashed into the burning mansion.

Gideon searched downstairs and Simon upstairs.

"Joshua! Jenna! Anyone here?" Simon hollered.

The entire upstairs hallway was in flames.

Simon heard crying coming from the linen closet. He rushed over to open the door, and was overjoyed to find Jenna alive, clutching her baby doll. She had kicked Sutton in the shins and ran away from him. When the fire had broken out, she hid in the closet.

"Uncle Simon, I am so scared!"

"I've got you. Now hold tight to my neck and close your eyes."

The flames now blocked the stairwell. He closed his eyes, too, and bolted through the fire. He managed to make it outside with just a few cuts and bruises.

Joshua picked himself up off the floor and staggered through the door. In the hall, all the family heirlooms, portraits, and antiques were ablaze. Annabelle's portrait was the only one left unscathed. He took it from the wall and fled, colliding with Gideon.

Donna remembered that the painters still had work to do on the third floor, and most of their supplies had been left upstairs.

Boom! The roof collapsed into the third floor. The ground shook as the massive stairwell broke free from the second-floor landing, separating the floors. Windows exploded, sending shards of glass through the crowd, and it was so hot the ice swan in the fountain melted.

Simon and Gideon had emerged safely outside. Joshua had broken his arm when the kitchen stairway buckled. A figure emerged from the rubble with fire down her back, and then collapsed at Carla's feet.

It was Toni, who had returned to her room for rest. Since the heart attack, she had been under strict orders to take it easy, and had left the reception around eight.

Carla plopped down and pulled the old woman into her lap.

"It's time to say goodbye. I'm going now, where I am wanted, up in the clouds to see my Gianni and Marie. Gideon, that favor you owe me—watch over my girls. In my private vault, you will find my journal, which will shed more light on the ways of The Order. Oh, baby girl, I am so glad I got to see you one more time." She touched Carla's face.

Donna was next to Carla, sobbing.

"I love you like my own, Donna Lord. And I'm glad I could call you family. Gianni is waiting." She looked over to Gideon. "Give Simon a chance. He's a good man." She took a deep breath and whispered, "I'm coming, honey."

Toni died in the arms of her beloved granddaughter, surrounded by all those she held dear. A tear-streaked Carla bawled as she cradled Toni in her arms. She kissed her on the forehead and threw Gideon's topcoat over her corpse.

Carla then felt what every Zorn had—the passing of magic. She had absorbed Toni's power, as Toni had her mother's before her.

Unbeknownst to the onlookers, Luna's evil face loomed above, sneering down on them. Her prophecy had been fulfilled once more, and its shockwaves would be felt for years to come.

"I'm sorry, Donna," Joshua said, face covered with soot. "I couldn't find Jenna."

His once-white shirt was as black as the tarred driveway.

"She's fine," Donna said. "She's sitting over there by Simon and Georgia." She pointed over to a table at the back of the tent.

"Thank God." He collapsed into her arms from exhaustion.

Donna hugged him close as they turned back to watch what was left of Windwood smolder.

In the wee hours of the morning, the fire was finally extinguished. As the firefighters sifted through the debris, a body with a piece of wood stuck in its chest was found.

"I think this is our second casualty!" the fireman shouted, over the truck engines and water being sprayed from the hoses.

"Put it over there with the other one." The captain pointed over to the body bag that contained Sutton.

The young man carried the corpse behind the fire truck so no one could see it, and laid it on the ground.

"Poor fellow." He pulled out the piece of wood lodged in its chest.

Then he reached for his lighter and pack of smokes in his front pocket.

The young firefighter felt the pain as the fangs sank into his neck. Then he relaxed as the pain turned to pleasure. The more the vampire sucked, the more her skin texture changed into that of a youthful woman with large brown eyes and long, flowing chestnut hair. She dropped the man like a ship's anchor, wiped the blood from her lips, and turned to Windwood.

"No, Iris, I will not let you." A sorrowful Annabelle appeared before her. "Not again."

"This time, dear sister, no one will stop me." Iris went straight through the apparition.

"No!" Annabelle cried, as she vanished.

Donna and Joshua hurried over to the hospital to see Brandon. Even though there hadn't been a change in his condition, they felt if they talked to him every day, maybe their voices would penetrate the walls of his brain.

As they got off the elevator, the floor was quiet, with no one in sight. They approached their son's room, and the RN who took care of him came up to offer her condolences.

"I just heard what happened. Are you two okay? Do you want me to get the doctor to look at you?" She looked at Donna, then Joshua.

"Thanks," he said, "but we've already have been looked at. All I want right now is to see my son. Is he any better?"

Joshua could tell by her expression that Brandon was the same.

Crash!, followed by the sound of broken glass, filled the corridor. The noises came from Brandon's room.

The trio darted down the hall, past the waiting room, almost tripping over the extra beds and heart monitors in the way. Joshua threw the door open to find the wall and windows blown out, and Brandon gone.

"Where's our son?" Donna stared out into the early morning sun.

It looked like the house of Windwood still had one or two secrets to keep.

THE END?

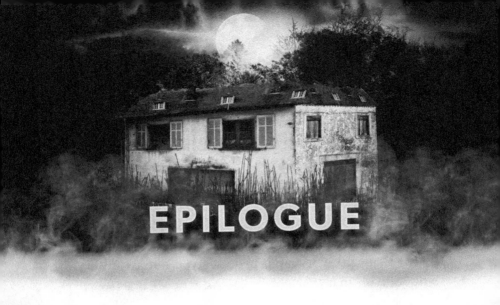

EPILOGUE

HE GOT OUT OF THE CAR AND STARED UP at what was left of the gray walls of Zorn Castle. The bulldozers had succeeded in knocking most of it down. The clouds covered the crescent moon, but a few beams escaped to shine on the Zorn coat of arms engraved above the entrance to the castle. From here, these evil bloodsuckers began their quest to dominate Bavaria and spread their malevolence across the globe.

It was here that his ancestor Captain Josef Wagner had decapitated them all. And it was here where he had returned to find the golden sarcophagus, along with the jeweled dagger, to destroy not just the Monarchs, but any other supernatural being.

"Where is it?" he called to the hidden figure who sat in the front seat, cloaked by darkness. "You better not be lying to me, Yannick." He held out his hand to reveal a trigger.

Once pressed, Yannick would explode.

"It's in the chapel. I am not lying, Tobias. I saw them put it there, with my own eyes." The figure got out of the car.

His skin was as white as the moon. His eyes were feline, and his fangs were visible under his lips.

"Move!" Tobias shoved him toward the entrance.

The once-grand castle, though burnt and crumbling, still demanded one's attention. But inside the chapel, with its holy relics, crosses, and saints that decorated the walls, it could do nothing to save the village from the carnage bestowed by the Zorn's.

The outside air blowing in from the holes in the wall made the hair on Tobias's neck stand up, and the stillness that surrounded the castle created an eerie atmosphere.

"Let's speed this up," he said. "I hate Bavaria, and would prefer to be back in my cozy hotel room in Berlin. The air here is, like, ten times worse than Beijing's on a good day. The evil is just dripping from the walls."

"Is the big bad vampire hunter afraid?" Yannick pulled a marble slab up from the floor. "It's right here!" He smiled, pointing to the hole in the ground where the sarcophagus should be.

"I'll show you how afraid I am when I cut you from the rectum up, and throw you to the wolves roaming the countryside."

Yannick's smile faded. Tobias bent down to look into the hole, and saw just that—a hole.

"Yannick, Yannick, Yannick. What am I to do with you?" He patted the vampire's back, taunting him with the trigger.

"I did what you asked me to. I even got you the vile of vampire blood you asked for. I could be executed by the Monarchs for helping a zombie."

"It's not here." Tobias kept his amber-eyed gaze locked on Yannick, who seemed to get even paler. "It looks like you're not going to see your four hundred sixty-third birthday." He went to press the button.

"It could've been moved to a town in the US called Solomon's Wake, after the Crimson Uprising. There are some still devoted to the Monarchs, who vowed to keep it safe while they slumber."

"Then where is the dagger?"

"I would imagine it's there, too." Yannick sighed.

"Oh, okay."

Tobias pressed the button and watched Yannick explode into a ball of fire before turning to ash.

"I told you not to lie to me."

He left the chapel, but not before burning down the rest of the castle.

Back in Stroudsburg, he was sitting at the local tavern called the Die Affen. He caught a glimpse of himself in the mirror above the bar, and wiped the speck of blood from his plump lips, pulled his long blond hair into a ponytail, and ordered a Gösser beer.

Although this was a minor setback, Tobias was determined to track down the sarcophagus and dagger, and finally make them pay for what they'd done.

The bar cheered as the news broke that castle Zorn burned. Some even ran out to watch, or went home to tell their loved ones. Soon, the town square filled as celebrations broke out all over Stroudsburg.

Tobias continued to drink his beer as he looked up at the TV again. He saw a news report about a fire at house called Windwood, in Solomon's Wake. He saw Donna and clenched his fists.

"I knew you'd turn up one day."

He guzzled his beer and slammed the glass down, pushed his stool in, and grabbed his keys before hurrying out the door He pulled the vile out of his glove box, and reached for a package of syringes he kept underneath his seat.

Tobias wasn't a filthy vampire, but he wasn't quite alive, either. To other immortals or magical beings, he was considered a zombie—not the flesh-eating, moaning, rising-from-the-grave kind depicted in movies and TV shows, with rotting flesh and missing limbs. Tobias was in the middle, neither alive nor dead. When he was spawned, he was left for dead. And instead of rising as a vampire, he stayed much the same except for his unquenching thirst for vampire blood.

The blood of the vampire gives him the beastlike strength that helps him take on these monsters, and it prevents them from reading and controlling his mind. So he can continue to wipeout every coven, den, and cofilin they call home.

Immediately, he felt the blood working. He grabbed the phone from his coat pocket and spoke into it.

"Cortana, get me directions to the airport. And get me any information you can about a town called Solomon's Wake."

He rolled down the window and sped off as the revelers crowded the street to watch castle Zorn burn behind him.

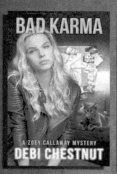

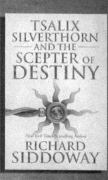

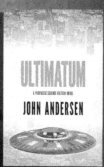

9 781952 404641